# THE PRISON
# IN ANTARES

# THE PRISON IN ANTARES

## DEAD ENDERS BOOK TWO

# MIKE RESNICK

an imprint of Prometheus Books
Amherst, NY

Published 2015 by Pyr®, an imprint of Prometheus Books

Cover illustration © Dave Seeley
Cover design by Nicole Sommer-Lecht

Inquiries should be addressed to
Pyr
59 John Glenn Drive
Amherst, New York 14228
VOICE: 716–691–0133
FAX: 716–691–0137
WWW.PYRSF.COM

19 18 17 16 15    5 4 3 2 1

Library of Congress Cataloging-in-Publication Data

Resnick, Michael D.
    The Prison in Antares / by Mike Resnick.
        pages ; cm. — ([Dead Enders ; book 2])
    ISBN 978-1-63388-102-0 (pbk.) — ISBN 978-1-63388-103-7 (e-book)
    I. Title.

PS3568.E698P75 2015
813'.54—dc23

                                                                2015026672

Printed in the United States of America

*To Carol, as always,*
*and to Rene Sears, for skill, friendship, and patience*

# 1

Nathan Pretorius stared at General Wilbur Cooper, who was standing in the doorway of his hospital room.

"How's it going?" asked Cooper.

"How's *what* going?"

"Your recovery, my boy," replied Cooper. "Your recovery."

"I'd tell you, but knowing you, you've probably spoken with every doctor I've got and know far more about it than I do."

"That's my Nate!" said Cooper, forcing a chuckle. "This is your third prosthetic foot—or is it your fourth?"

"I've lost count," replied Pretorius sardonically. "You keep sending me out, and they keep blowing parts of me away." He paused. "I'm stuck here, but you undoubtedly have a galaxy to run, so why not run it and leave me the hell alone?"

"You do me an injustice, my boy," said Cooper, trying very hard to look hurt. "I'm here to give you another medal."

"Leave it on the cabinet there," said Pretorius, indicating the structure. "In case it's escaped your notice, I'm not wearing my uniform."

"Not a problem. I'll hang on to it for another week or so, until you're up and around, and then we'll have a proper ceremony."

"So you came all the way over here from headquarters to tell me you're not giving me a medal today," said Pretorius. "Why do I have some difficulty believing that?"

"I came over to tell you that you and your Dead Enders did a first-class job in the Michkag affair."

"Is that what we're calling them now?"

"I thought it was your term."

"No you didn't," said Pretorius. "I'm due for some medication in another five minutes, so maybe you'd better cut through the crap and tell me why you're really here."

Cooper nodded his head briskly. "We've got a hell of a situation on our hands." He paused. "It's tailor-made for you and your Dead Enders."

"They're not mine," replied Pretorius. "And let me remind you that they're not yours either."

"Oh, they're yours, Nate. Can't break up a winning team."

Pretorius stared at the general for a long moment. "Are you *ever* going to get to the point?"

Cooper made a face. "Got a real stinker for you, my boy. A *real* stinker!"

Pretorius made no reply, and simply waited for the general to continue.

"You know anything about the Q bomb?"

"I know it's the reason we're losing the war against the Transkei Coalition in the Albion Cluster," answered Pretorius. "Or are they coming closer with it?"

"Well, yes and no," answered Cooper.

"Yes or no *what?*"

"Yes, they're getting closer with it, and no, we're not losing the battle . . . exactly."

Cooper paused again, and Pretorius stared at him. "Someday I hope they teach you to speak in paragraphs instead of sentences. We might save enough time to develop a defense against the Q bomb."

"How did you know?" said Cooper, surprised.

"How did I know what?" demanded Pretorius.

"That we've developed a defense against the Q bomb?"

"Good for us," said Pretorius. "Now that the war is won, I'm going back to sleep."

"We've lost it," said Cooper. "That's where you and your Dead Enders come in."

"They're not mine, and what the hell have you lost?"

"The defense, damn it!" snapped Cooper. "After a dozen years, we finally came up with a way to neutralize the Q bomb." He grimaced. "We used it against three attacks, and it worked. It actually worked!"

"So what's the problem?"

"The bastards managed to kill most of the team that created it, and they've kidnapped the one man who was the brains of the operation, Edgar Nmumba."

"But you still know how to neutralize the Q bomb?" said Pretorius.

"For the moment—they're pretty easy for our instruments to spot—but the real problem is that our solution is an incredibly complex and delicate mixture of hardware and timing, it doesn't allow substitutions, and there's every likelihood that even as we speak they're trying to pry his formulas out of him so they can change what goes into the Q bomb just enough to overcome our defenses."

"Can they do it?"

Cooper frowned. "Nobody knows. He volunteered to let our psychiatric team insert a number of incredibly strong, complex mental blocks, and theoretically they can't be broken by any means known or even conceived by us. But if there's a chance, and of course there is, we have to stop them before he gives them what they need." He paused, leaning against the rail of the hospital bed. "Nate, we haven't made the figures public, but they have delivered seventeen Q bombs, and we've lost an average of close to a billion people per bomb. We *can't* let them go back to using it."

"Why do I think I know what's coming next?"

"We *think* they're holding Nmumba in a prison buried deep beneath the ground on a planet in the Antares Sector, and we think he's still alive. What we know is that we've got to get him back before they can break him. That's where you and your team come in. I want you to rescue him and return him to us—and if you can't do that, then he's got to be killed before he can tell them what they need to know."

"I didn't enlist to kill fellow members of the Democracy," said Pretorius coldly.

"You didn't enlist at all," said Cooper. "You were drafted."

"The point is—"

"Goddammit it, Nate, the point is that if you have to kill one Man to save three or six or ten million others, let alone a billion, you'll do it and we both know it! You won't like it, and neither do we, but you'll do it."

Pretorius glared at him silently, because he knew that the general was right.

"The doctors tell me you'll be able to hobble around with your new prosthetic foot in another couple of days. You can practice with it while you and your Dead Enders are on your way to the Antares Sector."

"You don't want them," said Pretorius. "They have unique

talents that worked last time, on that mission in Orion, but this is clearly a different—and in ways more difficult—situation."

"You brought 'em all back alive and intact, and we don't know what we're facing here, except that it's a secure facility in an enemy stronghold, just like last time, so you'll take the same team."

"They're probably on five different worlds by now," protested Pretorius. "They're not military, remember."

"They're military *now*," said Cooper with a satisfied smile.

"You conscripted all five?" asked Pretorius, wondering why he didn't feel greater surprise or outrage.

"Last week. They're in the hotel across the street." He frowned. "All but one, anyway."

"Snake?"

"Sally Kowalski," replied Cooper.

"Snake," confirmed Pretorius. A grim smile played around the edges of his mouth. "I know where she's likely to be."

# 2

"**T**his way, sir," said the robot, walking smoothly down the prison corridor. It reached the end, turned left, walked past a row of heavy doors, each with a small viewscreen at eye level, slowed its pace as Pretorius limped after it, and stopped at the last door.

The robot looked into the room through the viewscreen, stood back as if in thought, then looked again, and finally turned to Pretorius.

"You may enter, sir."

"Thanks," said Pretorius, stepping into the cell as the robot ordered the lock to disengage.

The small, slender, wiry occupant sat up on her cot. "Well, look who's here," she said.

"Do you know how tired your government is of bailing you out of prison?"

"Oh, come on, Nate. It's only been four times. Well, five, counting today. And you must need me, so the bail money's well spent."

"What did you do this time?" asked Pretorius.

"Oh, hardly anything."

"It was *that* bad?"

"Buy me lunch and I'll tell you about it." Suddenly she smiled. "Well, the heroic parts, anyway."

"Come on," said Pretorius, walking out into the corridor. "And try not to steal any of the robots."

THE PRISON IN ANTARES

"You got a new gig, or you'd let me rot here," she said, following him.

"Rot here?" he repeated with a chuckle. "Have you ever seen a jail you couldn't break out of in two days, tops?"

"There was one on Altair III that took me a whole week," she answered with a grimace. "Do you need just me, or are there others?"

"The Dead Enders."

"Who the hell are they?" asked Snake. "They sound like a bad music group."

"I've heard some of 'em sing in the shower, and that's exactly what they sound like."

"So really, who are they?"

"You're part of them," said Pretorius. "They're our crew from the last mission."

"Talk about a mismatched crew!" she said, snorting in derision. Then she shrugged. "What the hell. We all came through it alive. And it'll be nice to see Pandora and Circe again."

"I'm glad you approve," said Pretorius sardonically.

"Is the critter back too?"

He frowned. "The critter?"

"The alien."

"Yeah, him, and also Felix Ortega."

"So we got a muscleman and a shape-changer."

Pretorius chuckled. "Close, but no cigar."

"I don't smoke anyway."

"Felix is more machine than man these days. He can lift a ton and break down any door anyone can build, but he's not doing it with muscles."

"Comes to the same thing," said Snake.

"Better," replied Pretorius. "Muscles get tired. Felix never does."

They reached the main office of the prison. Pretorius had to stop to sign a pair of documents, and then they were outside, walking between rows of towering angular buildings toward the hotel where the rest of the team was waiting for them.

"Just out of curiosity," he asked, turning to her, "how did they catch you this time?"

"Bad luck," answered Snake. "I managed to wriggle all the way up to the third floor of the Worsell Planetary Bank"—she pointed to it, three blocks away—"and suddenly some asshole up on four or five got cold and turned on the heat. Fucking vent must have hit sixty degrees Celsius before I could get out of it."

"So you got warm," said Pretorius. "That doesn't explain why—"

"I punched a hole in the ceiling and jumped down," said Snake with a bitter smile. "How the hell was I supposed to know that Old Man Worsell would be screwing one of his assistants on the desk right below me?" She shook her head, as if to rid it of the image. "Still, I got within fifty meters of the back exit before security showed up."

"Just as well," said Pretorius.

"What the hell are you talking about?"

Pretorius smiled. "I don't think even General Cooper's clout could have got you out if you'd actually stolen whatever it was you were there to steal."

"Idiot!" she muttered. "If I'd stolen it, I'd be five parsecs from here, lolling on a beach."

"You're not the beach type," replied Pretorius. "You might well have been five parsecs away, but you'd just be pulling off another heist there."

She considered his comment, then shrugged. "Probably," she admitted.

"Well, you can help pull off a heist for your government and maybe even get your record expunged for it."

She came to an abrupt stop. *"Maybe?"*

"All right," he replied. "Definitely."

"Damned straight," she said. "What are we stealing?"

"Let's keep walking. I don't feel like explaining it twice."

She pointed to a tavern. "Want to stop for a drink first?"

"Yes, I do," said Pretorius, continuing to walk past the tavern.

"Well, then?" said Snake, tugging at his arm.

"First I'll do what I *have* to do," he answered. "Later I'll tend to what I *want.*"

"I'll bet you were a fun guy before the military ruined you," muttered Snake, falling into step beside him.

# 3

**"H**i, Nate," said the half-man half-machine who still answered to the name of Felix Ortega. "We were betting on whether or not the Snake would escape before you paid her bail."

"How are *you* feeling, Nate?" asked Toni Levi, who operated under the name Pandora.

"Fine," said Pretorius, entering the elegant suite that boasted an exquisite display of alien art.

"No, you're not," said a blonde woman of such unearthly beauty that he still wasn't sure whether she was a human, a mutant, or an alien.

"I'm fine enough, Circe," said Pretorius firmly. He looked around. "Where's Proto?"

A brown cushion suddenly seemed to morph into a nondescript middle-aged man. "Right here, Nate."

"Try to keep looking like this while I'm here," said Pretorius. "It makes it easier to talk to you."

"Right, Nate."

"So what's going on?" asked Ortega. "It's been a month, and suddenly we've all been ordered to come to this suite."

"It seems the government was so happy with our last job that it's come up with another one for us," answered Pretorius. He was about to say more when there was a knock at the door. "Enter," he said, and the door irised to allow a slender young woman with flaming red hair into the suite.

"Hello," she said nervously. "General Cooper told me to come over and report to a Colonel Pretorius. Would that be you?"

Pretorius nodded. "Did he say why?" he asked.

"No," was the answer. "I got the distinct impression that you would be informing me of my assignment."

Pretorius cast a quick glance as Circe, who nodded her head almost imperceptibly.

"Okay," he said. "Have you got a name?"

"Iris Fitzhugh."

"Rank?"

She frowned. "I'm not in the service, sir."

Snake grinned. "What does he have on you?"

"I beg your pardon?" said the young woman, turning to face Snake.

"Don't worry about it," said Pretorius. "We're glad you're here. Probably."

"Probably, sir?"

"Depends on what your special talent is, Red."

"How did you know?"

"Know what?" asked Pretorius.

"Everyone calls me Red."

"I can't imagine why," said Pretorius, which precipitated a peal of laughter from the others. "Okay, Red, why are you here?"

"I told you, sir: General Cooper ordered—"

"I'm not 'sir,'" Pretorius interrupted her. "And what I want to know is *why* he ordered you to come here."

She frowned. "I have no idea, sir."

"Nate."

"I have no idea, Nate."

"Well, we'll figure it out," said Pretorius. "Have a seat, and welcome to the Dead Enders."

"Who the hell are the Dead Enders?" asked Ortega.

"You are not impressing the lady with your intellect," said Pretorius. "Red, this is Felix. He can crush a grape with just his thumb and his forefinger." She smiled. "He can do the same to a bowling ball with the same fingers. But sometimes his brain is a little muscle-bound."

"I'm pleased to meet you," said the woman.

"I'm glad someone around here is," muttered Felix.

"This mini-person here is Snake," continued Pretorius. "A fine acrobat, a contortionist without peer, and a thief without scruples."

"I disagree," said Snake.

"You have a peer, or you have a scruple?" asked Pretorius.

"With calling her Red. Name like that, you ought to call her Irish."

"*Are* there any Irish anymore?"

"What difference does that make?" replied Snake pugnaciously.

Pretorius turned to the woman. "Which do you prefer?"

"No one's ever called me Irish before. I *like* it."

"You've made a friend for life," he said, smiling at Snake. "Moving on, this is Toni Levi."

"Antoinette," Pandora corrected him.

"Right. But around here, she's Pandora."

"What a fascinating name!" said Irish. "May I ask what—?"

"What it means?" Pretorius finished her sentence. "She's our computer guru. There's no box of electronic secrets she can't open. Or at least, we haven't found one so far." He walked over to the blonde, who seemed to possess an otherworldly beauty. "And this is Circe."

"A Greek goddess?"

"Greek's as good a guess as any," said Pretorius. "No one knows where she comes from, and I'll give plenty of ten-to-one that she doesn't tell you either."

"What about the goddess part?" persisted Irish.

"Well, she's closer to that than to being Greek," acknowledged Pretorius. "She's our lie detector."

Irish stared at her intently. "A telepath?" she asked at last.

"An empath," said Circe.

"Comes to pretty much the same thing," said Pretorius.

"Not really," answered Circe. "Telepaths don't feel your anguish when you're terrified and scrambling for an answer."

"That's amazing!" said Irish. "On the other hand, I don't know if I'd care to have that particular ability."

"It can be more of a curse than a blessing," answered Circe.

"Yeah, I can see that," said Irish.

"Well, that's the team," said Pretorius.

They turned at the sound of a man clearing his throat. Pretorius turned and faced Proto.

"Forgive me," he said. "Here's our most recent member. His name, which I don't think anyone can spell, and which I'm sure I'll mispronounce, is Gzychurlyx."

Irish tried to form the word.

"We call him Proto," continued Pretorius.

"Proto?"

"For protoplasm."

She stared at Proto, frowning. "Protoplasm?" she repeated.

"Proto, show her what you really look like," said Pretorius, and suddenly the middle-aged man vanished, to be replaced by a shapeless lump of brown fur, perhaps six inches high and two feet in diameter.

Irish gasped and stepped back. "A shape-changer!" she exclaimed.

"Not quite," said Pretorius with an amused smile. He turned to Proto. "As you were."

The lump of fur was instantly replaced by the middle-aged man.

"He *is* a shape-changer!" insisted Irish.

Pretorius shook his head. "He's . . . I don't know . . . I guess you'd call him an image-caster. If you walk over and touch his shoulder or shake his hand, you'll find there's nothing there." She frowned and continued to stare at the alien. "Proto can make any being of any race we've discovered so far think that he's what he appears to be—and he can appear to be anything from a tiny insect to something that dwarfs the dinosaurs on Procyon VI. But those are all projected images. He's exactly what you saw: a little furry alien."

Irish frowned. "Machines don't think."

"I do believe you've figured it out," said Pretorius with a smile of approval.

"He can fool any living creature, but he can't fool a camera or an ID machine or any kind of scanner," she said.

"Right. Fortunately he remembers that, because it's awfully easy for the rest of us to forget it."

"I'm pleased to meet you all," said Irish. Another frown. "It makes me wonder what I'm doing here. I have no unique talent, not inborn like Circe or Proto, not acquired like Pandora."

"Oh, we'll figure it out soon enough," said Pretorius. "Cooper is a pain in the ass, but he's not a dumb pain in the ass. If he sent you here, he had a valid reason."

"How long have the Dead Enders been a unit?" asked Irish.

"We've been a unit for two months, maybe a little less," answered Pretorius. "We've had a name for about twenty hours—and we've had an assignment for maybe an hour and a half."

"I don't suppose you'd care to share with us?" said Ortega.

"I'd rather spend a couple of more minutes surrounded by happy faces," said Pretorius.

"*That* bad?" asked Pandora.

Pretorius shrugged. "Compared to what?"

"How about: compared to kidnapping the enemy's best general and replacing him with a clone?"

"You guys did that?" asked Irish.

"Barely," said Pretorius.

"Wow!" she said. "I'm in with experts!"

"Lucky experts," said Snake.

"Very lucky," added Ortega.

"But you pulled it off!" enthused Irish. Suddenly she frowned. "How many members of your team did you lose?"

"None," said Pandora. She jerked a thumb in Pretorius's direction. "Thanks to the genius here."

"*None?*" repeated Irish. "Suddenly I feel better. Awestruck, but better."

"Dumb luck," said Snake.

Circe shook her head. "We made our own luck. Or at least, Nathan did."

"Enough," said Pretorius. "I'm too old to blush."

"Fine," said Snake. "That's history anyway. What are we all here for this time?"

"Anyone here ever hear of Edgar Nmumba?"

He was greeted by a roomful of blank expressions.

"Left wing on the local murderball team?" suggested Snake sardonically.

"No such luck," said Pretorius. "Let me try another question. Has anyone here ever heard of the Q bomb?"

"Of course we have," said Ortega.

"We're not delivering a goddamned Q bomb?" demanded Snake. "I mean, we've got a space force to do that!"

"No, we're not going to deliver one. As far as I know, we don't have a single Q bomb in our arsenal."

"Then we're going to steal one from the Transkei Coalition!" said Snake.

"Snake, do you want to tell them what we're here for, or may I?" said Pretorius with a slight edge of anger in his voice that immediately caught her attention. She pressed her lips together and sat perfectly still.

"Okay," said Pandora. "Who *is* Edgar Nmumba?"

"He's a scientist," answered Pretorius. "More to the point, he's the genius who's created a defense against the Q bomb."

"A defense?" continued Pandora. "What kind of defense?"

"I don't know the technical details—nobody but Nmumba does—but I know it works. It detects them, it negates them, and it stops them from doing damage, which as you know can be devastating."

"It really works?" asked Circe.

"It has so far."

"I almost hate to ask the next question," she said.

"I don't blame you," said Pandora. She turned to Pretorius. "Okay, lay it on us."

"The Transkei Coalition has captured him," replied Pretorius. "He's got half a dozen mind blocks, put there by our best psychiatrists, but sooner or later they're going to break through, learn what he knows, and find a way to circumvent it." He paused while they assimilated the magnitude of the situation. "Those bombs take out close to a billion Men every time one makes it through our defenses. We have to get to Nmumba before they find a way past those blocks."

"And?" asked Snake, frowning.

"We rescue him and bring him back before they get what they want."

"There's got to be more to our orders than that," persisted Snake.

Pretorius nodded. "If we can't bring him back, we kill him."

"Makes sense," said Snake.

"Maybe it does, maybe it doesn't," said Pandora.

All eyes turned to her.

"How will we know if he's broken by the time we get there?"

Pretorius grimaced. "I don't know," he admitted. Suddenly he turned to Irish. "But I'll bet someone here does."

Irish nodded her head. "That's my specialty," she replied. "I've been working with posthypnotic suggestions and blocks for the past five years."

"Isn't that what Circe does?" asked Ortega.

Circe shook her head. "I read emotions, not thoughts. If he doesn't know he's been tinkered with, if he thinks he's giving us true answers to the questions we'll be asking him, I won't know if he's been fed a bunch of phony answers because *he* won't know."

"Then we *do* need you, Irish," said Pandora.

"Welcome to the team," added Proto.

"I just hope you're as good as Wilbur Cooper thinks you are," said Snake.

"*You* hope so?" said Irish seriously. "Believe me, *I* hope so even more." She looked around the room. "I've always thought I was pretty good at my profession—" she grimaced "—but having literally billions of lives depending on it . . . well, I find it unnerving."

"Cooper knows what's at stake," said Pretorius. "You wouldn't be here if you didn't have what it takes."

"I hope you're right, sir," said Irish.

"There are no sirs or ma'ams here. I'm Nate, you're Irish."

"Yes, Nate."

"I mean it," he continued. "We're going to be out of uniform, infiltrating enemy territory. One 'sir' could give us away."

She nodded. "Got it."

"We haven't got much time to waste," continued Pretorius. "I'll have at least a preliminary plan worked out by morning. We'll meet in this room an hour after sunrise, go directly to the spaceport, and take off. I'll make sure a ship is waiting." He turned to Irish. "The others know the procedure. Leave behind anything military you may possess—insignia, weaponry, anything that could possibly identify you as a member of the Democracy's armed services. We'll all be supplied with IDs, clothing, weaponry, whatever's needed, once we're aboard the ship."

"Yes, sir," said Irish.

Pretorius frowned. "What?" he said harshly.

"Yes, Nate," she said.

# 4

The ship was totally nondescript. A bridge, a galley, eight cabins, minimal armaments, no military insignia, a few scars from space debris, and a pair of lifeboats, each capable of holding four passengers.

The interior looked every bit as old and worn, but it had a few special features. Inside the shell of an old, decrepit computer was a new, state-of-the-art machine. The medical supplies contained nothing but bandages, painkillers, and antiseptics, but in the galley, inside a container labeled "candy," were a number of powerful medications that Irish felt they might need if indeed Nmumba was still alive and they succeeded in getting him onto the ship.

A military vehicle transported Pretorius and his crew from the hotel to the ship, waited until they had carried their minimal luggage aboard, and left.

"Proto, check the galley," ordered Pretorius. "Make sure we've got something you can metabolize."

"Right," said the alien.

"Irish, make sure we've got enough medications, and that they're the right ones."

"Yes, Nate."

"Pandora . . ."

"I selected it myself," she replied, indicating the computer. "It's exactly what we need."

"Make sure it's still there under all that camouflage and still functioning."

"Nate, our side is the Good Guys," said Pandora.

"You think Snake's the only Good Guy who collects what doesn't belong to her?" replied Pretorius. "Check it out."

"Yes, Nate."

He assigned minor duties to the others, and half an hour later they were ready to depart.

"Maybe now you really ought to confide in us," suggested Snake. "Where is the prison, how are we going to break in and then break back out, and what other little tidbits would you like to share with us?"

"First we have to pinpoint which world he's on," replied Pretorius. "So far all we know is that he's in the Antares Sector. Antares itself has three populated worlds, two of them terraformed, and the Sector has another fourteen. I'm going to assume he's on a planet that's orbiting Antares. They've got a hell of a garrison on Three, strong enough to patrol the whole system. The other two planets are Two and Six. Pandora will monitor all traffic and messages going to and from the system and see if we can get a fix on where they've stashed him. Even using the Bastei and McGruder Wormholes, it'll take us four, maybe five days to get there, and that's assuming we aren't stopped and don't have to divert." He turned to the alien member of the team. "Proto, did you study the holos I gave you?"

"Yes, Nate."

"Okay, show us what an Antarean looks like."

The middle-aged man morphed into an orange-skinned tripodal alien with remarkable swiftness.

"Note the ears," Pretorius said. "And the oval shape of the foot." He paused. "Any questions yet?"

His crew was silent.

"Okay," he continued. "Now let's see a native of Six."

"Aren't they the same?" asked Ortega.

"They're the same basic stock, but this is an Antarean whose progenitors have been living on Six for seventeen or eighteen generations," said Pretorius as Proto morphed again. "Note the elongated feet, and the much larger, cup-shaped ears. Is anyone likely to mistake a native of Three for an inhabitant of Six?"

There was a general shaking of heads.

"Okay, Proto, let's see a Two."

The alien morphed again.

"Ears and feet the same as Three, as you can see," noted Pretorius. "But the eyes are much smaller, which makes sense when you're that much closer to the sun, and the limbs, though jointed in the same places, are far leaner, due to the much lighter gravity. Are there any questions?"

Again, he was met by silence.

"Okay. Proto is at your disposal for the duration of the trip. Any time he's not eating or sleeping, he'll become any of the three prototypes you just saw until there is no doubt in your mind that you can identify each at first glance."

"Is there some reason why this is necessary?" asked Irish. "I mean, are we anticipating different reactions from different races?"

"Beats the hell out of me," answered Pretorius. "And since I don't know and you don't know, it makes sense to be prepared for any eventuality, even if the odds are that they'll all view us as the enemy, that they all have many of the same strengths and weaknesses, and that they probably even speak the same language. But learning how to spot them seems a better use of our time than playing cards, wouldn't you agree?"

THE PRISON IN ANTARES

"I'm sorry," said Irish, staring at the deck.

"Don't apologize. You've been working in a hospital. Now you're going to be working in a totally hostile environment, a war zone, and it makes sense that you prepare for it differently."

She nodded her head. "Yes, it does."

"Now, Pandora will be getting us a thorough readout on the worlds in question, the three circling Antares, and the other fourteen. We'll know the climate, the length of the days and nights, atmosphere, gravity, and any dangers the planets—as opposed to the planetary populations—offer to us. Any questions yet?"

"Yeah," said Ortega. "If they've moved him to a non-oxygen world, how do we get him out? We'll look mighty suspicious carrying an extra spacesuit with us."

Snake laughed aloud, and all eyes turned to her.

"You want to tell him, Snake?" said Pretorius.

"Felix, how do you think they got him to wherever they're keeping him in the first place, if it's not an oxygen world?"

"Damn, I feel dumb!" muttered Ortega.

Snake seemed about to agree with him, and Pretorius quickly spoke again. "All right," he said. "It would be nice if we could pinpoint where Nmumba's at and approach that world directly, but the likelihood is that even an unmarked ship like this isn't going to be allowed to approach without a reason, so I want a couple of you who aren't doing anything else—Snake and Irish—to find the closest worlds to Antares where we *can* land without getting blown out of the sky or arrested the second we touch down."

"Right," said Irish, and Snake nodded.

"Can't we just do it like we did with the Michkag job?" asked Ortega. "Sneak in aboard a supply ship?"

"It's possible," answered Pretorius, "but until we know where he is and what else is there, we can't count on it. Remember: when we had to sneak in and set up shop on Petrus IV during the Michkag mission, there was a garrison there that housed more than ten thousand soldiers, and supply ships came and went regularly. Now, maybe we'll find the same situation here . . . but maybe Nmumba's in a totally isolated place—an iceberg, a mountain, a cavern—with just a handful of guards, someplace that gets visited maybe twice a year by a very small supply ship."

"Okay, okay," said Ortega. "I'm sorry I asked."

"I'll be monitoring all communications from Antares and the nearby planets," offered Pandora. "If anyone lets drop where they're keeping him, rest assured we'll know."

"All right," said Pretorius. "We've got four or five days to pinpoint his location and fine-tune any plans we come up with. We might as well get going."

He nodded to Pandora, who ordered the ship to take off. It took them four minutes to emerge from the stratosphere, and then they switched to light speeds on their way to the Bastei Wormhole.

"Amazing things, these wormholes," mused Circe aloud. "When you hear the term 'light speed' you think nothing's beyond your reach—and then you realize that even at light speed you can travel for a thousand centuries and still not leave the galaxy. I wonder where we'd be if it weren't for these shortcuts."

"Back in the Spiral Arm and not at war with anybody," offered Ortega.

Circe shook her head. "I don't think so. Men have always found someone to fight with, even if only other Men."

"Sometimes I'd settle for that," said Snake.

"If they find a way to unlock Nmumba's brain and put it to work for them," said Pretorius, "you just may get your wish."

# 5

They were two days into their voyage, and in the space between their chosen wormholes. Pandora still hadn't been able to determine which of Antares's planets Nmumba was on, or even *if* he was on one.

"It's not enough to pinpoint a planet that can support human life," she explained to Pretorius. "Some have military garrisons, some don't. More to the point, they don't have to keep him on an oxygen world. I mean, hell, how many non-oxygen worlds have *you* been on? If they're only supplying him with oxygen and acceptable gravity in the one area they're keeping him, that makes it that much harder for him to escape, or for anyone to rescue him."

"I know," said Pretorius. "But start with the assumption that he's in the Antares system." He frowned. "You wonder how *any* life ever evolved there. The damned star is fifteen or twenty times the size of the sun."

"Antares Three is farther out than Jupiter is from the sun," answered Pandora. "Probably warmer than our tropics, too."

"Whoopie," muttered Snake.

"And you've been monitoring all their transmissions, and there's been no mention of Nmumba?" said Pretorius.

"That's right, Nate," replied Pandora. "But it's only been two days, and he's hardly a threat. They may not mention him until he breaks."

"Or dies," added Ortega.

"Not good enough," said Pretorius. "This isn't like the Michkag mission, where the only important thing was to get him into place totally unnoticed, even if it took an extra month. Nmumba could break any day. We can't waste too much time finding out where they've stashed him." He paused. "We're still in the Neutral Zone, right?"

"That's right."

"Okay. Take us to McPherson's World."

"It's a day out of the way," replied Pandora. "There are no wormholes or other shortcuts."

"It's worth it," replied Pretorius.

She shrugged. "You're the boss."

"What's on McPherson's World?" asked Irish.

"Nate's favorite whorehouse," said Snake with a grin.

"I'm being serious," said Irish, trying to keep her irritation in check.

Snake turned to Ortega. "Tell her, Felix."

Ortega nodded. "It's a whorehouse. The most famous in the whole damned Neutral Zone."

Irish frowned. "You're serious, aren't you?"

"They're serious," Circe chimed in. "It's the only brothel with a reputation that extends beyond the Neutral Zone."

"Kind of a No Man's Land," said Ortega.

"Except that it's more of a No Woman's Land, except for the staff," added Snake with a chuckle.

"We're really diverting to go to a whorehouse?" said Irish.

"Yes," said Pandora. "We'll be there in twenty-one hours, ship's time."

"And he does this a lot, does he?" persisted Irish.

"I'm right here," said Pretorius. "You don't have to pretend I'm not."

"I just . . ." she began, flustered. Then: "Never mind."

"I know you're going to have a difficult time believing it," said Pretorius, "but this may be essential to our mission."

"It was last time," agreed Ortega.

"Clearly I'm missing something," said Irish.

"Tell you what," said Pretorius. "Once we land you can come along with me."

"To a whorehouse?"

"To this particular whorehouse," replied Pretorius.

She shrugged. "What the hell. I've never been to one."

"Welcome to the Space Service," said Snake with a big grin.

Pretorius walked over to the control panel. "Land us just outside McPherson."

"The Tradertown?" asked Pandora.

"Yeah. They don't have a spaceport, unless they've built one in the last few months, so just find a nice empty space and set us down. You can get a readout of the temperature and oxygen content and the rest of it if you want, but it won't make any difference. Place hasn't changed in a few hundred years."

"A few hundred?" said Irish.

"That's right."

"How can you know that?"

Pretorius smiled. "I've been told by an expert."

Everyone else laughed at that, while Irish merely looked more confused. "Is anyone going to tell me what's so special about this place?" she said at last.

"We're heading for a Tradertown that was named for a man named McPherson," answered Pretorius. "In fact, the whole world is named for him, probably by himself. It's been in business for

THE PRISON IN ANTARES

seven or eight hundred years, give or take. No one knows why the hell he landed there. Not much grows, no one's discovered any fissionable materials, lot of dust storms, not much rain, not even much water. There's a rumor that no one's buried in McPherson's grave, that he had enough brains to leave the damned place after just a few years."

"Then why does anyone live there?" she asked.

"Almost no one does, except for the town of McPherson," said Pretorius. "And the residents are just there to serve the town's one major industry—Madam Methuselah's."

Irish frowned. "Madam Methuselah's?" she repeated. "I've heard of it. I always thought it was a legend."

"It's legendary, which isn't quite the same thing," replied Pretorius.

"I don't follow you."

He smiled. "The planet is as close to a hellhole as you can get and still be hospitable to half a dozen starfaring life-forms, including ours. So seven or eight hundred years ago an enterprising young blonde woman decided it might be the perfect place to open a business."

"A whorehouse," said Irish disapprovingly.

Pretorius nodded. "A whorehouse—one that catered to all the species that were able to reach the place. Over the centuries, as the clientele has become even more varied, so has the staff." He paused. "It's become a perfect No Man's Land. I know we talk about various quadrants of the galaxy being No Man's Lands, but a lot of them are totally unpopulated by *any* species. Madam Methuselah's caters to dozens of races, many of them at war with each other, but to the best of my knowledge there has yet to be a single physical altercation since its inception."

"Just so males of all these species can get their jollies?" she said disapprovingly.

"And females, too," said Pretorius. "They're not hampered by custom here."

"All right, females too," said Irish. "I assume we have some other purpose in going there?"

"A lot more gets exchanged there besides currency and bodily fluids," he said with a smile. "With any luck, this little excursion will save us the bother of pinpointing Nmumba's location, and since we've got to reach him before he breaks, it's worth the time."

Irish seemed lost in thought for a long moment. Finally she nodded her head. "Okay," she said. "I'll come along."

"How come you never asked me?" said Snake.

Pretorius chuckled. "I won't have to bail Irish out of the local jail after she picks the pocket of some two-ton creature with a foul temper."

"You hope," said Snake.

Pretorius nodded his head. "I hope." Suddenly he frowned. "You know, I think we're missing a bet here."

"What are you talking about?" said Snake.

"There are bound to be some Altairians at Madam Methuselah's, hopefully from all three inhabited worlds." He turned to Proto. "I want you to come along too. I know you can emulate an Antarean, but I want you to check out their uniforms, their insignia, anything that might have changed since the last time you saw one, anything that'll help you create a believable illusion of a member of any of the three variations of the race."

"All right," agreed Proto. "That makes sense."

"And don't come as a middle-aged man. I don't want anyone

thinking you're a customer. It wouldn't do to have one of them sidle up against you only to find out that what they see isn't there."

"What shall I go as?"

Pretorius looked around the deck. His gaze came to rest on Irish. "Her."

Instantly Proto appeared to be her identical twin.

Pretorius stared at the illusion, then shook his head. "No, you might get hit on. I think we'll be safer if you're an Antarean officer. A general. No Antarean serviceman or even officer is going to chat up a general."

Proto nodded, and before his nod was done he was a general in a dress uniform.

"Okay," said Pretorius. He turned to his crew. "We're as ready as we're going to be. Go on about your duties, grab some sleep before we land, and then let's get this show on the road."

# 6

It wasn't much of a world, eighty percent dirt and the rest dust. Almost all the water was underground, or at least elsewhere. The town consisted of a landing field, a boardinghouse, a message-forwarding station, a spare-parts shop for the more popular types of smaller spaceships, a general store that sold everything from dry goods to medicine to antique weaponry . . . and then there was Madam Methuselah's, which had a fame far out of proportion to both its size and clientele.

"That's it?" asked Irish, pointing to a frame building that was clearly the largest structure in the town, but seemed unexceptional in all other respects.

Pretorius nodded. "Hard to believe its fame has reached the Democracy and half a dozen other sectors, isn't it?"

"Clearly people don't come here for the ambience," said Proto.

"Tell me that in another ten minutes," said Pretorius with an amused smile. "Okay, no sense standing out here in the heat just staring at it. Let's go inside."

They climbed the three wooden stairs to the large veranda. The door sensed their presence and opened automatically, and then they were inside.

"My goodness!" said Irish, looking around. "Who would have guessed it?"

Females of more than a dozen races lounged in the main rooms, and Pretorius assured them that another thirty or forty were busy working at the moment. The walls were covered with exotic and erotic art—paintings, holographs, etchings—from dozens of worlds, and just ahead of them was a huge, elegant bar made of an alien hardwood that constantly fluctuated in color from a brilliant gold to a deep, rich mahogany.

"What's over there?" asked Proto, indicating a narrow passage that three Bodorians were entering.

"Drug dens," answered Pretorius. "They had three of them a couple of trips ago, but I haven't looked in maybe five years, so who the hell knows how many there are now. They don't serve anything too exotic there. Can't have a ten-foot-high Torqual or a two-ton Abegni deciding to tear the place apart."

"Could anything stop them?" asked Irish.

Pretorius nodded. "See those little purple critters?"

"I thought they were someone's pets," she said.

"They're Phorudorians," he said, "and those things that look like humps on their backs are natural weaponry that are every bit as deadly as laser pistols. Most of the clientele doesn't pay them any attention, which gives them an immediate advantage."

"Most interesting security I've seen in years," remarked Proto. "So how big *is* this place?" asked Irish.

Pretorius shrugged. "Maybe fifty rooms, plus anything they've added since we stopped here on the Michkag mission."

"They got a restaurant, too?" asked Proto.

"A small one, just for Men and closely related species," answered Pretorius. "They can serve intoxicants and stimulants to a hundred races, but the kitchen required to feed 'em all would take a building half this big."

"And this place has been here seven centuries?" said Irish.

"Probably longer. They say that Santiago himself visited it in its infancy. That's probably just a myth, but it sure as hell has been patronized by a few hundred dictators and kings, and more than its share of celebrities of all races."

"I'm surprised they cater to both sexes," remarked Proto.

"It's a big galaxy with a lot of tastes," replied Pretorius.

"And it's been in business all this time," said Irish, impressed.

"Right."

"When did Madam Methuselah name it after herself?"

"Right from the beginning, I assume," answered Pretorius.

"You mean the first one?"

He frowned. "The first *what*?"

"The first Madam Methuselah," said Irish.

"There's only been one," said Pretorius.

"Oh, come on!" she said with a smile. "She'd be eight hundred years old!"

"That's right," he replied without returning her smile.

"You're kidding!"

He shook his head. "No, I'm not."

"She must look like a moldering, desiccated corpse."

Pretorius smiled. "You think so?"

"Absolutely."

"See that blonde who just walked over to the bar? The one who's speaking to the Domarian?"

"Yes," answered Irish. "She's truly beautiful."

"Want to meet her?"

She frowned. "Why would I?"

Pretorius smiled in amusement. "That's Madam Methuselah." He enjoyed her surprised reaction for a moment, then signaled to the blonde, who walked over.

"Hi, Nathan," she said. "You're on another job, I presume?"

"Right."

"And that means you don't want to fertilize my frail flowers?"

"Alas, what I want doesn't enter into it," said Pretorius. "Madam, I'd like you to meet Irish, one of my crew."

Madam Methuselah extended her hand, and Irish shook it.

"You must enjoy brutally dangerous assignments, my dear. Our Nate has never accepted an easy one."

"Which reminds me," said Pretorius. "I need to speak to you, preferably not out here."

"My office," she said, nodding. "Bring her along. If you leave her out here, she may wind up working for me."

"Not likely," said Irish.

Madam Methuselah shrugged. "Bring her anyway," she said, and headed off to yet another corridor.

"Proto," said Pretorius, "stick around, and if any Antareans show up, make sure you can reproduce what they're wearing."

"Right," said Proto. "Pick me up here in the bar when you're done."

"It won't be long," answered Pretorius. He took Irish by the hand and led her through the corridor to a room at the end of it. The door sensed them and irised to let them through, and they found themselves in the most luxurious room in the brothel, an office with a solid-gold desk and the most elegant furniture Irish had ever seen. There was a platinum tray on the desk, with three crystal glasses filled with Alphard brandy.

"Take a drink and make yourself comfortable, Nathan," said Madam Methuselah. "You too, my dear."

They did as instructed and sat down facing her.

"All right," she said after a moment. "What seems to be the problem?"

"You don't know?" asked Pretorius. "That *is* surprising."

She frowned. "Of course I know. You want Nmumba. I was just being polite."

"You always are," he replied. Then: "You know where he is?"

She stared at him. "Of course I know."

"Okay," he said. "How much?"

"When have I ever charged you money, Nathan?"

He smiled. "I wasn't referring to money." He paused. "But when have you ever not charged *something*?"

"All right," she said. "If you get him out and return him to the Democracy, I will ask for a favor commensurate with the information I am about to give you. Deal?"

"As long as I don't have to break my oath to the Democracy."

"You won't," she said with a smile. "But you'll wish I'd asked for something that easy."

"Don't I always?" he replied.

"Deal," said Madam Methuselah. "Nmumba's a prisoner in the Antares system."

"The star system itself?" said Pretorius. "Not just the Sector?"

"The system itself."

"Which planet?"

"Give me a second," she said, touching a small diamond-studded bracelet on her left wrist, then stared at a tiny readout only she could see. "Antares Six."

"It's a big world," noted Pretorius.

"They're *all* big worlds in that system," she replied. "Antares itself is bigger than the orbit of Mars. Quite a bit bigger, in fact.

It'll probably go supernova in another couple of hundred thousand years."

"Then I won't worry about it this week," said Pretorius. "I'll need his exact coordinates."

"I'll have them sent to your ship. And have fun. My understanding is that the prison is almost two kilometers below the surface."

"What's the best way to approach it?" he asked.

She smiled. "Not in a Democracy ship, that's for sure."

"Okay," said Pretorius, getting to his feet as Irish followed suit. "That should do it."

"Are you sure you don't want to wait another half hour?" asked Madam Methuselah.

"Is there some reason why we should?"

"I saw your friend out there," she said with a smile. "In case it's slipped your memory, I'm the one who directed you to him the last time you were here, so of course I know where his talents lie. You doubtless want to know what the insignia of an officer from Antares Six looks like. There happens to be one with one of my frail flowers right now. He should be clothed and back in the bar in another twenty to thirty minutes."

"Thanks," said Pretorius. "We'll head back to the ship, but I assume you have no objection to him sticking around until the officer shows up?"

"Not as long as he buys a drink or two."

"I'll tell him on the way out."

He helped Irish to her feet and led her to the door.

"It was very pleasant meeting you, my dear," said Madam Methuselah. "If you ever get tired of the hero trade, I'm sure we can find a place for you here."

"Thank you," said Irish awkwardly, then fell into step behind Pretorius.

"Well," he said as they reached the bar, "what did you think of her?"

"I'm still trying to comprehend her age," admitted Irish.

"There's more to her than longevity," he said. "If there's anything of import going on anywhere in the galaxy and she doesn't know about it, then no one does." He smiled grimly. "That's one of the advantages of having the clientele she's got."

He signaled Proto to join them, told him to keep an eye out for the officer from Antares Six, told him to buy a drink, and ordered him not to imbibe it.

"Nate, I'm less than two feet high. I can't even lift a glass, let alone empty its contents."

"Damn!" said Pretorius. "You look so real I keep forgetting."

"I *am* real. I'm just not a six-foot-tall biped."

"Okay, stick around until the officer shows up, see what he's wearing and what his insignia looks like, and then come back to the ship. Try not to let him get a good look at you."

"Right."

Pretorius and Irish left the building and began walking toward the ship, which was almost a kilometer away.

"Well," he said, "you've had your first contact with the enemy. What do you think of it?"

"Enemy?" she said, frowning. "You mean some of the men we didn't see?"

"I meant Madam Methuselah."

"I thought she was your friend."

"If you live long enough," said Pretorius, "you're going to

learn that nobody except your teammates is your friend. You think Nmumba's captors are the only people she'd sell out? Hell, she'll sell me out just as fast if someone makes an offer."

Irish shook her head in wonderment.

"What is it?" asked Pretorius.

"Now I'm *really* amazed that she's lived eight hundred years. Or eighty." She smiled. "Or eighteen."

He returned her smile. "See? You're learning already."

# 1

**P**roto saw what he needed to see, and when he returned to the ship Pretorius debriefed him and then told the rest about what little had transpired.

"You want to wait for her to contact us?" asked Pandora.

"No," he replied. "She's in contact with people halfway across the galaxy. She won't have any trouble signaling the ship when she's found what we need to know." He paused thoughtfully for a moment. "I expect to hear from her within an hour, but just in case it takes her longer, stay in the Neutral Zone. Why dodge the enemy until we have to?"

"No problem," replied Pandora.

"And as long as we know we're heading to Antares, have your computer find the five closest Earth-type worlds."

"Right."

"Okay," said Pretorius, heading off to the galley. "I'm gonna grab something to eat."

"I'll join you," said Irish.

"Me, too," chimed in Ortega.

The three of them ordered their meals, then waited the requisite two minutes for the ship to manufacture and serve them.

"I don't know," muttered Ortega when he finally received his meal and began eating it. "It doesn't make any difference what I order—beef, pork, fish, eggs. It all tastes like soya products."

"And this surprises you?" said Pretorius.

"No. But it disappoints the hell out of me." He made a face. "Isn't there anything we can do about it?"

"Sure."

"Oh?" said Ortega. "What?"

"Develop a taste for soya products," replied Pretorius.

"Well, it's one way to keep my girlish figure," commented Irish, taking a taste of what passed for pie and pushing it aside.

"That's fine for you," said Ortega. "But I don't *want* a girlish figure."

Pretorius was about to comment when Pandora called to him from the bridge. "Communication from the Madam."

He got up, walked over to the control room, and confronted her holograph that floated just above the control panel. "You've got what we need?"

"Yes," replied Madam Methuselah, frowning. "It's not what I expected."

"He's alive?"

"Yes."

"And he hasn't broken?"

"I assume not," she replied. "At any rate, his imprisonment hasn't changed."

"Okay, where is he and what's unusual about it?"

"They've got a prison two kilometers beneath the surface," she began.

"I know," said Pretorius. "You told us about it."

"That's what's surprising," said Madam Methuselah. "He's not there."

"He's not on Six?"

"Oh, he's on Antares Six, all right," she replied. "But not in the prison."

Now it was Pretorius's turn to frown. "Okay, where is he?"

"In transit."

"Explain."

"Their miners have excavated a network of subterranean

tunnels across half the world," answered Madam Methuselah. "The surface is just too damned hot to work on, even for beings who have evolved and adapted to the place."

"Okay, they have a network of tunnels. So what?"

"Maybe he couldn't take the pressure at two kilometers, maybe there was some other problem down there. But instead, he's on a constantly moving vehicle—a prison car, you might call it—in the tunnels maybe fifty meters beneath the surface."

"And the network of tunnels extends across the whole damned planet?" asked Pretorius.

"Right."

"They've got to have more than one car moving at a time, maybe thousands. How do we spot the one we want?"

"I'm working on that," she replied. "I should have the answer within one Standard day." She paused. "But this is going to cost."

"Another undefined favor?" said Pretorius.

She shook her head. "I'm sorry, Nathan, but it's money this time. I'm going to have to do a little bribery."

"All right," he replied. "If it'll save time, just tell me who to—"

"Forget it," she said. "They'd sooner shoot you than look at you."

"But they'll deal with you?"

"I'm not a partisan," she answered.

"Okay. Let me know when you've got what we need and I'll have the money transferred to any account of your choosing."

The holograph vanished.

"Well?" said Circe. "Is that better or worse?"

"Who the hell knows?" replied Pretorius. "We don't have to fight our way two kilometers deep on a non-oxygen world and then back up. But on the other hand, we may have to hunt up an underground vehicle going God knows how fast and God knows where on that same world." He grimaced. "Maybe we should just kill Wilbur Cooper. He can't be as well protected."

"I'd volunteer," said Snake.

He stared at her. "Why am I not surprised?" He turned back to Pandora. "Well, one way or another we're going to Six. Find out everything you can from the computer—spoken language, written language, any alliance with any human or humanoid species . . . and especially, see if you can get us a map of what I'm going to call the subway system until we get a better term for it."

"Right."

"Proto, let me see a native of Six in uniform."

The alien instantly morphed into the desired species.

"Looks good," said Pretorius. "What rank are you?"

"Damned if I know," answered Proto. "The same as the officer in the bar."

"Let Pandora run your insignia through her computer."

"Right," said Proto, walking over.

Pandora had the machine scan him, then waited a few minutes for it to come up with an answer. "It is almost the equivalent of a captain," she announced at last.

"Almost?"

"They have three levels of officer between their lieutenant and colonel. This one's closest to a captain."

"Okay," he said. "We can't expect Proto to learn the whole damned language, and besides, we don't want him to have to explain away an accent. Find him a couple of simple phrases: Yes, sir; no, sir; right away, sir; things like that."

"Right," agreed Pandora.

"What do the rest of us do?" asked Irish.

Pretorius smiled. "Just be glad I haven't given you any orders yet," he said. "I assure you that's due to change."

"Well, clearly I can't apply my expertise until we rescue Nmumba," she said, "but I'll be happy to do anything that's necessary to effect that rescue."

"And I'll be asking you to," he replied. "But until we know where he is, or where he's likely to be, and how best to get to him without getting him or all of us killed, you might as well just relax."

"And once we hear from Madam Methuselah again, you'll develop a plan of action?"

"One thing you can count on," said Snake in amused tones. "Whenever you ask him what that plan of action is, he'll tell you he's working on it. You'll be lucky to get any details three seconds before the bad guys start shooting at you."

"Oh, come on, Snake," said Circe. "He brought us all back alive. What do you suppose the odds were against that?"

"I didn't say he wasn't lucky," replied Snake. "I said he wasn't talkative."

"If I have a choice," said Irish, "I'll take luck."

"Ship approaching," announced Pandora.

"Registration?" asked Pretorius.

"Nothing we've ever seen before."

"Okay, it's a Neutral Zone. As long as he's not showing his weapons, pay him no attention. He's probably just on his way to McPherson's World."

"That place is a gold mine," said Irish.

Circe smiled. "You're undervaluing it."

Irish considered the remark, then nodded her agreement. "Platinum."

The ship ignored them and proceeded to its obvious destination.

"Don't leave the Neutral Zone until we hear from Madam Methuselah," Pretorius instructed Pandora.

"I know," was her reply.

"And scramble whatever we send her."

"Right."

"In fact," continued Pretorius, "we'll move the money the long way around."

"I don't understand," said Pandora.

"Once we know where she wants it, send the message in code to a space service bank and tell *them* to transfer it. They'll have better protections for something like that than we do."

She nodded her head. "Right. Got it."

Circe walked over to the galley. "I think I'll have some tea."

"I'm dying to see you work," remarked Irish. "I've never seen a living lie detector before."

"I like to think I'm a little more than that," said Circe. "But I do have one thing in common with lie detectors."

"Oh?"

Circe nodded her head. "Yes. If the subject believes what he's saying, I can't detect that he's lying. Remember: I'm an empath, not a telepath."

"And I'm an image-projector, not a shape-changer," added Proto.

Pretorius smiled. "We're a unit of almosts and not-quites."

"Except for you," said Circe to Irish. "You're exactly what you're purported to be."

"She'd damned well better be," Snake chimed in. "I don't want to risk my life bringing Nmumba back if he's already given them what they want."

"On the flip side, you don't want to kill him if he hasn't," said Ortega. He smiled at Irish. "That's what we've got *her* for."

Irish realized just how much depended on her, and suddenly she wasn't hungry anymore.

# 8

"It's taking her longer than I'd have thought," remarked Circe, checking her timepiece.

"Damned planet's ten times the size of Earth," replied Pretorius. "It could take her a couple of days to pinpoint where he is, or what his route is." He paused. "Well, there's no sense just sitting around waiting. She told us something else, too." He turned to Irish. "Remember?"

"That we couldn't approach Antares in a Democracy ship," she replied.

"Right," said Pretorius. "She didn't have to be a genius to figure that out. Hell, we're at war with the Transkei Coalition, and they're part of it. There's no way we can disguise this one, so we might as well go about getting a ship that won't get us blown out of the sky when we approach Antares."

"Just a minute," said Snake. "If Proto is able to appear as an officer from Six, the guy must have had a ship there. Why don't we just steal it?"

"Yeah," Proto chimed in. "I mean, we know he was there."

Pretorius shook his head. "No, we can't cause her any trouble. Get one of her customers killed there—either the officer or just some concerned citizen—and she might never deal with the Democracy again." He paused. "Besides, there are seven of us, eight once we grab Nmumba and make our way back to base. I saw *one* officer from Antares Six, not eight. The likelihood is that his ship wouldn't be able to accommodate us all, even if we could steal it with no repercussions."

"I hadn't thought of that," admitted Proto.

"Maybe that's why Nathan is in charge," said Circe with a smile.

"I suppose we could just enter Coalition space, get as close to Antares as we dare, attract a ship, and kill or capture it," said Pretorius, "but I can think of twenty things that can go wrong, most of them fatal. It's too damned chancy." He turned to Pandora. "Find us a planet or system near the edge of the Neutral Zone where we can reasonably expect to find some Antareans, preferably nonmilitary."

Pandora began issuing orders to her computer, then looked up. "Do the Antareans have to be from Antares Six?" she asked.

"It's preferable. Why?"

"Because it's got a population of a couple of million, while Antares Two has maybe eighty million and Antares Three's got upward of ten billion."

"Okay, I see your point," said Pretorius. He lowered his head in thought for a moment, then looked up. "Hell, they've got to be used to seeing ships from other planets in the same star system. Sure, any ship that's equipped to handle us and comes from any of the Antares planets should do the trick."

"That makes it a little easier," said Pandora, still bent over her computer. A moment later she looked up. "Does it have to have military insignia?"

"I think we're better off without a military ship," replied Pretorius after considering it for a moment. "I'd like the armaments, but there are dozens of Antarean and Coalition protocols we're unaware of, and if we give a wrong answer to a military unit or spaceport we could get blown to bits." He paused, considering their options. "No, the one thing we don't need to do is get into a shooting war with any part of the Coalition fleet, either at Antares or on the way to or from there. See if you can find us a ship, within twenty percent of this size, and I don't know how the hell you can measure fuel consumption with your computer, but I'd like to think that once we leave Antares we won't have to renew the nuclear pile or whatever the hell it's using until we get back to the Democracy."

"All right, I'll see what I can do," said Pandora.

"And while I'm thinking of it, try and find a ship with a computer that can do pretty much what yours can do. What's the point of having the best hacker in the Democracy if all she's got is the equivalent of an adding machine and map reader?"

"Nate, there's just so much I can scrutinize before they know they're *being* scrutinized, and that blows the whole operation."

"Okay, okay," said Pretorius. "Why am I telling *you* what to do? Just let me know when you've found us a vessel."

"Hopefully without too many soldiers guarding it," added Ortega.

They sat around making small talk for a few minutes while Pandora kept issuing orders to the ship's computer. Finally she turned and faced the rest of them.

"Okay, I've found what we need," she announced.

"What have you got?" asked Pretorius.

"Miga, the third planet in the Brynne system."

"Where is it?"

"About six light-years this side of the Coalition's border," said Pandora. "But it's very near the Trodok Wormhole—at least, I think that's how it's pronounced—that'll get us more than halfway to Antares."

"And what makes this world the one we want?"

"First off, it's an oxygen world, pretty much the same content as Antares Six, a little thin, but breathable. It's a farming world, and a reasonably productive one, so there's a constant flow of ships in and out of it. Right now there are two ships from the Antares system, one from Two and one from Six, each about the right size, one on the ground, one docked at an orbiting hangar. There's quite an active Tradertown where the one on the ground is, maybe five hotels and guesthouses, a few bars, the usual."

"Sounds good," said Pretorius. "How soon can we get there?"

"If the damned Billermein Wormhole will just stop moving for another few hours, I can have us there in seven Standard hours," answered Pandora.

"Put us in gear and let's get moving," he said.

"Hell," added Ortega, "even if the two Antarean ships are gone, they figure to have more shortly."

"They'd better *not* be gone," said Pretorius.

Ortega looked at him questioningly.

"Don't forget," said Pretorius. "We don't know what they're doing to Nmumba, or how much longer he can hold out."

"If he hasn't broken," added Snake.

"If he hasn't broken," agreed Pretorius.

# 9

hen they were still two light-years away, they were able to bring up an image of Miga, a nondescript little world, the third of five planets circling the G-type yellow star of Brynne. It had a single mountain range, a freshwater ocean, a few major rivers and a number of minor ones. It possessed a Trader-town with a population of about ten thousand, and half a dozen even smaller villages—headquarters for the farming communities, actually—and not much else. There was no gold beneath its surface, no fissionable materials, no diamonds, and not enough silver to bother with.

Because it was in the Neutral Zone it was populated primarily by Men or their mutated descendants, plus a few other races, none of them members of the Democracy or the Transkei Coalition.

"So what do you think?" said Ortega, staring at the readout that Pandora had transferred to a screen for all of them to see.

"Looks like a world," replied Pretorius. "Nothing special to its name that I can tell."

"Then this is the place we want?" asked Pandora.

"Yeah, we're almost certainly not going to find anything more to our liking, especially this close to the Coalition." Pretorius stared at the figures. "Total planetary population, 17,273. And they draw a couple of ships a week?"

"At least," said Pandora.

"Must have a shitload of robots and machinery to produce that much," he said. "What are their major exports?"

"Mutated grains that are geared to the Antarean Three and Six digestive systems," she replied.

"Okay," said Pretorius. "Start checking out the ships. Are they all Antarean, or are there some others from within the Coalition? And are the ones that are clearly Antarean all military?"

"And if not," added Snake, "are they accompanied by the military?"

"I'm checking," said Pandora.

"If you can access their records for the spaceport and the hangar, go back a month and see every kind of ship that's gone there, transacted some business, and then gone back into the Coalition. I'd like to see if we can confiscate something other than a small military vessel. If we have to establish visual contact with anyone, Proto will look like . . . well, like Proto in his natural state, and the rest of us are clearly Men."

"Give me a couple of minutes to check."

"I have a question," said Irish.

"Shoot," said Pretorius. Suddenly he smiled. "You should pardon the expression."

"Does it make much difference what kind of ship we steal?" she asked. "I mean, military or commercial?"

"You ask that as if they're all sitting in a line waiting for us to appropriate one of them," responded Pretorius. "We'll take what we can get, and improvise from there. There are advantages and disadvantages to both."

"Since I've never been on a mission before, may I ask what they are?"

"If we swipe a military ship, we'll almost certainly have to kill the captain and crew to stop them from reporting it," said Pretorius. "Also, we're likely to be hassled a lot less in space. Once we touch down on Antares Six, or even approach it, we're going to have to come up with a reason why our video communications system isn't working, because if they get a look at us in control of an Antarean military vessel, it'll take 'em about three seconds to give the order to open fire on us."

"Then clearly we want a commercial ship," said Irish.

"Not necessarily," replied Pretorius. "If it's a commercial ship, we're likely to be stopped and boarded by any military vessel that finds us suspicious, or is just out to impress its superiors, or just wants to grab some grain or whatever the hell they think we're carrying."

"Not a plethora of happy choices," commented Circe.

"If there were, they'd have given the job to someone else," said Pretorius.

"And those are our only choices?" persisted Irish.

"No," he said. "We can try approaching in this ship."

"Don't be silly," said Snake. "They'll shoot the second they spot us."

"Not if we're offering to surrender."

"To *what?*" she demanded.

"If I think there's a chance we'll be incarcerated where they've got Nmumba stashed, it's an option I at least have to consider."

"So assuming they don't kill any of us on the way to the prison, you think eight of us, including Nmumba, can break out of jail where he couldn't alone?"

"I didn't say it would be easy, or even possible," replied Pretorius. "I said it's an option, and it's my duty to consider all our options."

"Good," said Snake. "Let's consider sitting out the war on Calliope or some other pleasure planet and let the Democracy develop another Nmumba. I mean, hell, if he can neutralize a Q bomb and we've got close to a trillion citizens, let them find someone else who can."

"I'll take it under consideration," he said with an amused smile.

"Got it!" said Pandora, staring at her computer.

"And?" replied Pretorius.

"There are two cargo vessels in orbit, another parked in the orbiting hangar. One military ship at the local spaceport, but I don't think we can fit more than three of us into it, four tops . . . and even given that Proto's true shape takes up almost no space, there are still six of us."

"Any other ships approaching it?"

"Not at the moment," answered Pandora, "at least not that I can spot."

"Can you hack into their spaceport's computer without being spotted, and see if any other military ships are expected?" asked Pretorius.

She shook her head. "I don't think so."

"What does that mean?"

"Just that it's a more sophisticated machine than you'd expect for such a little world," replied Pandora. "I'm not saying that it's military. I mean, hell, it's in the Neutral Zone, so why would either side's military give it such a complex and expensive machine? I'm just saying that I don't think it's worth taking a chance."

"You're the computer expert," said Pretorius. "I'm sure as hell not going to argue with you."

"Then do we proceed?"

He paused in thought for a moment. "The military ship's too small to be transporting anything but its crew, and maybe some knick-knacks they pick up in town, right?"

She nodded. "Whatever a knick-knack is."

"So they have no overt reason to stick around. Maybe they're refueling, more likely they're grabbing drinks or a meal."

She looked at him expectantly.

"I know time is of the essence, but so is surviving. We'll stay where we are for another six hours, hope they've gone, and proceed to Miga. If they're still there, we'll try to blow them apart before they know what hit them, and then we'll have to pacify the locals while we steal a ship." He paused. "I don't know about the rest of you, but I'll be much happier if they've left before we show up." He leaned back on his chair. "Wake me in five hours."

# 10

"**S**o what have we got?" asked Pretorius as the image of Miga filled the viewscreen.

"The military vessel's gone, and there's only one ship worth stealing," answered Pandora, checking her computer. "It's a large, powerful vessel of Antares Six registry. Definitely not military."

"Good," said Pretorius. "We don't need to take on a large warship. How much crew does it hold?"

She shrugged. "It's large, but it's clearly not a passenger ship. I'd say it holds ten, possibly a dozen."

"And it's in the Tradertown's spaceport?"

"Right," replied Pandora. "As near as I can tell, they stopped off for some r-and-r. There's nothing in the town that requires a ship with that kind of power."

"Okay," he said. "That sounds like what we're after. Take us down. Once we've got it we can equip it with our weaponry and your computer, and it won't alert or scare any Antarean navy ships. Take us down, and park us as near our target as possible." He looked around the deck. "Felix, Proto, Circe, you're coming with me." He paused, then shrugged. "You too, Irish. Maybe you can learn something from one of these bastards that'll help you when we get our hands on Nmumba."

"What about me?" demanded Snake.

He shook his head. "You stay with the ship."

"Why?"

"You want a valid reason or the real one?" asked Pretorius.

"Both."

"The valid one is that if we have any problems and they figure out which ship is ours, your job is to protect it and Pandora long enough for her to take off, get into orbit, and await orders."

"Yeah, that's valid," agreed Snake. "Bullshit, but valid." She glared at him. "Now what's the real reason?"

"Same as always," he replied. "You're the best thief I ever saw as well as the best escape artist, but you simply can't keep your hands in your pockets, and I don't need the added hassle of protecting you when they catch you robbing the till."

"What makes you think they'll catch me?" she demanded without bothering to deny his basic assumption.

"You don't know what kind of security they have, or what kind of sensory perception some of the races there will have," answered Pretorius, "and even if you swipe some cash, this is a Tradertown, not a city. If they find some money's missing, they'll shoot you as you run to the ship."

"Not if I don't run in a straight line," she replied. "And we could use some local currency."

He looked amused. "The only currency we'll be able to use will be Antarean. Do you plan to rob the guys whose ship we're stealing?"

"Why not?" said Snake.

"I've got one hundred credits that says she can pull it off," said Ortega.

"Oh, shut up, Felix!" said Pretorius irritably.

"You really don't think I can do it?" demanded Snake.

"Probably you can," he acknowledged. "But I'm not interested in probablies, and I'm not willing to bet five lives on it. You're staying on the ship, and that's an order."

"Okay," she said. "But you're a fool."

"I've been called worse," he replied. "Okay, Pandora, let them know we want to land, get whatever coordinates and permissions you need, and take us down."

"Excuse me," said Irish as the ship touched down, "but I have a question, doubtless based on my inexperience."

"Ask," said Pretorius.

"You mentioned Snake robbing the Antareans," she said. "That implies that we're going into the town, since your reasons would be invalid if we were gaining access to their ship immediately after we land."

"Right," he said.

"That's my question," she said. "If we want their ship, why are we going into town?"

"We don't want any survivors contacting the Antarean military and warning them to be looking for a ship of this description and registry," answered Pretorius.

She frowned. "So you're not hunting them up to question them or evaluate their strength?"

He shook his head. "We'll question them if we can, but the end result's going to be the same." She seemed about to say something, but he held a hand up to silence her. "We're at war, remember? And they've got a prisoner who can save literally billions of lives if we can get to him before they break him."

"I'm sorry," she said awkwardly.

"Don't be. You're new to this, and asking questions is how you learn."

"Okay," announced Pandora. "We're cleared to land and are about to begin our approach. They've given us a spot about six ships away from the one we're after."

Pretorius frowned. "That makes it a little more difficult, but what the hell."

"I don't follow you," said Circe.

"I was thinking if we could land right next to the ship we could transfer most of the armaments and the computer without being spotted, but we can't be seen doing that much walking back and forth from half a dozen ships away. We'll keep our ship and transfer everything in deep space or on a totally empty planet once we take control of the Antarean ship."

"How many of them are in the town and how many are still on the ship?" asked Ortega.

"How many are in the town is just guesswork," answered Pretorius. "We don't know how many the ship is carrying. But Pandora can tell us how many are still onboard."

"In a minute," she said. "I'm still making course adjustments." After another thirty seconds or so, she began manipulating the computer again. "There are three living entities onboard."

"Three Antareans, right," said Pretorius.

She shook her head. "Two Antareans."

"What's the third thing?"

"I can't tell from the readings," she replied. "It could be anything from a prisoner to a pet to a non-Antarean passenger."

"Big? Little?"

She studied her computer. "Maybe eighty pounds."

Pretorius turned to Ortega. "So if we only see the two Antareans when we board it, keep an eye out for something with teeth or pincers that may be lurking in a bulkhead." He turned to Irish. "That goes for everyone. I'm telling Felix, because with his physical equipment, real and artificial, he'll be first in line when we board it."

"Okay, we're through the stratosphere, entering the atmosphere, and should touch down in three minutes," announced Pandora.

"Proto, time to become an officer," said Pretorius. "Make him a native of Antares Two."

"Why Two?" asked Irish as Proto's image changed.

"Because he doesn't speak a word of Antarean," answered Pretorius. "Hopefully they have different dialects on different worlds. And since our prey isn't military, maybe they'll leave him alone if he's an officer and projects a nice, haughty air."

"Makes sense," she said, nodding her head. "I'm learning."

They fell silent then, watching the planet growing huge on the viewscreen, which then adjusted and began homing in on the Tradertown. In another minute the buildings and streets were visible, as was the spaceport, and shortly thereafter they touched down.

"All right," said Pretorius, walking over to the hatch. "I have no idea how long we'll be, but don't contact us. I'll contact you if we need anything." He turned to Snake. "Grab a weapon and kill any Antarean that tries to enter the ship."

"What about something other than an Antarean?"

"Keep him or them covered, have Pandora disarm them, and wait for me to get back."

"Always assuming you live long enough to come back," said Snake.

"Always assuming," said Pretorius, climbing down the stairs to the ground. He waited for his four companions to join him, and then began walking into the town.

"Shit!" muttered Ortega. "It's all bars and restaurants. We're gonna look mighty suspicious looking into every one of them."

"We won't have to," said Pretorius. He activated his communicator. "Pandora?"

"Yes?"

"That's the only Antares Six ship in the port, right?"

"Right," she answered.

"Okay," he said. "Have the computer locate the ones that aren't on the ship."

"Working on it."

After a minute he spoke again. "It's taking a while."

"Their physiology is very similar to natives of Antares Two and Three," she replied. "I don't want to send you into the wrong den of iniquity." There was a brief pause. "Okay, got 'em. They're in . . . damn, I can't translate or decipher the name. Walk to the first cross street. I'll keep the channel open."

Pretorius and his crew followed her instructions.

"Now look to your left," she continued. "Do you see a building, on the far side of the street, maybe thirty meters from you?"

"Yes."

"Has it got a door wide enough to accommodate you and Felix entering side by side?"

"Right."

"Okay, that's the spot."

"Thanks. Over and out." Pretorius put his device back into a pocket. "You heard her," he said. "That's the joint."

"How do you want to handle this?" asked Ortega.

"We'll kill them," said Pretorius, "but I'd much prefer not do it in front of the population if we don't have to. No sense alerting the locals, or having one of them contact the ship we want."

"Then why are we here at all?"

"There's a difference between killing them and neutralizing them," answered Pretorius. He turned and stared at Proto. "Damn, you look real! I wish to hell you could speak their lingo." He continued staring, his brow furrowed. "Well, we might as well *try* to do it without killing them all. Proto, lose your lower jaw." The jaw vanished. "No, not totally. As if you'd been shot there. Not recently. An old war wound. It blew away part of your jaw and crushed the rest, so no one can reasonably expect you to speak clearly."

"Then why am I still in uniform?" asked Proto as he made the adjustments Pretorius had asked for.

"Maybe you're a scientist or an engineer. It doesn't matter. They can't question you, because you can't answer them." He began walking to the side of the building. "This place got a back entrance?"

"It must have," said Circe.

"Okay. Felix, go around back and wait there. When they finally come out, put them all out of commission, swiftly and silently."

"Right," said Ortega, heading off.

Pretorius turned to Proto. "I'm going in with Circe and Irish first. It wouldn't do for us to be seen as your companions, even in the Neutral Zone." Proto nodded his head in agreement. "I still don't know if it's a bar or a restaurant, not that it really matters. Give us a minute to get settled at a table, then come in, hunt up our Antareans, act distressed, and signal them to follow you out the back door, as if there's something there you want them to see."

"I have a thought," said Proto. "Won't it work better if I enter from the back, as if I've just seen whatever it is I want them to see?"

"I *like* that!" said Pretorius. "Much better idea. Felix will know it's you because of the uniform. If there's any doubt, talk to him in Terran. He knows the sound of your voice."

"Right," said Proto, heading off.

"And give us a minute or two to get settled."

"Why, if you're not coming out back with or after them?" asked Proto.

"Because I want Circe there when you try to get them to follow you," answered Pretorius. "If there's any chance that they're not buying it, or that they see through your disguise, that something's not right physically, she'll know and wave you off."

"I hadn't thought of that," admitted Proto. "Okay, I'll take a few minutes."

He began walking around the building, while Pretorius and the two women entered what turned out to be a tavern, populated by half a dozen races, half of them of human stock, the rest more reptilian—and sitting at a table in the corner were five Antareans.

"How close do you have to be?" asked Pretorius in low tones.

"Anywhere in the room will do," answered Circe.

He led them to a table, and they all sat down. The Antareans shot them some hostile glances, but otherwise ignored them. Then, after perhaps two minutes, Proto, appearing distraught in his Antarean guise, entered the tavern from behind the bar, and walked swiftly to the middle of the room, looked around until his gaze fell on the Antareans, walked over, and began gesticulating.

They simply stared at him for a moment. It was clear they didn't understand what he wanted, and clear that he couldn't speak with part of his jaw misshapen and the rest of it missing. Pretorius kept waiting for him to slam a fist into the table and find some way to demand they follow him, then remembered that his entire body beyond the lowest eighteen inches was an illusion and he *couldn't* slam his fist into anything.

"Are they buying it?" whispered Pretorius to Circe.

"Yes," she replied. "They're confused, but I assume that's because they don't know quite what he wants. None of them doubts that he's an Antarean officer, or that he's truly unable to speak."

Finally Proto took a few steps to the back door, turned, gestured for them to follow him, and repeated the procedure three times until they finally rose from their chairs and did indeed follow him out the back door.

"Well, that's that," said Pretorius. "Let's give Felix a couple of minutes, and then we'll go out and meet them."

"I'm surprised we haven't heard a sound yet," said Irish.

"Felix is a walking armory," said Circe. "He's not only as strong as four or five men put together, but all those mechanical parts double as weapons."

"He's a good man," said Pretorius. "Not the brightest member of the team, God knows, but absolutely fearless, and loyal to a fault—along with being a killing machine *par excellence*." He got to his feet. "We might as well go. If he hasn't disabled or killed them by now we're in real trouble."

The three of them paid for their unfinished drinks, walked out the front door, waited a moment to make sure no one else was leaving, then walked around to the back of the building, where they found Ortega and Proto standing over the five Antareans.

"Dead?" asked Pretorius.

Ortega nodded. "No trouble, Nate. Two of 'em had weapons in their hands as they walked out the door, but I took care of that."

Pretorius looked around. "There's a small storage shed over there. Let's move the bodies before someone trips over them."

Ortega carried three at once, then came back for the other two.

THE PRISON IN ANTARES

"I'd help you," said Pretorius, "but I'd probably end up dragging him, and why leave tracks?"

"I doubt that Irish or I could even budge one," said Circe.

"Not a problem," said Ortega. "That's what you've got me for."

"All right," said Pretorius. "There's two more on the ship. It'd be stupid to leave any other witnesses. Let's take care of them and get the hell out of here."

Five minutes later they came to the Antarean ship, and Pretorius contacted Pandora.

"They still there?" he asked.

"Two Antareans and a *something*," she confirmed.

"Okay. Talk to you in a few minutes." He turned to Ortega. "No change. Go in first and—"

"Kill them," said Ortega.

"No sense taking chances," agreed Pretorius. "And if they ever catch us, they won't hang us any higher for killing seven than killing five."

Ortega climbed the stairs to the hatch and entered the ship. Within twenty seconds he called back that both Antareans were dead.

"Okay," said Pretorius. He turned to Circe, Proto, and Irish. "Follow me, and remember, there's still something alive in there. A pet, an alien of a different race, *some*thing."

The four of them entered the ship, which was minimally more spacious than their own vessel, and began looking around the bridge.

"Can you sense where the other one is?" Pretorius asked Circe.

She shook her head. "Not yet, Nathan."

"Not much weaponry," noted Pretorius. "I wonder if the computer is worth a damn?"

"Beats me," said Ortega.

Circe frowned and leaned against a bulkhead.

"Are you all right?" asked Irish.

"Just a little dizzy spell, I think," she replied.

"You want to sit down?" asked Pretorius.

"No," said Circe, still frowning. "Maybe a drink of water." Then: "The Antareans *do* drink water, don't they?"

"Yeah, they do."

"Then one of these cabins much have at least a sink," she said, reaching for a door handle. "I'll just get a sip and I'll be just—"

As Circe opened the door there was a hideous growl and something dark and scaly hurled itself at her, jaws spread apart, needle-sharp teeth closing on her throat, ripping through the flesh. She screamed and fell backward, blood spurting straight up, as the creature raked her shoulders and torso with razor-sharp claws. She uttered one more gurgling scream and shuddered convulsively, as Ortega pulled the creature from her and pulverized it with a single blow atop its head.

Pretorius and Irish knelt down next to Circe, looking for some sign of life. Finally Irish shook her head.

"She's gone," she said.

"Damn, that was fast!" muttered Ortega.

Pretorius kept searching for a heartbeat, but couldn't find one. Finally he looked up at Ortega.

"I'm not going to bury her on an alien planet," he said. "Find something to wrap her in. We'll jettison her into space after we're out of this system and before we enter Coalition territory."

Ortega nodded his head, and Pretorius contacted Pandora to tell her what had transpired.

"So much for never losing a team member," remarked Snake in the background.

# 11

"**W**hat the hell happened?" asked Pandora as Pretorius and his party returned to the ship.

"Watchdog, watchcat, watch-*something*," muttered Ortega.

"She was uneasy, but she couldn't spot it," added Pretorius.

"But if she was an empath, surely she could sense that something wanted to kill her," persisted Pandora.

"I don't know," said Pretorius. "Maybe it was so alien she couldn't read it. Maybe it felt eager or happy to attack someone." He shrugged. "These things happen."

"You don't sound all that upset by it," said Snake.

"Of course I'm upset," replied Pretorius. "We *needed* her. You know that from the Michkag operation. It's not as if human empaths grow on trees."

"You're upset that we no longer have an empath," persisted Snake, "not that a friend has died."

"*Shut up!*" snapped Pretorius. "Of course she was a friend. This is war, goddammit, and people take risks in war, and sometimes those risks don't work out."

Nobody spoke for a long moment. Finally Pandora spoke up.

"What now?" she asked.

"Now we find a meeting place in space, well beyond this solar system, and I go back to the Antarean ship."

"Can you work the controls?"

He merely stared at her.

"All right," she said uncomfortably. "Sorry I asked."

"I'm going over there now," he announced. "Once I'm at the controls I'll establish radio contact with you, we'll hit upon a meeting place, and we'll get the hell off this dirtball." He looked around the deck, then pointed to Irish. "You'll come with me."

"Right now?" she asked.

"Right now. We'll transfer your gear when we transfer everything else."

Pretorius stood by the hatch, waited for her to climb down to the surface, then followed her.

"I don't know anything about flying a ship as big as our own, let alone one with alien controls," said Irish as they walked to the Antarean ship.

"I know."

"Then why—?"

"You don't want to be there when they talk mutiny," said Pretorius.

Her eyes widened. *"Mutiny?"*

"Nothing will come of it," he said. "Snake's the loudest of them, but they probably all have to vent, and it's better that they do it in private."

"I don't understand," she said.

"My reputation—I didn't ask for it, and I never believed in it— is that I never lose anyone on one of these missions. It's bullshit, of course. I've lost my share of subordinates. But they seem to have convinced themselves that if we could all live through the Michkag caper nothing could kill any of us, and now they're coming face-to-face with the fact that we're not immortal and we're preparing to pull off a jailbreak in an alien military prison."

"I see," she said softly.

He sighed. "I know: You can't have considered that you might die on this mission either. Well, if we're smart enough and careful enough, you'll live to tell about it." Suddenly he smiled. "Except that it'll almost certainly be classified, and they'll lock you away for a long time if you *do* tell about it."

They arrived at the Antarean ship, boarded it, and Pretorius seated himself at the control panel.

"I've seen worse," he said, quickly figuring out how to power up the ship and open radio contact with Pandora.

"Everything working?" she asked, her holograph appearing right in front of him.

"No problem," he said. "Pick a spot, maybe two light-years out, and feed the coordinates to this ship. Then wait for me to take off—I assume the ship's in working order and that I won't have any trouble, but if I'm wrong I don't want you millions of miles ahead of me—so once this vessel's away, give us five minutes and then follow us."

"Right," she said. "Give me just half a minute here." She looked down at her computer, which was not part of the holo image. "Okay," she said a few seconds later. "Your ship knows where it's going now. Take off whenever you want."

"Now's as good a time as any," he replied. "Over and out."

He uttered some orders to the ship, cursed when he realized it didn't respond to Terran, entered his destination on the alien control panel, and then felt the surge as the ship took off.

"You doing okay?" he asked Irish.

"Yes," she said. "They wouldn't really mutiny, would they?"

"No, of course not," he said. "They just want to bitch and grieve, and since I'm the object of one and the cause of the other, it's best to give them a little time to get it out of their systems. We've got to be a well-coordinated unit when we finally go into action."

She smiled ruefully. "It feels like we've already been in action."

He returned her smile. "Spoken like someone who's spent her professional life in a lab."

"Which I have. Well, a lab and a hospital."

"I just hope you have to prove how good you are," said Pretorius. She frowned. "You do?"

He nodded. "It'll mean he's still alive, and hasn't overtly joined the enemy."

"I must seem terribly green to you," said Irish.

"We'll put some other color on you before we're done," he replied.

In a few minutes they had reached their rendezvous point, and in another three hours they had transferred their computers and the bulk of their weaponry to the Antarean ship.

"I hope it'll all work," said Pandora when they were done.

"It's already working," replied Pretorius.

"Different power sources. I just hope it doesn't damage the computer."

"Or the guns," added Snake.

"Well, we'll find out," said Pretorius.

"You don't seem very worried," noted Ortega.

"Would worrying help?" asked Pretorius.

"Probably not, but I do it all the time anyway."

"So we're all here and all tied in to the power," said Pandora. "What do we do now?"

"The first thing we need is a map of the subway, or whatever we're calling it," replied Pretorius. "It's a big planet. We can't just hope he shows up on our instruments."

"There must be dozens of maps on Three," said Pandora. "Maybe I can find a way to tie into one."

"There's also thousands of defense weapons on Three," said Pretorius. "I know we're in an Antarean ship, but that doesn't mean we can't be scanned and boarded, especially if we can't show that we're there for a purpose."

"So we go to Six?" said Pandora.

"We go to Six," he confirmed.

"And then what?"

"That depends on what we find there," answered Pretorius. "We need to locate, not a subway station, at least not one that's just for boarding and exiting the vehicles, but something that controls them—controls their power, their routes, their destinations, whatever."

"How do we do that?" asked Ortega. "I mean, for all we know, there's no public transportation at all. The whole system might be military."

"If it is, that will be to our advantage," said Irish, and all heads turned to her.

"Would you care to explain?" said Pandora.

"If it's public transport, the system will go anywhere that the inhabitants live," she said. "But if it's entirely military, it will have far fewer routes and destinations. More dangerous, to be sure, but fewer."

"Makes sense," admitted Ortega.

"Yes, it does," agreed Pretorius. "But it's totally hypothetical. We have to learn what the hell this system does, who and what it transports and to where."

"So we still need a map," said Snake.

He nodded his head. "We still need a map."

"So where do we get one?"

"We head to the Antares system, hope nobody challenges what is obviously a ship that's at least of Antarean origin if not ownership, and when we can determine where the hell a map might be, either Pandora finds a way to transfer a copy to our ship's computer, or we send our best thief in after it."

"Thanks a heap," said Snake grimly.

"It'll be on a computer," said Pandora. "Sooner or later everything is, and sooner or later every computer's security can be breached."

"That's fine in theory," said Pretorius. "But all we've got is sooner, not later. Every day we don't locate and grab Nmumba is another day they have to break him."

"We won't know until we find the right computer," said Pandora.

"*If* we can find it," he corrected her.

They reached the Antares system two days later—and they found the right computer an hour after that.

# 12

"**G**ot it!" announced Pandora.

"Good!" said Pretorius. "Where is he?"

She smiled and shook her head. "I've got the map, Nate. The tunnels, as it were. Now I have to find out where all the vehicles are, and finally which one is holding Nmumba."

"And then get him out," added Proto.

"Oh, I think we ought to let Nate do *something* or he'll feel useless," said Snake, and none of them could tell if that was her idea of humor or if she was still bitter over the loss of Circe.

"Well, start with the basics," said Pretorius. "Fueling stations. Any entrances and exits on the surface. If these things traverse the whole planet—yeah, I know, we don't know the directions or durations of their routes—but *if* they do, they're going to have to stop for more than fuel. Food, for instance. Maybe even for air." He sighed deeply. "Find out what you can—and while you're at it, see where the biggest military base is, on or beneath the surface."

"Just the biggest?" asked Pandora. "They may have a dozen or more."

"Just the biggest. Nmumba could make the difference between either side winning or losing this damned war. They're not going to give him to the second string." He paused, frowning. "But they may try to disguise that. Once you find the base, see what other bases they're in contact with, and which vehicles as well."

"I'll do my best," replied Pandora. "But this could take more time than you think, or than we have."

"If you can think of a shortcut, or can find something Irish or Snake can do on one of the other computer terminals, be my guest," said Pretorius. "You can't use Felix. He could think he was tapping in a code or an order and break the machine with those metal muscles of his."

"What about Proto?"

Pretorius smiled and shook his head. "What you see isn't what you get." He nodded to the alien, who immediately stopped projecting the image of a middle-aged man and became the very real cushion-like being that he was.

"Sorry," said Pandora. "I'm so used to seeing him . . ."

"I know. We all forget." He stood up and walked over to the galley. "Okay, do what you can. In the meantime I'm going to see if I can convince this alien kitchen to make some coffee or the equivalent."

"I'll join you," said Snake, walking after him.

It took Pretorius three wasted cups of various liquids to conclude that the Antareans had no interest in coffee or anything remotely like it, so he simply ordered what passed for a pastry and sat down. Snake sat down opposite him.

"I thought you were hungry," he said.

She shook her head. "No."

"All right. What is it?"

"I've been thinking about it . . ." she began.

"Oh?" he said, wondering where this was leading.

"Yeah," replied Snake. "And I've decided to forgive you."

Pretorius frowned. "For what?"

"Circe."

"I don't need your forgiveness," said Pretorius harshly. "It wasn't my fault, and if you were using what passes for your brain, you'd know it."

"You don't understand," she said.

"Enlighten me."

"Why do you think we all agreed to this mission?"

"You were conscripted and had no choice," he replied.

"You think I had to stick around after the Michkag caper? You think Pandora couldn't have rigged orders transferring her to some other world? We stuck around, and agreed to come on this mission, because if you could bring us all back from the last one alive, given the odds we faced, we figured you could do it again."

"Everything went like clockwork on the Michkag mission," replied Pretorius. "Do you know how rare that is?"

"Yes," said Snake. "But we know how rare *you* are, and we trusted you to bring us all back again."

"I appreciate the trust, but not the intelligence behind it," he answered.

"Anyway, I forgive you. Probably we all do." Suddenly a rueful smile crossed her face. "Except maybe Circe."

"I didn't think you even liked her."

"I didn't especially," admitted Snake. "Hell, I don't like anyone, not even you. But I like the thought of coming back alive."

"Well, hang onto that thought, because this one looks every bit as dangerous as the last one, and we already know it's not going as smoothly."

She seemed about to comment, thought better of it, and got up from the table without another word. A moment later she and Irish were standing by the computer while Pandora gave them instructions for tracking the tunnels.

Ortega walked into the galley a few minutes later, figured out what commands were required for some well-cooked meat, and sat down.

"Once we land, we got to program this thing for beer," he said.

"And coffee," added Pretorius.

"Damn, I miss *our* galley."

"This one's safer."

"Safer?" repeated Ortega. "It can't even cook human food."

"Yeah," agreed Pretorius. "But we can orbit Antares Six in it without getting blown out of the sky."

"Well, there is that," admitted Ortega. He took a mouthful, chewed vigorously, made a face, and swallowed. "So what are we gonna do when we pinpoint Nmumba?"

"Rescue him, hopefully. Or possibly kill him."

"I mean, how do we plan to go about it?"

"It all depends on what Pandora finds and what we can improvise from that."

"Do we snatch him while he's on the car or derail it—always assuming it runs on rails—or what?"

"Damned if I know," said Pretorius. "Like I say, it depends on what we learn. Also, it's at least remotely possible that he's not even in the tunnels anymore. Someone had to see our ship back on Miga. If they contacted the military on any of the three inhabited Antares planets, they may already have removed him. I'm sure the entire network wasn't built just to keep anyone from snatching Nmumba, so it'll probably keep in motion without a hiccup or a glitch, and we won't know until we board the damned thing, whether in motion or derailed, always assuming it has rails, and indeed there's no reason to assume so." He paused. "I know time is of the essence, but we just don't know enough yet, and the dumbest thing you can do in enemy territory is just plunge in hell for leather without knowing exactly what you're doing and what lies in wait."

Ortega sighed deeply. "You're right, of course." A self-deprecating smile crossed his face. "If I'd been in charge of the Michkag mission, I think I'd have got us all killed."

"I think I've got something here," announced Pandora over the intercom.

"Wonderful," muttered Pretorius. "I may get us all killed yet." He got up, left the galley, and walked over to where Pandora was sitting at the control panel.

"I've got the network pretty mapped out," she said, staring at a screen that had nothing but incomprehensible symbols on it. "There are no tracks, no metal that we can follow as it winds around the planet a quarter-mile deep, but because they dug it out of solid rock, the sensors are able to pick up differences between the tunnels, which have some atmosphere, and the surrounding rock."

"Just looks like gobbledygook to me," commented Pretorius.

"I'll have a map up in another minute or so," answered Pandora. "If I did it now, before the sensors completed the survey, it would look like the vehicles were running into walls." She hunched over the machine, her fingers moving swiftly, her commands sounding more like alien exclamations. Finally she looked up. "Okay, I told it to create a map that we can read, and to put it on the viewscreen."

And as she said the words, a map of a large section of the planet appeared, crisscrossed and honeycombed with literally hundreds of tunnels. She uttered one more command, and the planet began turning on its axis so they could see and follow the tunnels all the way around it.

"Very good," said Pretorius.

"That was the easy part," answered Pandora.

"Oh?"

She nodded. "You want the hard part?"

"Might as well."

She uttered two more commands, and suddenly tiny figures were streaking through the tunnels.

"One hundred and thirty-seven different vehicles moving all the hell over the planet," she said. "The trick is to figure out which one Nmumba is on, because it stands to reason that we're only going to get one crack at him."

The computer beeped, and she looked down at the symbols.

"Make that one hundred and forty-one," she said.

# 13

They'd spent almost two hours tracing the routes of the vehicles, which Pretorius persisted in thinking of as trains, without much success. They eliminated twenty-three vehicles where Pandora's computer couldn't find any trace of anything alive, and six more that clearly were carting oversized animals from one location to another. That left more than one hundred vehicles, and from the ship's distance in space the computer couldn't tell a human from any of the varieties of Antareans.

"Maybe we're looking at this the wrong way," said Pretorius, staring at the screen.

"Oh?"

He nodded. "According to Madam Methuselah, and she's never misled me yet, they've got him on a train that's perpetually in motion."

"It sounds good," said Snake. "But it has to stop every now and then, either for fuel, or for food for the crew, or just to let another vehicle finish crossing in front of it."

"But some of the other vehicles haven't stopped since we've been tracking them," noted Irish.

"I know," said Pretorius.

"Then what are you driving at?" asked Pandora.

"The thing we're overlooking is that this is a *prison* train. It's got valuable cargo, more valuable than the Antarean equivalent of cattle or furniture. So valuable that it stands to reason that they expect someone to break into the train, or blow up the tracks or whatever it's running on, or stop it and break a prisoner out in some other way."

"So?" said Ortega, frowning.

"So they're going to do the best they can to hide their route," said Pretorius.

"How the hell much can you hide in a subway tunnel?" asked Ortega.

"Maybe a little more than we've been supposing," said Pretorius. He turned to Pandora. "Can you program the computer to pinpoint the one train—well, one or two or however few; who knows how many prisoner trains they've got—that doesn't repeat its route, that varies it?"

"Varies it how often?" she asked.

"Once the machine's programmed to look for variations, all you have to do is plug in the time frames, right?" he replied. "So start with thirty minutes, then an hour, then an hour and a half, and so on."

"Okay," she said. "But it could take a few days. I mean, some of the routes may encircle the planet, and we might not know until they make two complete loops that they're not varying their routes."

"Anything's possible," answered Pretorius. "But I think it's more likely that it'll change tracks, so to speak, every few hours, and probably change guards at the same time. You wouldn't want to dump them off half a world from home, and why pay to keep and house them if they're just working regular shifts?"

"It sounds logical," she said.

"But?"

"But we're dealing with aliens, and who the hell knows what they think is logical?"

"Point taken," said Pretorius, "and if you or the computer can come up with a better way, we'll use it, but we've got to start *some*where."

"Okay," said Pandora, turning back to the controls. "Give me a couple of minutes."

"Why don't we just shoot and see who shoots back?" suggested Ortega.

Pretorius smiled. "First, they're all a quarter mile under the ground. How the hell are they going to shoot back, even if any of our weapons can get through to them, which I doubt? And what do you do if four or five ground stations return fire? They'll know we're enemies, they'll be able to identify the ship and summon help, and we still won't have a clue which train Nmumba's on."

Ortega seemed about to argue, then changed his mind and fell silent.

"I have a question," said Irish.

"Ask," said Pretorius.

"If Nmumba is as valuable as we know him to be, wouldn't they go out of their way to make the prison train look like every other one?"

"It's possible," admitted Pretorius. "But if they did, we're out of luck, because it could take months to spot the proper train. So we have to assume that the prison train is handled differently. And there's every likelihood that it is, because first, they're not expecting anyone to go looking for it. He was put here because they figure any rescue attempt will be made two miles deep at the jail. And then there's another likelihood, which is that they don't really expect humans to have commandeered an Antarean ship so quickly, without their being warned of it." He paused. "To tell you the truth, I don't know which alternative is more likely . . . but I do know which is easiest for us to accomplish our mission, and sometimes that's all you have to go on."

"I didn't mean to annoy you," said Irish.

"You didn't annoy me," said Pretorius. "I want you to question anything that doesn't make sense to you, and if you get a lousy answer, point it out."

"Unless they're shooting at us," said Snake.

After two more hours the computer started chattering, Pandora spoke back to it, the others all listened to what sounded like an incomprehensible dialogue, and finally she looked up and turned to them.

"We've pinpointed a vehicle that has changed its route twice," she announced. "The computer couldn't be sure after just one course change, but now it tells me that there's a ninety-three percent chance that it is indeed altering its route every fifty minutes or so."

"What kind of readings can you get from the train?" asked Pretorius.

"Six living beings," she answered. "Until we can get closer, probably below the surface, it can't differentiate the readings."

"But we *will* know before we attack that Nmumba's on it?" persisted Pretorius.

"We'll know if *some* human is on it," said Pandora. "But since I don't have Nmumba's exact readings, we won't know for sure that it's him until we board and enter the thing."

"Okay," said Pretorius. "I keep calling it a train. You call it a vehicle. I assume tracks, but for all I know it's rolling along on concrete or maybe even floating above it. I assume guards will be positioned at each end, but they may not be. I need to know exactly what the situation is before we act."

"Agreed," said Pandora.

"And we can start by finding out how the hell to get underground to begin with," he continued. "Surely the ship can't fit. I doubt that the little space sleds can. So once we've plotted his route—and yes, I know, it's subject to change—how do we get to the spot in the tunnel where we can either board the thing or stop it?"

"'Easy' is not in our lexicon," said Snake with a grim smile.

"Neither is 'fail,'" responded Pretorius. "Because if *we* fail, so do maybe billions of civilians."

# 14

"**I**t'd be nice if people could live on the surface of the damned planet," muttered Snake, studying the map the large screen was displaying. "Then we could just track them until we found someone who was taking the train."

"If anyone *does* take it," replied Ortega. "I mean, hell, it's clearly not going to any desirable location, not on this world."

"Oh, there'll be underground cities, or at least colonies," said Pretorius. "Remember, we know there's over a million Antareans living here, and that they've been here long enough to mutate slightly. And they wouldn't have built thousands of miles of underground tunnels or whatever the hell they are, just to endlessly transport the occasional prisoner." He turned to Pandora. "Are you getting *any* human readings at all?"

"I'm trying to," she answered. "The trick is finding the damned trains. Finding the tunnels is easy."

"We could encourage them," said Ortega.

"Oh?" replied Pretorius. "How?"

"Drop some bombs over the tracks. If they think we're trying to reach Nmumba, they might rush him to the far side of the planet, and if Pandora's looking for that . . ."

Pretorius sighed and shook his head. "Stick to being the strong guy we know."

"What's wrong with—" began Ortega.

"We're not in a military ship," answered Pretorius. "Do anything unusual—and I'd have to say that dropping bombs is a bit out of the ordinary—and they'll blow us to pieces in about two seconds."

Ortega frowned. "How can they, if they're all a quarter mile or two miles under the surface?"

"I'm sure they have weapons on the surface. They surely have weapons on the planet's moons, weapons that can be directed from the moons or from the planet." He paused. "Do you need more reasons, or will those suffice?"

"Okay, okay," muttered Ortega. "But if they're that well protected, I don't see how we're gonna rescue this genius."

"Ask me in two hours," said Pretorius.

As it happened, it only took an hour and thirty-six minutes.

"I've found him!" announced Pandora at that time.

"You're sure?"

"Well, I've found a Man," she replied. "I assume it's him. I'll have a better readout in another couple of minutes." They were all silent as she manipulated and studied her computer. "Dental matches, and he's got a platinum plate in one of his legs. That's our boy, all right."

"How about blood type?" asked Pretorius.

"Can't do it from up here, Nate," said Pandora. "That's like asking if his DNA matches."

"Okay, we'll assume it's him. Now that you've pinpointed him, I assume we can follow the train's progress, wherever it goes?"

"Yes, absolutely."

"Check the direction it's going," said Pretorius, "and see if there's any part of the route where, once it's committed, it can't divert for, say, an hour."

She put the question to the computer.

"Yes, there is. About two hundred and sixty miles from here, it'll enter a . . . I don't know what to call it; a *tunnel,* I suppose . . . where there won't be any branches for another seventy-two miles."

"So we'll want to gain access to the train shortly after it enters that area, and make our getaway, such as it is, before it's gone another seventy miles."

"You're going to have to be more precise than that, Nate," said Pandora.

"Oh?"

She nodded. "Let's say you get off at Mile Sixty-Seven. Then what?"

"I hadn't considered that," said Pretorius. "Getting off is just the first step. We still have to reach the surface, and get back to the ship." He paused. "Okay, where *should* we get off?"

"I suppose it depends on how well-guarded Nmumba is," said Pandora. "If you can access the train, get to him immediately, and leave without incident, there seem to be—*hatches* is clearly the wrong word; make it *routes*—routes to the surface at the twenty-third and fifty-first miles, give or take. Failing that, you actually reach—I can't call it a *station*—make it a loading *platform*—at Mile One Hundred Twelve. There's clearly a pathway to the surface there, but it's just as clear that you'll have to fight your way *to* the surface, since unlike the others it's not deserted."

"So if we can get access to the train, we definitely want to get Nmumba off it before it's traveled fifty miles?" said Snake.

"That's if we get onto it when it's entered the area with no forks or branches," said Pretorius. "That's our ideal boarding spot, but it's always possible that we'll have to board when it's moved farther along." He turned to Pandora. "How fast is it moving right now?"

She checked. "About seventy-five miles an hour."

"Okay. Where can we touch down in the landing sleds and get right down to the level of the tracks or whatever the hell it's riding on?"

She put the question to the computer, which pinpointed a spot on the planet's surface that looked like every other spot.

"How many alien life-forms are guarding it?"

She asked again, then looked up with a puzzled frown. "None," said Pandora.

"That's too easy," said Pretorius. "The damned place must be booby-trapped." Then he shrugged. "What the hell, it makes no difference. We have to chance it. Every minute we wait is one more minute they have to break him." He turned back to Pandora. "Can you get us a schemata of the trains—what size they are, how to board them, what the atmosphere is like?"

"On the train?" she asked.

He shook his head. "It'll be normal—well, normal for *us*—on the train," he replied. "They don't want to asphyxiate Nmumba before he talks. No, I mean in the tunnels."

She checked. "Nothing there to hurt your skin. I'd say just take breathing apparatus, and something to protect your eyes."

"One final question: there have got to be some military ships in the vicinity, either to protect whatever the hell they're transporting on the trains that aren't carrying Nmumba or to shoot down anyone who's come to rescue him. Where are they, how many are they, and what kind of weaponry are they carrying?"

Pandora studied her computer one last time. "You're going to have a hard time believing this, Nate, but we're the only ship in orbit around the whole damned planet."

"You're reading it wrong."

She stepped back and gestured toward the computer. "Be my guest."

He grimaced and shook his head. "I apologize. You're the best there is. If you say there's no ships, there's no ships." He frowned. "But *why?*"

He was still wondering when he, Ortega, Snake, Irish, and Proto boarded a space sled and began descending toward the planet.

# 15

**"S**o where *is* it?" said Snake, peering ahead.

"We're going to have to trust Pandora and the instruments," answered Pretorius. "If we could see it from here, or even from just a mile above it, it'd probably be the best-guarded hole in the ground you ever saw."

"What makes you think it isn't?" she asked.

"We know what kind of weaponry the Antareans use, and the sensors couldn't spot it," said Pretorius. "That doesn't mean we won't be spotted, so Felix, keep alert. If there's anything down there, don't give it a chance to shoot first."

"Right," said Ortega.

"Is there anything I can do?" asked Irish.

"Plenty," said Pretorius. "But first we have to get our hands on Nmumba." He turned to Proto. "Okay, we know you can't fool their instruments, but assuming we get past them, there's got to be some Antareans on the train. Time to change into one." He paused. "You studied their uniforms?"

"Yes," answered the alien.

"They'll never believe a general traveling without underlings," continued Pretorius. "I think maybe a colonel or the equivalent, and make sure the insignia identifies you as security, something that just lets you look at them as if they were insects when they start questioning you about what you're doing there."

"I'll have to," said Proto. "I don't speak the language."

"None of us do," replied Pretorius. "Snake, pass out the t-packs. Most of the people we met in the Tradertown spoke some form of Terran, and that won't be the case from here on."

She opened a box she had carried onto the sled with her and handed out tiny translator mechanisms to each member of the team.

"They're set for Antarean, right?" said Ortega, attaching his to a metal shoulder blade.

Pretorius couldn't restrain a chuckle. "Wouldn't be much use if they weren't."

"Just checking," said Ortega. "It wouldn't be the first time I didn't know what the hell an enemy was saying."

"Not on any mission with me," replied Pretorius.

"No, not with you," admitted Ortega. "But it's made me a little cautious about these things."

"All right," said Pretorius. "Proto, where the hell is yours?"

"Right here," said Proto, indicating the image of his foot. "Remember, I'm just projecting a picture, so to speak. My image can't support any physical objects."

"Okay," said Pretorius. "Keep it hidden. Remember: you're an Antarean, so obviously you don't need a t-pack. And by the same token, don't speak, because if they've got half a brain between them they'll see that your lips don't match the sounds, and that the words are coming from your boots. Just look important and arrogant. Don't speak to us, not in Terran, not in any language, for the same reason. We don't want them spotting where the sound is coming from, even though you can make it match your lips in Terran."

"Are you sure we're even going to encounter any Antareans?" asked Proto.

"Somewhere below us is a Man who's changed the balance of

power in the war," said Pretorius, "a man that our government will do anything to rescue. Wouldn't *you* guard him?"

"How are we going to get onto or into this train or whatever it is?" asked Snake.

"I've been considering that," answered Pretorius, "and I think the one thing we *must* do is board it while it's moving. If Pandora can track it from space, surely they've got stations on and under the planet that are tracking it every second. If we stop it, or even slow it down perceptibly, it's like broadcasting that we're trying to steal their prisoner."

"Fine," replied Snake. "So we can't slow it down or stop it. It's going sixty or seventy miles an hour, and if it has any windows, which I doubt, they're going to be sealed." She stared at him, frowning. "So how do we board it?"

"I'll show you when we get there."

"What's wrong with telling us now?"

Pretorius smiled. "I don't want half of you to decide to quit and go home."

Irish noticed that no one smiled back.

"So how will we tell when we're over the hole or whatever the hell it is we're aiming for?" asked Ortega.

"Pandora's programmed it into the sled," answered Pretorius. "It's one of the few things we don't have to worry about." He checked his watch. "We should be approaching it in another five minutes."

They rode in silence for the next three minutes, and finally they could spot their destination on the viewscreen.

"Good!" said Snake. "For a while there it looked like we were just going to go headfirst into the planet."

"I'd tell you to check your weapons," said Pretorius, "but of course Proto can't lift a weapon and Snake just uses her knife, and Felix *is* a weapon." He smiled. "Very odd crew." He handed a burner to Irish. "Here," he said. "I hope you know how to use it."

She looked at the laser pistol as it lay flat on her hand as if it were some alien creature. "I've never fired one in my life."

"Here's the firing mechanism, here's the safety," said Pretorius, pointing to them. "Hopefully everything will go smoothly and you can make that same statement tomorrow."

"Passage coming up," announced Ortega as the sled slowed. "Looks like it goes straight down."

"It does," replied Pretorius. "Almost half a mile."

"So are you ready to tell us what the hell we're doing next?" asked Snake.

"I'd like to check it out first, just to make sure our information is correct, or see if we have to improvise," said Pretorius. "But what the hell, we're here, there's no turning back, so let's hope it's correct." He paused as the sled entered the chute that led down to the tunnels. "It's true that the trains, vehicles, cars, whatever the hell they are, average seventy-five miles an hour, but like I say, that's their *average.* They'll go up to ninety or so on straightaways, but like any vehicle they have to slow down for turns, and the reason we chose this chute is that it's a couple of hundred yards from a turn of almost ninety degrees."

"A right turn?" said Ortega.

Pretorius shrugged. "Right, left, it depends what direction it's coming from. But it's going to have to slow down to a crawl, whether it's on tracks or even floating above the tunnel floor, and that's where we'll board it."

"From the top, through a window, a door, or what?" asked Snake.

"We're going to have to play it by ear," answered Pretorius. "We'll have about twenty minutes to take up our positions, and we'll do so in such a way that, however the vehicle is constructed, at least one of us can enter it."

"And what about the rest of us?" said Ortega.

Pretorius walked to a box on the floor and opened it. "This is a super-strong and super-lightweight cord. We'll all be attached to it." He held up a small metal object. "And this mechanism will reel us in before the thing can pick up speed after rounding the corner." He paused. "Now this is *essential.* Since we don't know who's going to gain entrance first, you're going to be attached directly to each member of the team. Each attachment will have a little red mark on it. To detach it, you just touch the mark. You'll detach from everyone but the one who's inside the vehicle." He looked at each of them in turn. "If you don't touch those marks within seconds, you're going to be dragged along in the wake of a vehicle or train that's approaching ninety miles an hour."

"Let's see them now," said Snake, "so if we have any questions we can ask them before we're all hooked up to them."

"Fair enough," said Pretorius, passing the cords around.

"Seems simple enough," remarked Snake after examining hers, and the others agreed. "I assume that pressing the white dot reels us in?"

"Right," he answered. "And remember: Once we've gained entrance, our only concern is finding Nmumba. If he's alive, it'll mean he hasn't told them what they want to know yet. If push comes to shove, if it's clear that we're going to fail . . ."

"You mean *die*," said Snake.

He nodded. "If it's clear that none of us are going to get out of this alive, our only obligation is to kill Nmumba before they can break or turn him. Is that understood?"

They all nodded.

"All right," continued Pretorius. "Since it's clearly a prison train, we can assume there are no passengers, no innocent bystanders. Every being on the vehicle except Nmumba is an enemy and is expendable." He sighed heavily. "There's no sense taking prisoners anyway. It's an enemy train on an enemy world. Where the hell would we stash 'em?"

"So how many cars is it?"

Pretorius shrugged. "It's about fifty meters. Hard to imagine any single thing that big making a right turn, but who the hell knows? It could be half a dozen cars, or one long car that's jointed. Or something we haven't considered yet." He paused. "Any more questions?"

Silence.

"You forgot what may be the most important one," he continued.

"What was that?" asked Irish curiously.

"Can you breathe the air?"

"Surely not in the tunnels," she replied. "Not if the chutes are open to the surface."

"Right," said Pretorius. "So we're all taking oxygen with us."

"How about on the train?" asked Ortega.

"I assume it's breathable, but just in case they've got Nmumba hooked up to an oxygen supply, keep your breathing apparatus. And according to our readouts, the temperature is a bit chilly, but well above freezing."

"What about gravity?" asked Proto. "I hate to ask, but it affects me more than it does you."

"Pretty much Deluros VIII Standard," answered Pretorius. "Maybe a tad heavier. Ah!" he said as the ship touched down. "We're there. Felix, grab the cords. Everyone, hook up your oxygen and let's go."

They all climbed out and found themselves in a totally round tunnel with a diameter of some thirty feet. The ship immediately rose and hovered in the shaft, hidden from view.

"Okay, where's the turn?" asked Snake.

"Maybe half a mile in this direction," replied Pretorius, pointing down the tunnel. "Let's get started."

"No tracks," noted Ortega.

"No marks on the floor, either," said Pretorius. "I have a feeling that it probably floats, if that's the right word and I suspect it isn't, a couple of feet above the floor."

"How are we doing on time?" asked Proto.

"About ten minutes," said Pretorius. "Figure seven. Who the hell knows if it speeds up every now and then?"

"As long as it slows to a crawl on the turn, who cares?" said Snake.

"All right," said Pretorius, pulling his end of the cord out of the box. "Let's start getting ready. Remember, the white marks reel you in, and the red marks detach you, so position them where you can touch the red marks instantly."

"Well," said Snake, once she'd hooked herself up to the cord, "no sense all of us standing in the same spot. Felix, make me some handholds up to the ceiling."

Ortega aimed his prosthetic left hand, which doubled as a

burner, and created handholds and footholds every two feet, up to the ceiling.

"Give 'em a couple of minutes to cool off," he said, "or you'll burn your hands."

"The hell I will," she said, slipping the cord up to her wrist, pulling a pair of gloves out of a pocket, and putting them on. She tested the new holes in the wall, then scampered two-thirds of the way up to the roof of the tunnel.

"Can't you go any farther?" asked Ortega.

"Of course I can," replied Snake. "But why do I want to spend the next few minutes hanging upside down? I'll climb the rest of the way when we see or hear it approaching."

"I'd blast a hole right in the middle of the floor," said Ortega to Pretorius, "but if the damned thing has wheels it could wreck it."

"Play it safe," replied Pretorius. "We can't take any chances with Nmumba."

"What should *I* do?" asked Irish.

Pretorius frowned. "There's no sense standing on the other side of the tunnel, since whether Snake, Felix, or I manage to get into the vehicle, you'd be dragged underneath it. You might as well stand right next to me."

"And what about me?" asked Proto.

"It's never going to stop for an officer on foot in a tunnel," answered Pretorius. "That's too damned far-fetched. And while I see a pair of hands at the end of two powerful arms, that's all an illusion and you can't grab anything." He lowered his head in thought for a few seconds, then looked at the alien again. "I've never tried this before, but the *real* you isn't any bigger than a pillow. Can I lift you?"

"Probably," said Proto.

"Let me try."

"Go ahead."

Pretorius began reaching down, then stopped. "Get rid of the illusion," he said. "I don't know where you start and end."

An instant later Proto's true shape appeared, and Pretorius lifted it.

"Forty pounds," he said. "Maybe fifty. Yeah, that can work." He set Proto back down on the floor.

"*What* can work, if I may ask?" said Proto.

"If there's an open window, I can toss you through it." He stopped and stared at the alien again. "I don't see any hands or feet. I assume you have a top and a bottom, that if you land in much the same position you are now, it won't do you any internal damage."

"I don't think so," answered Proto. "No one's ever lifted and thrown me before."

"Well, it's probably not on your job description," said Pretorius wryly. "But the military teaches us to improvise."

"And you'd better start improvising soon," said Pandora's voice. "The train will reach you in about forty seconds."

# 16

It wasn't quite a train, at least not the kind they had imagined, because it consisted of a single car—a flexible car some fifty meters in length that was able to curve with the tunnel as it approached the turn. There were a few windows, widely spaced and barred.

"Got it!" yelled Snake from where she clung to the tunnel's ceiling. An instant later she released her hold and dropped from sight as each of the others hit the white marks on their cords and Ortega grabbed Proto and tucked him securely under an arm.

Despite its flexibility the train slowed to a crawl as it maneuvered around the right-angle turn, and by the time it was picking up speed Snake's teammates had joined her on the roof of the vehicle between a pair of raised air ducts.

"Can you see in?" asked Pretorius.

"Not a damned thing," replied Snake. "I don't think these ducts go down to the floor of the vehicle, which is to say we won't be trapped inside them if we enter the thing through them. But they do go down a few feet, and unless someone decides to stand right under them there's absolutely nothing to be seen."

"The damned train's going to be going full speed in another half minute," noted Pretorius. "We'd better enter right now. We could get blown off while we're maneuvering to get inside forty or fifty seconds from now." He turned to Ortega. "Pull the duct's cover off, Felix."

He drew his weapon in the few seconds it took Ortega to

remove the top of the duct and hurl it over the side of the vehicle, and lowered himself, feet-first, to the floor. There were three uniformed Antareans standing nearby. All three were dead before they even knew Pretorius was among them.

He looked at the blank walls and realized that though the single vehicle was close to fifty meters long, it was divided into compartments, with a broad aisle traversing the middle of the car from one end to the other. He gestured to his companions to join him, then remembered that he'd have to catch Proto, which he did.

"What now?" whispered Ortega.

"Now we find out where the hell they're keeping him," answered Pretorius, also whispering. "And we do it quietly, since if they hear a ruckus they might just kill him."

"And you don't think they heard you kill these three bozos?" asked Snake, gesturing to the fallen Antareans.

Pretorius shook his head. "The burner just makes a low humming noise, they never got a shot off, nobody screamed. I think we're okay."

"Lots of doors," said Ortega, opening the door to their compartment and looking down the corridor. "We can't just start busting each of 'em down."

"No," agreed Pretorius. "But—" he pointed at some grates in the ceiling "—we know they've got a ventilation system. My guess is that it runs the length of the vehicle." He pointed to a small grate on the ceiling. "Fortunately we've got a reasonably accomplished sneak thief with us who also happens to be a contortionist and doesn't panic in tight spaces."

"Damned right I don't," said Snake.

"You ready?" asked Pretorius.

"Stupid question," she said, walking over. "Give me a boost."

Pretorius was about to lift her when Ortega pushed him gently aside. "She'll never reach it short of standing atop your head." He picked Snake up. "Ready?"

"Ready," she replied.

He literally tossed her straight up. She reached out, grabbed the edge of the vent and pulled herself up.

"No lights or beams," cautioned Pretorius.

"Spare me your platitudes," she replied, starting to ease herself along the vent.

"What now?" asked Irish.

"Now we wait and hope she can make our job a little easier," answered Pretorius.

"I don't suppose she can rescue him all by herself."

He shook his head. "Seems doubtful, since they had three armed men—well, Antareans—in this compartment, which hasn't got any prisoners and isn't a galley. Still," he added with a shrug, "with aliens you never know. Some of them think like us. Others would sacrifice their lives for the equivalent of a cup of coffee, or go to war over an object that's identical to three hundred other objects that they couldn't care less about."

"Almost all my experience has been with Men," said Irish.

"That's okay," replied Pretorius. "That's what you're here for."

"I'm sure this is old hat to you," she continued, "but I find every aspect of it exciting."

"Facing alien soldiers who want to kill you is a lot of things," he answered with a grim smile, "but old hat isn't one of them. The reason I keep drawing these assignments is because I'm pretty good at keeping us *out* of danger." He sighed. "Or I was, until we lost Circe."

"I'm sorry," she said.

"Don't be. It wasn't your fault."

The vehicle slowed down briefly for another turn, then picked up speed again. A moment after that Snake reappeared, dropping lightly to the floor.

"Well?" said Pretorius.

"The aisle seems to be the dividing line. You're on the crew's and security's side of it, with living quarters, a dormitory, and a galley. There are eight long narrow cells on the other side of the aisle."

"Eight cells doesn't make it from here to the front," noted Pretorius. "What else is there?"

She shrugged. "Whatever it is, it doesn't need ventilation. The shaft stopped after the eight cells. At least, I assume they're cells. I couldn't see much, but they all looked empty."

Pretorius frowned. "If you didn't find Nmumba, then Pandora was wrong."

"Of course I found him," said Snake. "That's why I came back."

"You might have mentioned it," said Pretorius. "Where is he?"

"From here, sixth cell on the left." She paused. "Well, actually I didn't see him at all . . . but there were four armed Antareans in it, and there weren't any in any of the other cells, so that's got to be where they're keeping him."

Pretorius grimaced. "We might as well assume he's there. I can't see us breaking into seven empty cells without drawing a little more attention than we want." He turned to Proto. "Okay, time to become an Antarean."

No sooner had the words left his mouth than the alien had projected an image of an armed, uniformed Antarean officer, the equivalent of a colonel.

"Looks damned good!" said Ortega. "Could have fooled me!"

"And me," added Irish.

"But will it fool *them*?" asked Proto. "If Pandora is right, and she almost always is, this vehicle hasn't stopped for days. Won't they know what officers are on it?"

"They might have their doubts," agreed Pretorius. "But if you outrank them, do you think any of them is going to challenge you to your face?"

"I hope not," said Proto. "I can't wear a t-pack without giving myself away, which means I won't know what they're saying."

"Not to worry," replied Pretorius, pulling out a small device. "I had Pandora program three or four lines into this thing. They're all gruff commands: *Attention, Silence,* and *Leave Us.* Touch a different spot and you get a different command. Run through it a couple of times until you're comfortable with it." Since he couldn't see Proto's true shape he bent over and placed the device on the floor next to the "Antarean officer's" foot, and it vanished from sight almost immediately.

Proto activated it and played it three times, listening intently.

"Can you mouth the words?" asked Pretorius.

"Yes."

"Hopefully that's all you'll have to do." He turned to Ortega. "Felix, go up and down the aisle and kill any guards or prison warders who are in their compartments."

"Right!" said Ortega, walking to the compartment's door.

"And Felix?" continued Pretorius.

"Yeah?"

"Silently."

Ortega nodded and crept out into the corridor as the door closed behind him.

THE PRISON IN ANTARES

"Okay," said Snake. "When Felix returns we walk down there and Proto enters the cell and orders them out, and they obey him and we kill them as they leave. Then what? We're all in a prison cell speeding away from a ship at ninety miles an hour on a planet we're at war with."

"You forgot to mention that we don't have any food or water," said Pretorius with a smile.

"You've got to have some notion of how we're getting off this damned train," she continued. "How'd you like to share it with us?"

"This particular route has only been used by this one prison train since Pandora's been tracking them," answered Pretorius. "Once we've got our hands on Nmumba, we'll go up front and do whatever's required to reverse course. The odds of running into another vehicle on this route are minimal."

"Uh . . . avoiding another train is the *easy* part," said Snake. "What about the rest of it?"

Pretorius pulled another tiny cube out of a different pocket. "This one's programmed to tell the driver or engineer or whatever the hell he is that he can reverse course or die." He paused. "Now, just between you and me, the likelihood is that this thing hasn't *got* a driver, but once we get to the control room or whatever it's called, we'll have Pandora take control of it from the ship."

"I've got a question," said Irish.

"What is it?"

"If Pandora can take control of this thing from the ship, why didn't you have her do it immediately?"

"Because we want Nmumba alive," said Pretorius. "What do you think would happen to him the second the vehicle came to a stop and started reversing course with no announcement to that effect from a higher-up that they trust?"

She nodded her head. "I hadn't thought of that," she admitted. "I'm new to this. I'll learn."

"I'm sure you will."

They waited in silence for almost five minutes, and finally Ortega crept into the compartment.

"All dead?" asked Pretorius.

"All of 'em on this side of the aisle. You didn't want me going into the cell side, right?"

"Right," agreed Pretorius. "I guess we're ready. Proto, sixth cell on the left. I'll knock for you, since you don't actually have any hands. They'll spot you and open the door. Step in, give your three or four words, and if they buy it, step aside and let them walk out. We'll be waiting for them." He turned to Snake. "How many were there?"

"Four that I saw, but there could be more."

"That could be a problem," said Pretorius. "By the time the fourth has left the cell, they'll know who or what's out here. If any of them shout a warning, whoever's left inside will probably try to kill Nmumba."

"Leave it to me," said Snake.

They turned to her questioningly.

"You walk in to take one or two of them out, they'll see you and kill Nmumba instantly. But I'm so small to start with, if I slide in on my belly with my burner in my hand, I can probably get two or three quick shots off before they even know I'm there."

Pretorius nodded. "Okay, it's worth a try." He looked around. "Any other questions?"

They were silent.

"Then let's get this show on the road. Proto, lead the way."

They walked quietly down the aisle, until they came to the sixth door on the left. Pretorius reached out and pounded his fist against it.

It irised a moment later and Proto stepped through.

"Attention!" commanded the voice he had hidden on his person.

Six Antareans stood at attention, and Proto stared arrogantly at each in turn. Then he placed his hand to his mouth, as if rubbing it, and issued the command: "Leave us!"

The Antareans seemed confused. They didn't respond aggressively, but they simply didn't respond at all.

"Leave us!" came the command again, as Proto's image glared at them.

Three of the Antareans saluted and walked out the door. Ortega made short work of them, but not short enough, because one of them screamed. Even as the sound left his lips Snake was sliding across the floor. Her first shot melted the eye of a fourth Antarean, who collapsed while she was firing at the fifth. The sixth got his weapon out, but before he could take aim and fire, Pretorius nailed him with his screecher, and he collapsed before the onslaught of solid sound.

"Thank goodness!" said a voice off in a corner, and they turned to see an emaciated and badly bruised Edgar Nmumba sitting on the edge of a cot, staring at them. "I'd given up all hope."

"Irish, get him on his feet and stick with him," ordered Pretorius. "Felix, drag those bodies in here. The damned aisle can't stay empty forever. Sooner or later someone's got to walk down it—from the engine, from some room that was locked, from some other cell. Snake, pick up all their weapons, then melt any you don't want keep."

"Right," she said, gathering the weapons while Ortega gathered the bodies.

"Proto, you might as well keep that identity until we're out of here. It won't register on the security cameras, but if we run into any more Antareans between here and the control room, an officer is a handy thing to have."

Nmumba's eyes widened as he started at Proto. "You mean you're *not*—?"

"No," answered Proto.

"Amazing!" said Nmumba weakly.

"Not half as amazing as what you've accomplished," said Pretorius, "and what you're going to continue to accomplish as soon as we get you home."

"I'm just grateful that you've saved me from those . . . barbarians!" said Nmumba.

"I've heard 'em called a lot of things," replied Pretorius, "but 'barbarian' isn't one of them. After all, they invented the Q bomb."

"You don't have to live in the dirt and wear rags to have the ethics of a barbarian," said Nmumba.

Pretorius nodded. "True enough. How are you coming on those bodies, Felix?"

"One to go."

"Okay, get him in here and we'll be on our way."

"Home?" asked Nmumba.

"Eventually," said Pretorius. "First we have to get off this damned train and get back to our ship." He looked around. "Everybody ready?"

There was a general murmuring of assents.

"Okay. Snake, you didn't get any farther than the next two cells, right?"

"Right."

"Then since we don't know what's ahead, we'll let Proto lead. Felix, take up the rear in case anyone comes up behind us. Irish, there aren't enough of us to surround you and Nmumba, but try to keep at least one of us in front of you and one behind you, whatever the situation. Let's go."

They walked down the aisle, past eight more compartments—soldiers' quarters that matched the ones they'd already passed—on the right, and a solid wall on the left.

"What's in there, do you suppose?" asked Irish. Indicating the wall.

"Who knows?" said Pretorius. "Storage. Power plant for this and half a dozen other trains. Hard to guess with aliens."

"I wish I could help you," said Nmumba, "but I haven't been out of my prison car, or cell, or whatever you wish to call it, since I was brought aboard."

"That's all right, sir," said Pretorius. "It's not that vital." *I hope.*

"Please call me Edgar. 'Sir' is too formal—" a weak smile "—especially for a man who's been in the same prison outfit for weeks. Actually, the one thing I know *isn't* behind that wall is a laundry."

Pretorius smiled. "We'll give you a full day just to lounge in a bathtub when we get back to the Democracy, Edgar."

"I'm sure I can use it," replied Nmumba.

"Coming up to it," announced Snake as they came to a door that blocked the aisle.

"Okay," said Pretorius. "Same routine as last time. Use the

recording to bring 'em to attention and then tell 'em to leave—always assuming there's anyone there to give orders to."

"Right," acknowledged Proto.

"Felix, you and Snake take care of anyone who walks out of there. Irish, hang back with Edgar until this is over."

She nodded and led Nmumba back down the aisle as Pretorius pushed against the door. It irised, just like the last one, and Proto entered—and found himself facing three members of a race he'd never seen before.

Shit! thought Pretorius, ducking back out of sight behind Proto. They're not Antareans! Will they even understand him? And then: Wait a minute. If they're on this train, of course they will.

They jumped to attention at Proto's command, and he gestured that there was something out in the aisle he wanted them to see. Pretorius positioned himself to the side of the doorway, and after two of them had stepped out he quickly walked through and dispatched the third one with his screecher while Ortega and Snake quickly and efficiently killed the other two.

"Damn!" muttered Pretorius a moment later. "I can't make heads or tails of this control panel." He looked around. "That thing's got to be a communication device." He began fiddling with it until Pandora's voice came through loud and clear.

"Will you please stop changing the frequency every five seconds?"

"Gladly," said Pretorius.

"How is it going?"

"We've got Nmumba, and we're in the control room, but I don't know how the hell to bring this thing to a stop and reverse course."

"Stay on that frequency and let our computer tie into the train's," she said.

"I won't touch a thing."

A moment later they could feel the vehicle start to slow down, and shortly thereafter it came to a stop.

"Now you want to go back to where you boarded it, right?"

"Right," said Pretorius. "But if you stop there, if we just abandon it while we get onto our sleds, someone's going to know something's very wrong even sooner than they should. Can you slow it even more that it normally slows at that corner, give us time to get safely off, and then reverse course again? Maybe double the speed for half an hour or so until it gets to where it's supposed to be at that time, then let it go at its normal speed until someone notices that it's not stopping or speeding up or responding?"

"I can do that," she answered. "But they might notice sooner, Nate. I mean, if I can track it from up here, surely they can track it."

"Yeah, but they'll try to communicate with it before they come looking to see what's wrong, and we can be off the damned thing in twenty or thirty minutes, and up to the ship in ten more. Once we're out of the system, we don't give a damn what they find."

"Okay," she replied as he felt the vehicle picking up speed as it raced to the point where they had first encountered it.

The rest of the ride constituted the only uneventful few minutes they'd spent since landing, and shortly after exiting the vehicle they were on their sled, streaking through the stratosphere to rendezvous with their ship.

# 17

"**W**here to?" asked Pandora when they were all back aboard.

"I don't imagine our ship is still available," replied Pretorius. "I think we'll just head back into the Democracy. We'll signal them when we're still in neutral territory so they know not to fire at us."

"Will they believe you?" asked Nmumba.

Pretorius smiled. "Hell, no. *I* wouldn't. But they won't shoot if we don't give them any reason to. They'll surround us, and either board us or escort us to the nearest base, with their weapons trained on us all the way. Once we're landed, or at least in orbit, they'll satisfy themselves that we're who we say we are, and hopefully they'll supply us with a better ship than this to go the rest of the way and report to Cooper."

"Cooper?"

"General Wilbur Cooper," said Pretorius. "Our boss. The reason you're off that train."

"Ah!" said Nmumba. "I owe him an enormous debt of gratitude. How can I ever repay him?"

"You've already repaid him about a billion times over," said Ortega.

"I just did what any citizen would do," replied Nmumba.

Pretorius shook his head. "You did what no other citizen could do. That's why the Transkei Coalition grabbed you."

"Sorry to interrupt," said Pandora. "But am I taking the quickest route or the safest?"

"We've already got our man," answered Pretorius. "Might as well go the quickest. Worst comes to worst and they blow us apart, they can't get what they want from him." He turned to Nmumba, who suddenly looked nervous. "Don't worry about it, Edgar. They have no reason to attack an Antarean ship, which is what this is." He chuckled. "We're actually in more danger once we reach the Democracy if we can't pick up a neutral or Democracy ship along the way."

"Yes, I can see that," said Nmumba. "I'm sorry if I seem like a wide-eyed kid, but this is all new to me."

"Never served in the military?" asked Snake.

"I was a civilian scientist attached to one of the labs back on Deluros VIII," he replied. "I had military credentials, of course, but I didn't wear a uniform."

"Hell, you can go to work naked for all I give a damn," said Snake, "as long as you keep destroying Q bombs."

"It took me three years to come up with an effective method for spotting, tracking, and disabling them." He allowed himself the luxury of a smile. "Thank God I don't have to reinvent it each time!"

"So if I told you I'd busted off part of the extender on my metal hand, that'd be outside your field of expertise?" suggested Ortega.

"I'm afraid so."

"Ah, well, I'll get a new one back in the Democracy."

"I have a question," said Nmumba.

"Ask away," replied Pretorius.

"What happened to the Antarean officer who was with you? Was he killed?"

"No."

"Surely he didn't stay behind!"

Pretorius grinned. "He's right here on the ship."

Nmumba looked around. "Where?"

"You're looking at him."

Nmumba frowned. "I don't understand."

"Proto, do your trick for the gentleman."

The figure of the middle-aged man instantly morphed into the Antarean colonel.

"Well, I'll be damned!" exclaimed Nmumba. "A genuine shape-shifter!"

"Not quite," said Pretorius.

"Then I still don't understand."

"I'll explain it to you," said Irish, leading him to an empty cabin. "We have to have a long conversation anyway."

"And while she's explaining it to you, I'm going to grab some lunch," said Pretorius, getting to his feet. "Or is it dinner?"

"Who the hell cares?" said Snake, heading to the galley. "I'll join you."

"I could do with a meal too," said Pandora, joining them. "The ship will warn us if I'm needed."

Pretorius ordered the Antarean equivalent of a sandwich and a beer, made a face as he took his first bite, and made another one as he washed it down with a swallow of what passed for beer.

"Awful stuff," he muttered.

"Once we're back in neutral territory, I can touch down and change the galley's contents," said Pandora.

"Good thought," agreed Pretorius. "But let's give Miga a wide berth. Someone's got to have reported this ship as missing by now."

"To say nothing of its crew," added Snake.

"All right," agreed Pandora. "I'll try to hunt up some world populated by Men. It might make getting a different ship a little easier."

"Good," said Pretorius.

He took another bite of the sandwich, and made another face.

"Hard to win a war eating shit like this," said Snake, nibbling around the edge of her own sandwich. "Damned lucky we didn't have to do much fighting down there in the tunnel."

"Sometimes lucky is better than good," offered Pandora.

Pretorius frowned. "We *didn't* do much fighting down there, did we?"

"You killed six Antareans and three members of some other race," noted Pandora. "I'd call that a lot."

He shook his head. "Not for the most valuable prisoner in a war that involves close to a trillion on each side. *Think!* This is a guy who, if they break him, they win the goddamned war." He paused. "If we got our hands on Nmumba's equivalent, an Antarean who, say, could create a bomb we had no defense for, would *we* guard him with just six Men?"

There was a brief pause as they considered what he had said.

"Now that you mention it . . ." replied Pandora.

"Would we put him on a vehicle that didn't have half a hundred defense mechanisms built into it?" he continued. "Why didn't anyone or anything attack our sled when it was descending to the tunnel? And why did we emerge so close to the only turn where we could board a vehicle that was otherwise going too fast?"

"What are you getting at?" demanded Snake, frowning.

"I was so busy concentrating on the mission, I hadn't realized it until just now," he said.

"Realized *what?*"

"It was too easy," said Pretorius.

# 18

Pretorius sat on his cot in his cabin. Seated opposite him, on an obviously uncomfortable chair created to accommodate the Antarean bulk, was Irish.

The door was closed.

"It certainly didn't seem easy to *me*," she was saying. "I was terrified."

"You've never seen action before," he replied. "And killing the enemy in battle is never easy. I'm just saying that this particular prisoner should have been *much* harder to reach, and all but impossible to free. There are something like seven or eight billion Antareans in this system, plus some alien allies. Why were only six of them guarding him?"

"Well . . . the train . . ." she began.

He shook his head. "We reached the tunnel without anyone trying to stop us . . . and we reached it very near the one place where we were able to board the damned train." He paused. "They've got what's supposed to be an impenetrable jail two miles beneath the surface. Why wasn't he there?"

"I don't know," said Irish. "Maybe the gravity?"

"I had Pandora check it out when we thought he might be there, before Madam Methuselah gave us his location." He frowned. "Which reminds me: I have to let her know, far from owing her, *she* owes *me*. And she'd better get a new informant for this system."

"So are you trying to say he's *not* Edgar Nmumba?"

"I'm saying that he might not be," answered Pretorius. "We

need an expert to determine whether he's the real McCoy or not. That's why you're here in the first place."

"I'll do my best."

"Good," he said. "I just wanted to alert you to the fact that there are now two possibilities, not just one. The one you were prepared to find was whether or not he'd broken, whether he'd talked and they'd somehow tinkered with him so we wouldn't know it. But now the other possibility is that he's not Edgar Nmumba at all." He stared at her. "The end result is the same: whether he broke or whether he's a ringer, we need to know, and act upon that knowledge. But the method of finding out if either is the case may differ, and you need to know that."

"And do the others know?" asked Irish.

"Which he is? No, of course not. You're the expert."

"No, I mean, do they know about your suspicions?"

"Yes. You'll have three, four, maybe even five hours of sessions with him every day, but the day is a lot longer than that, and I want everyone watching and listening and analyzing when you're not around."

"All right," she said. "Is there anything else?"

"No, that covers it."

"I'll do my best, Nate."

"Okay, we're done. Let's go back out before Snake accuses us of having an affair."

They returned to the main deck, and shortly thereafter Irish took Nmumba off to a cabin to continue running mental and emotional tests on him while Pretorius rejoined the others.

"So what do you think?" asked Ortega.

Pretorius shrugged. "I don't know. That's what we've got an expert for."

"Well, he's not armed, so even if he's a ringer, what harm can he do?" continued Ortega.

"Oh, come on, Felix," said Snake. "For one thing, he can crash the ship. Or signal for help while we're in Coalition territory. Or just kill the oxygen and die with the rest of us."

"Just be aware of what he *may* be, and don't be obvious about keeping an eye on him," said Pretorius.

"I can do sixteen or eighteen hours here at a stretch," said Pandora, "but eventually I have to sleep."

"When you do, let me know and I'll sit in."

"Nate, you don't know how to run this vessel." She looked around the deck. "Hell, none of you do."

"Yeah," said Pretorius, "but Nmumba doesn't know that. Just put everything on automatic and show me how to respond to an alien signal if one comes in. I'll just sit here, and he'll assume I'm piloting it."

Pandora considered what he said and smiled. "You know, he probably will, at that."

"Okay," said Pretorius. "The rest of you, spend your spare time learning everything you can about Nmumba from the computer. What was his home planet's major spectator sport, what were the best teams, anything like that. Then, without being too obvious—that especially means you, Felix—let drop that you rooted for such-and-so a team, and who did he like? Anything like that, anything at all that could trip him up."

"And if he's the real thing?" asked Proto, who was back in his guise as a middle-aged man.

"Then either they broke him and put him back together, or he's one tough son of a bitch who hasn't told them a thing. And if that's the case, if he really *is* Edgar Nmumba and not a ringer, then Irish better be as good as she's supposed to be."

They spent the next two hours learning what they could about Benitara IV, Nmumba's home world. Irish emerged first, and Pretorius promptly walked up to her.

"How's it going?" he asked.

She shrugged. "It's too early to tell. He *seems* all right, but of course if the Coalition expected us to rescue him they wouldn't have chosen a mental weakling."

"When can you make a definitive call?"

"I don't know. Three days, four days." She paused. "Of course, if he blunders, if he lets something drop that he shouldn't, then I'll know right away. But if I just use normal means, and he doesn't make a mistake, then it'll be a few days before he either makes that mistake or shows me that he's been telling the truth and there are none to make."

"Okay," said Pretorius. "In the meantime we'll be doing a little low-level testing of our own."

She shrugged. "He told me that he expects you to, that he'd do it if he was in your place. He says he didn't break, but too many lives depend on our taking his word for it."

"Then we won't disappoint him."

"All right," she said. "I'll tell him he can come out now. I explained that I had to report to you first."

Pretorius nodded his assent. "Go ahead and get him. Whatever happens over the next couple of days, we might as well head out of the Coalition's territory and back to the Neutral Zone. If he's legit, we're on our way home. And if we find out he's not, then we'll kill him right on the ship." He paused, then added: "Let's see just how hard the Coalition pursues us."

She waited to make sure he had nothing further to say, then went to her cabin, ordered the door to iris, and escorted Nmumba back to the main deck.

"Getting hungry?" asked Snake.

"It's been a long time since I've had a *real* meal," said Nmumba. "They only gave me enough to keep me alive."

"I wish I could cook you up a silverwing, but we're stuck with the equivalent of soya products until we can get some new supplies."

"Not a problem," he answered. "I've never had silverwing."

"I thought people on your world—"

"I know you're testing me," he interrupted her mildly. "And in your place I'd do the same thing. But the silverwing is not native to my world, and I've never eaten one."

"I'm sorry," said Snake. "I meant silverthorn."

He smiled. "Now *those* I like." He sighed deeply. "I haven't had one in, oh, it must be fifteen years. They didn't import them to Braxus II, and they were just too expensive on Deluros VIII."

Ortega brought up the subject of murderball, which was popular through the galaxy. Nmumba didn't have a rooting interest, didn't even know the leading players in the various leagues, let alone his planetary team . . . but as he explained, he'd been much too preoccupied with his scientific studies and then duties to spend any time on such frivolous pursuits as sports.

Pandora decided to take her down time, and Pretorius seated himself at the control panel.

"How am I doing so far?" asked Nmumba.

"I beg your pardon?" said Pretorius.

"I know you've all been testing me. It's what I'd do in your position."

"Good answer."

"So how *am* I doing?"

"You're still alive," said Pretorius. "And we're disinclined to give second chances."

"Good!" said Nmumba. "Then perhaps I can start relaxing."

"Be our guest. You know where your cabin is."

"Yes, I do," he replied. "But by relaxing, I meant, well, unwinding. Perhaps with something to read."

Pretorius tossed him a couple of ear inserts. "There's a simple extension of the computer in your cabin. Just tell it what book you want to hear, and if it's in the ship's library it'll . . . oh, shit! I forgot. This isn't *our* ship." He grimaced. "It's *our* computer, but it's not tied in to the master computer on Deluros anymore. Couldn't take the chance that anyone or anything scanning the ship might catch that." He uttered a brief command, then gestured to the screen. "What we've got is Pandora's personal library," he continued, indicating a list of perhaps four hundred titles. "Pick the one you want."

"Not a problem," answered Nmumba. "I haven't seen *any* book in months." He got to his feet. "I think I'll listen to it while I'm lying down." He paused. "You don't mind if I cast some tranquil scenes on my wall?"

"*I* don't have to look at 'em," said Pretorius. "Be my guest."

"I *am* your guest," said Nmumba with a smile as he began walking to his cabin. "Your very grateful guest."

Then he was in the cabin, and the door had snapped shut behind him.

"Well?" asked Pretorius. "Anyone got an opinion?"

"He seems okay to me," offered Ortega.

"I don't know," said Snake. "I mean, hell, we've hardly spent any time with him when we weren't running for our lives." She paused for a moment. "If anything, he seems too calm."

"She never trusts anyone," said Ortega.

"That's why I'm still alive," she responded.

"He *does* seem calm," said Pretorius. "It could be because of his weakened condition, or all the drugs they probably fed him to loosen his tongue. Or maybe he's just a damned good actor." He turned to Proto. "What do *you* think?"

"I am not human myself," answered Proto. "Other than physical features I wouldn't begin to know what to look for."

"Point taken," said Pretorius. "Well, we'll just keep an eye on him. And on the goddamned pursuit."

"Is there any?" asked Snake.

"Not that Pandora or I have been able to pick up," he answered. "They've got to know by now that he's gone."

"Then why—?" asked Ortega and let the word hang.

"See what I mean?" replied Pretorius. He turned to Irish. "I hate to say something like the fate of a few hundred million Men is in your hands," he began, "but the truth of the matter is that the fate of a few hundred million Men *is* in your hands. This is your ball game. Even if he's truly Nmumba, even if he can pass a DNA test, that doesn't mean he's not working, willingly or unknowingly, for the Transkei Coalition." He shrugged. "It's up to you."

"I'll do my best," she said.

"I know you will," answered Pretorius.

"It just damned well better be good enough," added Snake.

"And on that happy, supportive note, let's grab some lunch," said Pretorius. "No one's coming at us. The computer will alert me if I have to get back here in a hurry." He stared at it. "Damn! I wish Pandora was here now."

"What is it?" asked Irish tensely.

"I want it to tell me if Nmumba is closer to it than I am, and I don't know how."

"Why should that matter?"

"It depends on where his loyalties lie at this minute, on any posthypnotic suggestions they may have planted," replied Pretorius. "If he's been programmed to sabotage anyone who rescued him, I don't want him near the computer."

"We'll just keep watch," said Irish.

"Oh, hell, I'll grab my meal and eat it at the controls," offered Ortega.

"And drool all over them," said Snake.

"Okay, *you* sit there," he responded.

"No, you're a lot less approachable for anyone who doesn't know the two of you," said Pretorius. "You sit there, Felix."

"What do you mean, 'for anyone who doesn't know us'?" demanded Ortega.

Pretorius smiled. "She fights dirty."

Ortega considered the answer for a moment, then nodded. "Yeah, I'll sit there."

Irish stared at the oversized Ortega, who was almost fifty percent machine, and the diminutive Snake, who could fold herself to fit into a small overnight bag, and the alien Proto, who could project the most terrifying shapes and images but in truth was barely twenty inches high, and not for the first time she wondered just what kind of crew she'd become part of, or what she would have to do to ever fit into this odd group known as the Dead Enders.

# 19

The ship was nearing the boundary between the Transkei Coalition and the Neutral Zone. They'd been traveling for almost two days without incident, and Pretorius, who had expected immediate pursuit, was finally beginning to relax.

"The damned train ran without stopping the whole time we tracked it," he was saying during breakfast in the galley. "They've got to have found the bodies by now, but we've passed maybe forty other Antarean ships since we left the planet with Edgar. They're at least a day behind, and even if they alert the military out near the border, they don't know what kind of ship they're looking for."

"I think we should change ships once we hit the Neutral Zone," said Snake.

"I agree," said Pretorius. "No sense making it all the way to the Democracy only to have some would-be patriot blow us apart." He turned to Nmumba. "Well, let's have the bad news."

"Bad news?" repeated Nmumba with a puzzled expression.

"By now they know we've got you. Clearly you didn't tell them everything you know or they'd have killed you. So how long before they build a Q bomb that you *can't* neutralize?"

"Whatever they make next, it won't be a Q bomb," said Nmumba with certainty. "They'll need an entirely new principle. My method will neutralize any variation of what they've been using."

"What do you *think* they'll come up with next?" persisted Pretorius.

Nmumba smiled. "Since it will require an entirely new principle, one that hasn't been tested or even theorized yet, I can't even hazard a guess, except that it will be totally different, probably in its effect as well as its detonation."

"I'm not following this," said Snake. "Give us an example."

"The Q bomb can vaporize a continent in a matter of seconds," answered Nmumba. "It is, in effect, an absolutely huge blast. The next one may be totally silent, but might poison the atmosphere of an entire world, or create an instant ice age, or quickly dry up every drop of water—always assuming the population needs water, and about eighty percent of the inhabited worlds do. Or it may escape detection by coming to the planet in three or four discrete parts, none of which creates any problem or sets off any alarms until they join a day, a week, or even a month later." He paused. "As I say, different principles."

"I'd say we got you out of there just in time," said Ortega. "Who the hell knows how close they are to that shit?"

"It'll take more than me to come up with defenses against all those possibilities," replied Nmumba. "I was incredibly fortunate to have stumbled on the principles governing the Q bomb at the same time they were developing it."

"We'll settle for that," said Pretorius.

"Uh . . . better not relax or celebrate too soon," said Pandora, studying her instrument panel. "A military vessel's approaching."

"Can they read Edgar's DNA from beyond the ship?" asked Pretorius.

"I doubt it," replied Pandora. "They'd have it on record, but they can't read it without taking some kind of sampling, however miniscule."

"Maybe they're looking for him, maybe they're not," said Pretorius. "But we're Men in enemy territory, and the goddamned ship isn't armed!"

"So what do I do?" asked Pandora.

"Give me a second to think," said Pretorius. "How far are we from the Neutral Zone?"

"In a straight line, maybe fifteen hours."

"Okay, what's our alternative to a straight line?"

"There's a wormhole about half an hour away," she said. "We can beat them to it, might even outrun their weaponry . . ."

"But?" he said. "There's a 'but' in there."

"But it's not mapped on this ship's computer. It's there, but I don't know where it leads."

"Head for it, full speed."

"You're sure?" she asked.

"Consider the alternative," he replied.

The ship sped forward, and they all gathered to watch the viewscreen, even though the wormhole was invisible.

"How are we doing?" asked Pretorius after ten minutes had passed.

"They're just following us, as if they're curious about why we'd head for the wormhole," answered Pandora. "They're not in hot pursuit."

"Figures," he said. She looked at him questioningly. "They don't know we're humans," he added.

"Of course," she said.

"Stay on course anyway," he said. "If we slow down now, they're bound to want to know why we were headed for the damned thing."

"Right."

Two minutes later the military ship gave them an order to stop.

"Ignore it," said Pretorius.

Two minutes after that, the ship began firing.

"We seem to be just beyond their range," said Pandora. "I think we'll make it to the hole."

"Will they follow us?" asked Ortega.

"Not likely," replied Pretorius. "First, if this damned hole isn't on our charts, it might not be on theirs either, and for all they know they'll emerge in the Democracy. More to the point, if we emerge first, and of course we will, we can be waiting to blow them away. They don't know for a fact that we're not armed."

They reached the wormhole in another four minutes, and the military ship turned away just before they entered it.

"Well, that's that," said Pretorius.

"Hell, maybe we'll luck out and emerge in the Neutral Zone," said Snake.

"Or maybe even the Democracy," added Ortega.

"Let's just hope we can dope out our position when we're finally out of it," said Pandora. "We're a little low on food, and while I haven't visited the hydroponics section, we're not producing oxygen in the quantities I'd like. We've not about to asphyxiate, but we really should add to the plants. I'd hate to emerge in a totally unpopulated sector."

"You mean we *might?*" asked Proto.

"If you've got a way to chart a wormhole before you come out the other end, I wish you'd share it with us," said Pretorius.

"How long might it take to find sources of food?"

"It depends on what's at the other end of the hole," said Pretorius.

"And plants?" continued Proto.

"Same thing."

"You don't make it sound very urgent," commented Nmumba.

"We're safe for the moment," replied Pretorius. "*That* was urgent."

"I've got to get back to the Democracy," said Nmumba.

"You will."

"Quickly," he continued. "I learned some things there, things that might be vital."

"We'll do our best," said Pretorius. "The main thing is, we're out of Coalition territory." He paused and frowned. "At least, I hope we are."

They traveled through the wormhole for six hours, and emerged . . . *somewhere.*

"We're sure as hell not in the Democracy," announced Pandora, studying her instruments. "Not in the Coalition either, as far as I can tell."

"When should we know?" asked Pretorius.

She shrugged. "Once we get a fix on the major stars, it shouldn't be too long. Ten minutes, I hope. Certainly no more than half an hour."

After thirty minutes had passed, Pandora looked up from her panel.

"Still no luck," she announced.

"What the hell is going on?" muttered Pretorius.

They found out what the hell was going on in another fifteen minutes.

"As near as the computer can tell," said Pandora, "that wormhole chucked us three-quarters of the way across the galaxy. Probably things live here, but we've never contacted them or run into them. Officially this is one hundred percent empty space."

"So what do we do now?" asked Snake.

"Only one thing we *can* do," answered Pretorius. "We go back through the wormhole."

"*What?*" demanded Nmumba.

"No choice," said Pretorius. "No Democracy ship has ever been in this region. We don't have charts on any other wormholes, and if we try to go home through real space, it'll take us about seven hundred and fifty thousand years at light speed to get there."

"Great minds think alike," replied Pandora. "I've already reversed course and headed back to the wormhole."

"But the Antareans will almost certainly be waiting for us!" protested Nmumba. "There *must* be a faster way back to the Democracy."

"You're the genius," said Pretorius. "You tell us one, we'll give it a shot. I'm not anxious to go right back into a hole where the enemy might be waiting for us at the other end."

"Can a neophyte offer a suggestion?" said Irish.

"Sure," said Pretorius.

"Except for getting home your mission is accomplished," she said. "You've *got* the man you came to get. Why not find a habitable planet and set down on it for a month before going back? By then they should have giving up waiting for us to reemerge."

"Makes sense," said Pretorius. "If he didn't break, and you say it looks like he didn't, no one's going to be exploding any Q bombs."

"I *like* that idea," agreed Pandora, and Snake nodded her approval.

"*No!*" shouted Nmumba.

All eyes turned to him.

"We can't wait! I *have* to get to Deluros!"

"Irish makes sense," said Pretorius. "They'll be watching that hole for days, especially if *they've* ever mapped it. They'll know we have to come back out or die of old age in the farthest reaches of the galaxy. This will lower the odds against us."

Nmumba shook his head. "It's unacceptable. I *have* to get to Deluros!"

"You'll get there," said Pretorius irritably. "You just won't get there this week."

Nmumba began pacing around the deck, ranting that he couldn't wait, that his information was vital. He bumped against Ortega, and when he'd resumed his original position he displayed the burner he'd removed from Ortega's holster.

"I'm through arguing," he said, pointing it at Pretorius. "You—" he nodded his head toward Pandora "—get us to the Democracy."

"The only way I can do it in our lifetime is through the wormhole," she answered.

"Then take it. We can't wait."

She looked at Pretorius, who nodded his consent.

"You!" he said as Snake began reaching for her screecher. "Drop it!"

Snake seemed to consider his order for a moment. Then, with a shrug, she dropped the weapon so close to her that she could reach him if he tried to collect it.

"Speed it up!" Nmumba ordered Pandora. "I'm not going to die on this goddamned ship!"

"Who do you think wants to kill you?" asked Pretorius.

"Me," said Snake with an evil smile.

"I have no time!" snapped Nmumba.

Suddenly he frowned, as if he couldn't comprehend something, and then he pitched forward on his face, to reveal Irish standing behind him with a burner in her hand.

"I . . . I've never fired one before," she said weakly. "Not even on the practice range. It's just part of the gear you gave me."

"You did fine," said Pretorius, walking over and kneeling down next to Nmumba's body. "Yeah, he's dead. What the hell got into him?"

Nobody had an answer.

"You know," said Pretorius, "maybe we spent too much time worrying about his head. Pandora, tell Felix how to manipulate him so you can scan his whole body."

"Right," said Ortega, walking over and waiting for Pandora's instructions.

And three minutes later they found it.

"Fascinating," said Pandora. "A microscopic bomb, attached to his liver. Evidently he could set it off by some set of physical manipulations."

"What kind?" asked Pretorius.

"I don't know. Could be anything from biting the inside of his lip to purposely stubbing a toe. The wiring is all biological, so there's no way to tell." She paused. "I'll tell you something else, too. He's got no spleen and no pancreas . . . and I don't mean they were surgically removed."

"So he *was* a ringer."

She nodded. "And not even a human one."

"What was his big hurry?" asked Snake. "He could blow himself up just as easy in a month or a year."

Pandora shrugged. "It could be half a dozen reasons. Maybe the thing was operative only for another week or two. Maybe whatever triggered it was just natural enough that he wasn't likely to go a couple of months without doing it." She paused. "Whatever it was, it clearly had a definite time frame and he was afraid of that."

"He's not the only one," said Pretorius. "Felix, jettison the body."

As Ortega carted the body off, Snake turned to Pretorius. "So is our mission over?"

"That's what we've got to find out," said Pretorius. "And where we're going, I don't think we're going to find anyone anxious to tell us."

# 20

"**Y**ou look worried," noted Pandora as Pretorius stood beside her while she had the computer plot a course to the wormhole.

"I am," he said, frowning. "I can't believe they don't have three or four ships posted at the other end of the wormhole, and our vessel doesn't have a single weapon, not even an old-fashioned pulse cannon." He shook his head. "I'm willing to take risks, but this isn't a risk, it's suicide. Hold our position."

She instantly instructed the ship to remain stationary.

"All right," he said. "Let's find out exactly where the hell we are. And it wouldn't hurt to pinpoint a couple of habitable worlds in case we have to replenish our food supplies."

"Habitable but uninhabited," added Snake from a few feet away.

"If possible," agreed Pretorius.

Pandora nodded and began manipulating her computer.

"You know," said Ortega, "there's got to be more than one wormhole. Look how many we have in the Democracy."

"True," replied Pretorius. "But the trick isn't just finding them, it's knowing where they go. It's a big galaxy, Felix."

"Got an oxygen world," announced Pandora. "Ninety-four percent Standard gravity, air a little thin but breathable, and almost no neutrino activity, which implies that it's either uninhabited or at least an agricultural world."

"How far away?" asked Pretorius.

"We can reach it in two days, three at the outside."

"Let's go—and keep hunting for wormholes the whole time."

"I'll hunt for them," replied Pandora, "and I'll find them. But I don't know what good they'll do if they haven't been mapped."

"We'll start traversing them," answered Pretorius, "and sooner or later we'll come to a section that the ship knows, that's been mapped, and then we'll find a wormhole that'll put us near Antares, but *not* where they'll be waiting for us."

"May I offer an observation?" said Irish.

"You're a member of the team," said Pretorius. "Of course you may."

"I think there's at least a possibility that they're *not* looking for us to return," she said.

"Oh? Why?"

"Because there's a chance they think they've fooled us and that we're on our way, in however roundabout a fashion, to the Democracy."

"Good point," acknowledged Pretorius. "You could very well be right." He sighed deeply. "But it's not worth risking the ship for. Let's at least try to find another approach to Antares before attempting it."

It took three more hours, but finally Pandora announced that she had pinpointed their location.

"So where are we?" asked Pretorius.

"Believe it or not, we're smack-dab in the middle of the Bellini Cluster."

He frowned. "The Bellini Cluster? That's got to be seventy thousand light-years from the Democracy, and almost as far from the Coalition."

"Aren't wormholes wonderful?" said Snake dryly.

"Has any Man ever been out this way?" asked Pretorius. "Which is to say, has anyone charted it?"

"I'm still checking."

"Well, one way or another, we'll get back to Antares," said Pretorius. "If we want to."

"If we *want* to?" repeated Ortega. "What are you talking about?"

"Use your brain, Felix," said Pretorius. "What do we know about the dead man?"

"That he wasn't Nmumba."

"Right. Now, what do we know about the real Nmumba?"

"That he's buried two miles deep in that prison," said Ortega.

"And how do we know that?" asked Pretorius.

"Because Madam Methuselah—" Ortega frowned and fell silent.

"Right," said Pretorius. "She's never misled me before, but if she was wrong about this guy, she could be wrong about the very existence of a two-mile-deep prison." He paused. "I've been considering the possibility, and I think we've at least got to confirm it before we invade enemy territory again."

"So do we go back to her?" asked Snake.

"We at least let her know that her informant was either wrong or lying to her, and then we play it by ear from there." He paused. "They've got a pretty good description of this ship, so we're going to want a different one. Hopefully something with some armaments, just in case. After all, if we determine that Nmumba is there, they're not going to ignore a ship that approaches the sixth planet this time. They *wanted* us to steal the ringer and take him back with us, but they're not going to want us to get anywhere near the real McCoy. Which is another reason why I don't want to turn up in Coalition territory in this ship."

"Okay," admitted Snake. "It makes sense."

"Got something!" announced Pandora.

"Oh?" said Pretorius. "What?"

She frowned. "I always thought it was a myth."

"*What* was a myth?"

"Nothing," she said, frowning. "It actually exists."

"You want to start at the beginning?" said Pretorius.

"We're maybe ten hours from the Chryenski Wormhole," replied Pandora. "Ever hear of it?"

"No."

"I think I did," said Irish. "A very long time ago, when I was a little girl. I think it was part of a nursery rhyme."

"Okay, we're ten hours from the Chryenski Wormhole," said Pretorius. "What makes it so special, or so mythical, or so whatever-it-is?"

"It'll take us to within three light-years of Sol," said Pandora.

"*Earth's* Sol?"

"That's right."

"Isn't there something already taking up that space?"

"Centaurus," she answered. "But like everything else in the universe, it's rotating on course. The likelihood of a collision is maybe a billion-to-one against."

"Seems reasonable," Pretorius opined.

"It is."

He stared at her. "That's not enough to make it a myth or a nursery rhyme. What else can you tell us about it?"

"The woman who mapped it more than a millennium ago, a Lieutenant Chryenski, is the only person who traversed it. Once she came out near Sol, she decided to go visit our birthplace, maybe see how some of the cities had evolved."

"Makes sense," said Pretorius.

Pandora smiled. "She thought so too."

"Are you *ever* going to get to the point?" he asked irritably.

"She went to Earth," answered Pandora. "But it was a dinosaur-infested Earth of ninety million years ago."

"Are you saying this damned wormhole isn't just a hole in space but a hole in time as well?"

"Yes."

"Shit!" he muttered. "We can't use it."

"Yes, we can," said Pandora.

He shook his head. "We'll go to Antares from Sol, and show up ninety million years before Nmumba was born."

She smiled. "Chryenski did a little exploring and experimenting once she realized what had happened. If her written record is to be believed, it's an anomaly that only affects this wormhole and one other, one that leads from Sol to the Albion Cluster."

"You mean every other wormhole kept her ninety million years in the past, but the one to the Albion Cluster put her back in the present?" asked Pretorius.

"Back in *her* present," confirmed Pandora. "Remember, her voyage occurred a thousand years ago."

"But we know our way around the Albion Cluster," said Pretorius, trying to control his enthusiasm. "If we go to Sol and then to the Cluster and we're back in the current time, we know how to get to the Transkei Coalition from there. Hell, we can trade ships there, or purchase one. They'll honor Democracy currency, and I should be able to get Cooper to transfer the money. Then—"

He was still making plans as Pandora aimed the ship at the Chryenski Wormhole.

# 21

They emerged just beyond the Oort Cloud, much closer to Sol's system than they had anticipated, but nothing untoward happened as a result of it.

"Looks pretty much the same," remarked Snake as Pandora threw an image of Earth and the Moon on a viewscreen.

"You've been there?" asked Irish.

"No," said Snake, shaking her head. "Hell, I don't think I've ever met anyone who *has* been there. But I've seen enough drawings, photos, and holos of it."

"It only has one moon," noted Ortega.

"How the hell many did you expect?" asked Pretorius.

Ortega shrugged. "I dunno. It wouldn't be the first planet to lose a moon or two."

"Continents look a little different," said Snake. "I suppose that's proof that we're back where we figured to be." She paused. "Damn, I'd love to stop by long enough to see a T. Rex."

"That's for paleontologists," said Pretorius. "Our job is freeing Nmumba."

"Or terminating him," added Snake.

He nodded his agreement. "Or terminating him." He turned to Pandora. "Okay, find the hole we need and let's get to the Albion Cluster."

"Right," she said. "Good-bye, Mom."

"Mom?"

"The mother of the human race," said Pandora.

Within a few hours, ship's time, and ninety million years, give or take, real time, they had left Sol far behind and emerged in the Albion Cluster.

"What friendly planet are we closest to?" asked Pretorius.

"In miles or time?" asked Pandora.

"Time, of course."

"I can get us to Tsung Lo IV in about five hours, using the Killebrew Wormhole."

Pretorius nodded his approval. "Do it." He turned to Ortega. "Felix, check out our supplies—*all* our supplies: weapons, food, medications, everything—and see what we need to pick up." He paused. "Everything but fuel."

"Pandora's going to check that?"

"She could if we needed to, but we don't. We're dumping this ship, remember?"

"Right," said Ortega, who clearly didn't remember, but just as clearly didn't much care.

"I don't know anything about Tsung Lo IV," said Irish. "What's it like?"

"Oxygen world, pretty much Standard gravity," answered Pretorius. "Snows a lot."

"Are we looking for another Tradertown?" she asked.

He shook his head. "Tsung Lo's a little more civilized than that. Got a population of maybe a couple of hundred million, mostly humanoid. Three or four major cities, none of them close to each other. Lot of gold, silver, and platinum beneath the surface. It began life as a mining world."

"Began life?" she repeated. "What is it now?"

"Economic center, financial center, banking center, call it what you will. Not much activity that you can see, but in good years they all get rich."

"A world like that should have whatever kind of ship we need," said Irish.

"It will," replied Pretorius. "They won't manufacture it, but they can usually supply anything you want to buy." He frowned. "Hopefully within a day or two. They're still working on the real Nmumba. I don't care how strong he is, how well-conditioned our psych boys have got him, sooner or later everyone breaks. Or dies."

"We might kill him ourselves," interjected Snake.

"We might," agreed Pretorius. "But if we do, we'll know whether or not he's told them what they need to know. If we find him dead, we won't know that until they start dropping Q bombs again." He paused again. "And on that happy note, let's grab some breakfast, or whatever meal's coming next, before we hit the hole. I've eaten when traversing a long one, but I always feel a little, well, flimsy when I eat in a wormhole."

"Sounds good to me," said Ortega.

"I've eaten," said Proto, who had his own needs and his own food supply, "but I'll join you."

"Me, too," said Irish, walking toward the galley.

"I'll join you later," said Snake.

"You're not hungry?" asked Irish.

"Starved," replied Snake.

"Well, then?"

"Got to do my exercises," explained Snake. "No one's asked me for any of my specialties yet, but when they do—and Nate *always* does—I've got to be in shape."

"May I watch?" asked Irish.

Pretorius chuckled. "I hope you have a high tolerance for boredom."

Snake smiled. "What he means," she explained, "is that these aren't push-ups or leg lifts or anything that's the least bit interesting to watch. I'm not an athlete. Well, not primarily. I'm a contortionist. I fit in, and move through, places that no one else can fit in or move through." She pointed to a box against a wall. "My first exercise is to get into that thing and stay there for fifteen minutes." She chuckled. "Not exactly the kind of thing I can charge admission for."

"Okay," said Irish. "I admire anyone who can do that, but I think I'll eat with the rest."

"I'll be there in another forty-five minutes," promised Snake. "I know, I know—you'll all be done eating by then. But what the hell, the chairs are comfortable, and you have nothing else to do, so you can stick around and talk to me while I'm eating."

"That presupposes that anyone wants to talk to you," said Pretorius with a smile.

"I love you too," said Snake, walking over to the box. "And the whole time I'm in there, I'll be thinking of ways to torture you."

"More ways than you've already thought of?" he asked.

"You make me feel creative," she said, opening the box, and folding herself into it.

"Amazing!" said Irish.

"You think *that's* amazing, you should see her in action," said Ortega.

"Isn't that what I'm seeing now?"

Pretorius smiled. "It's more like *in*action."

Pandora walked over and joined them. "We're in totally uninhabited territory," she said, "and we're heading to neutral territory, so I don't see any reason not to put the ship on automatic and grab a meal."

"Long as you're back at the controls before we hit the wormhole," said Pretorius.

"I'll be there," she said. "That's Standard Operating Procedure. But to tell you the truth, I don't know why. Once we're inside a wormhole I can't maneuver, can't turn around or change directions, can't break out through what passes for a wall, so why bother?"

"Beats me," admitted Pretorius. "But I think until we learn more about them than that they go from here to there, we'd better follow the procedure."

"Well, they *are* useful," said Pandora. "From what I've read, there was a time, when we were just moving out into space, people were sure that achieving light speeds was the answer to exploring the galaxy." She smiled. "That was before they figured out that if you doubled our average life span, we could still explore about a tenth of one percent of the galaxy at light speeds."

"Thank God for wormholes," said Ortega.

"We needed a lot more than wormholes," added Pretorius, "but they were a vital first step. I wonder how many we blundered into before we developed the technology to spot and chart them?"

"A few hundred, I'd guess," said Pandora.

"I do remember reading or hearing that we'd colonized about forty worlds before we learned to spot and use the wormholes," offered Irish.

"Just think," said Pretorius. "Without them, we could be back on Earth beating the hell out of each other instead of fighting creatures who smell colors and excrete bricks."

"Do I detect a note of cynicism?" said Pandora with a smile.

"Part cynicism, part regret," said Pretorius. "I'd have been in the military either way. And there are days I think it might be nice to face off against creatures that aren't out of your childhood nightmares."

"Oh, come on, Nate," said Pandora. "Most of them aren't."

"True," he admitted. "But enough of them are."

They fell silent then, perhaps considering what Pretorius had said. Ten minutes later Snake burst out of her box, stretched for a few seconds, and walked into the galley.

"Damn, that's tiring work!" she said. "Too bad we didn't stop by Earth when we had the chance. I could eat a horse—or a small dinosaur!"

# 22

They emerged without incident, and within three minutes Pandora was able to locate their position within the Albion Cluster.

"Closest populated planets?" asked Pretorius.

"Brysk V, Tchemni II, and Moltoi," she replied. "We can reach any of them within a day."

"I assume it won't come as a revelation when I admit that I've never heard of any of them," he said, and Snake chuckled at his remark. "Any of them habitable by Men?"

"All three," she answered. "I thought that was what you meant."

"None of them allied with the Democracy or the Coalition?"

"No, none of them."

"Any of 'em got a population of one hundred million or more?" asked Pretorius.

"Moltoi has close to three billion."

"Humanoid?"

Pandora studied the computer, then shrugged. "Mildly."

"How about the other two worlds?"

"Brysk V is an agricultural world, colonized by a race known as the Kapcrodi. Less than fifty thousand population."

"And the other?"

"Tchemni II has a native population of five million. They have some agriculture, some mining, some relatively unsophisticated industry."

"Okay, get us to Moltoi," said Pretorius. "And show us what a native of the world looks like."

"We'll be there in nine hours and six minutes, ship's time. Two wormholes. And now for a resident."

She manipulated the computer, and a moment later an inhabitant of Moltoi was cast on the screen.

"Average height, five feet three inches. Average weight, one hundred twelve pounds. Legs are jointed as hocks, not knees, and it locomotes on all four limbs, though it stands upright."

"Damned inefficient," remarked Irish.

"Efficient enough to dominate this world and colonize half a dozen others," replied Pandora.

"If this is a male, just how small are the females?" asked Snake.

Pandora checked her computer, then looked up with a curious frown. "There *are* no females."

"What?" demanded Snake.

"And this character," continued Pandora, indicating the figure on the screen, "isn't actually a male."

"So they only have one sex?" asked Ortega.

"You haven't been paying attention, Felix," said Pretorius. "They don't *have* sexes."

"So how do they make little Moltois?" continued Ortega.

"As near as I can tell, they reproduce by a form of budding," answered Pandora.

"What fun is that?" said Ortega.

"Have a baby and then tell me about it," said Snake.

"You say they've colonized other worlds," said Pretorius. "I assume they're not at war with anyone?"

"Not at the moment," said Pandora.

"So we should be able to contact them and land without incident?"

"I assume so," replied Pandora. "Still, you never know."

"Okay," he said. "Now have the computer see if it can find out who they trade with, and especially if they have any treaties or reciprocal agreements with any of the Coalition worlds."

This time it took the computer almost five minutes.

"They trade with eighteen Coalition worlds," announced Pandora. "And I assume your next question is: Do they trade with any of the Antares planets? And the answer is yes, they trade with the third one—the big one."

"Good," said Pretorius. He smiled. "Actually, my next question was going to be: Do they trade with any Democracy worlds?"

She manipulated the computer again, then looked up. "Twenty-six of them. Including—" she frowned—"Earth."

"Clearly they don't use the same wormhole," replied Pretorius with a smile. "Mighty few triceratops were known as interstellar traders."

"This is serious, Nate," said Pandora. "If someone wants to go to war with Earth, someone who knew the coordinates and effects of that wormhole, they could destroy all life on the planet before anyone had evolved to stop them."

"Forget about it," said Pretorius. "We've got to concentrate on Antares and Nmumba."

"But—" began Pandora.

Pretorius smiled at her. "Think it through," he said. "If at any time between now and the goddamned heat death of the Universe someone goes back ninety million years ago and wipes out all life on Earth, what's the logical outcome?"

"Oh, of course!" she said, laughing.

"Well, *I* don't get it," complained Ortega.

"Felix," said Pandora, "if they wiped out all life ninety million years ago, *we* wouldn't be here talking about it."

"Sonuvabitch!" he muttered as the logic of it struck home.

"All right," said Pretorius. "Pandora, make contact with Moltoi, explain that we're from the Democracy despite having leased a Coalition vessel on a neutral world, and that we'd like to land and see what they've got to sell or trade."

"They're going to want to know what world we're from, maybe even what financial entity we're associated with."

"Might as well say Deluros VIII," answered Pretorius. "It's our capital world, so of course they'll have heard of it."

"And about the additional information?"

A smile spread across Pretorius's face. "Tell 'em we work for Cooper Enterprises, and if they need any contact information, give 'em General Cooper's private ID."

"You're sure?"

"Why should he sleep the sleep of the innocent when we're out here risking our necks for him? Yeah, I'm sure."

"I *like* that idea!" said Snake enthusiastically. "And no matter how much it pisses him off, he'll go along with it."

"It'll also drive him crazy wondering what we're doing in the Albion Cluster," added Ortega.

"Anyway," concluded Pretorius, "handle it that way. I recommend that the rest of you get some food and rest before we land."

"Surely you're not expecting any trouble on Moltoi," said Irish.

"No, I'm not," said Pretorius. "But . . ."

"But?" she repeated.

"But in my experience, that's exactly when you run into it."

# 23

They landed at a regional spaceport on Moltoi without incident, spent fifteen minutes clearing Customs with Proto registering under his true name and race (and appearance), rented rooms at a guesthouse for bipedal humanoids, and met in the lobby after unloading their minimal luggage. Proto had once again assumed the form of a middle-aged man, and since they had just landed and been cleared, no one considered him anything out of the ordinary.

"Okay," said Pretorius. "Our first duty is to get a different ship, one the Coalition won't be looking for. We'd like to buy it, but we'll steal it if we have to."

"Should we be discussing it right here in the lobby?" asked Irish, looking around at the multitude of different species, including some armed, uniformed Moltois.

"Just keep your t-packs turned off," replied Pretorius. "I doubt that we've got any Terran speakers in the vicinity. If you see someone concentrating on some device that *might* be a t-pack, then we'll find a different place to talk."

"I'm sorry," she said. "I'm new at this."

"You're doing fine," said Snake, patting Irish on the shoulder.

"Yes, you are," Pretorius confirmed.

"So what kind of ship do we want?" asked Proto.

"We'd much rather have a Coalition ship than one that's local to the Albion Cluster," answered Pretorius. "And we definitely don't want an Antarean ship. We don't know all their codes. That's probably forgivable in most Coalition members—they've got a *lot* of worlds—but not in a ship that's registered to any of the Antares planets."

"So how do we choose a ship?"

Pretorius looked at each member of his team in turn. "I think," he said at last, "that we'll send the two of you who look least like Men to scout out the spaceport and see what's there. Proto, you've had a chance to study the Moltois; you can appear as one." He turned to Ortega. "Felix . . ."

"I'm a Man, damn it!" growled Ortega.

"You're a Man on a mission and will do whatever's required to accomplish it," said Pretorius. "I know one of those arms extends a few extra feet of impenetrable metal. When you get to the spaceport, lengthen it. One of your eyes is artificial. Can you make it glow, or seem to spin inside your head?"

"No," said Ortega. "But I can do *this.*" And suddenly an eight-inch telescope extended from his right eye socket.

"Good," said Pretorius approvingly. "I won't ask you about each of your enhancements. Just put as many on display as you can when you get to the spaceport."

"All right," replied Ortega. "But can I ask what this is all about? We're just scouting out ships."

"We'd like to buy or rent one," answered Pretorius, "but if we have to steal one, it'll make the next few days much easier if they're not looking for Men."

"Okay," said Ortega with a shrug. He turned to Proto. "Let's go. The sooner we find what we're looking for, the sooner both of us can stop feeling like freaks."

Pretorius was grateful that Proto didn't reply "Speak for yourself,"

and the two of them walked out the front of the guesthouse and caught
a public transport that took them the two miles to the spaceport.

"What about the rest of us?" asked Pandora.

"If we're going to pick up an alien ship, we're going to need
supplies," said Pretorius.

"I know, I know," said Snake. "I'll take care of it."

She began walking to the exit.

"Does she have any of the local currency?" asked Irish.

Pandora and Pretorius merely smiled.

"Why should this be any different than Deluros VIII?" he said.
"I don't remember the last time she paid for anything. Hell, I'll bet
*she* can't remember it either."

"What if she gets caught?"

"Then if they know who she is, she'll be in a secure cell and I'll
have to bail her out."

"And if they don't know?"

"She'll pick the lock and be back here a few minutes later," said
Pretorius. "Now, what else are we likely to need?"

"Weapons?" suggested Irish.

He shook his head. "I'd like some weaponry on the ship, but
there's no way it's going to win a battle against a fully armed military
ship. As for personal weapons, it's my finding that anyone, human or
otherwise, is usually more efficient with weapons they're familiar with
than with those they've just picked up. Look at the Moltois. Their
fingers are ten or twelve inches long, they've only got two per hand,
plus what looks like a misshapen thumb. Any weapon that's made for
them is going to take more adjustment on our part than we're going
to be able to make with any degree of comfort or efficiency."

"So what do we three do now?" asked Pandora.

Pretorius shrugged. "Grab some lunch, if we can find a joint that serves food we can metabolize."

"I saw a restaurant that had a lot aliens in it," noted Irish. "Just up the street a bit."

"I hesitate to call that winding, uphill-downhill thing a street, but lead the way," said Pretorius.

"Why would they create it like this," said Irish as she led them out the door. "The ground is flat. Why build hills into the street?"

"You'd have to ask a Moltoi," replied Pretorius. "You can go crazy trying to make sense of alien cities. Like over there, for example." He pointed to a building. "Three stories high. In good repair. Windows on the third floor. No balconies, but platforms without railings, so if someone slips or trips he falls twenty feet to the ground. Of course, that presupposes that he can gain access to the third floor and its almost-balconies, because I don't see any doors or any other means of ingress."

"I used to go crazy trying to make sense out of alien cities and structures," said Pandora, "because they obviously made sense to the races that built them. In the end all you can do is shrug and say, 'Well, they're alien.'"

"It does make you wonder why we get into wars with them," added Pretorius. "Theoretically neither side should want anything the other side covets, but somehow that's never been the case."

"I took a few courses in alien psychology before I specialized," said Irish. "They had certain principles—generalities, really—and more exceptions than you can imagine." She smiled. "I was originally going to train for Alien Contact. After a year I realized that it was all guesswork, and I decided to study something where I could realize tangible results."

"Is that the place?" asked Pretorius, indicating a restaurant about fifty feet ahead.

Irish nodded. "Everyone on this world's an oxygen breather, but the clientele in this place seem less dissimilar to us and more diverse than most of them."

"A Glenarite, an Atrian, a couple of Bortais," commented Pretorius. "Yeah, they're close enough. If they like the food, we probably won't, but at least it won't kill us."

They entered the restaurant, walked over to an empty table, and sat down.

"Damned uncomfortable chairs," remarked Pandora.

"You won't be thrilled with the eating implements either," said Pretorius with a grin.

A gleaming metal robot approached them. "I am your server," it announced. "I am conversant in thirty-four languages and dialects."

"Do you speak Terran?" asked Pretorius.

"Yes," replied the robot.

"And do you take Democracy credits?"

"No, we do not."

"How about Willow IV tardots?"

"I must check," said the robot. It fell silent for a few seconds as it tied into whatever computer was controlling it. "Yes," it announced, "we accept tardots."

"I can't read your menu," said Pretorius.

"One moment," said the robot. It fell silent again, and suddenly the alien script was replaced by Terran.

They ordered the simplest dishes, those least likely to upset their digestive systems, and then surveyed their surroundings a little more thoroughly.

"I only see two citizens of the Coalition here," noted Pandora. "I hope that doesn't imply that there are very few on Moltoi."

"Why?" asked Irish. "I didn't think we'd want anything to do with them here."

*"Think,"* said Pretorius.

She stared at him, then lowered her gaze to the table for a few seconds. "Oh! Of course!" she said, looking up with a grin. "We need a Coalition ship. So naturally we'd like a broad selection."

Pretorius returned her smile. "We'll make a saboteur out of you yet," he said.

"I thought this was a rescue mission."

"It is," he replied. "But you'd be surprised how few of the enemy stand aside and let us rescue their prisoners."

"Point taken," said Irish, as the robot returned and set a tray of drinks on the table.

"What's this?" asked Pretorius.

"Flavored water," replied the robot.

"Why flavored?"

The robot was silent for a few seconds as it contacted its control.

"Men do not like the taste of our unfiltered water," said the robot. "If this is unsatisfactory, I can bring a concoction that is said to resemble lemonade."

"You lost me at 'concoction,'" said Pretorius.

"And me at 'resemble,'" added Irish.

"We'll settle for the water," said Pandora.

The robot retreated, but returned less than two minutes later with their meals.

"Not as bad as some I've had," commented Pretorius, taking a taste.

"I hope we don't have to eat this stuff too often," said Irish.

"If there's anything edible in this town, rest assured that Snake will find it," said Pandora.

They finished their meals, lingered over their water for a few minutes, and were just about to return to the guesthouse when Ortega and Proto, who was once again appearing as a Man, entered the restaurant and walked over to join them.

"I knew you'd be at one of these hash houses," said Ortega. "What's good?"

"You mean, what's less bad?" corrected Pandora.

"Are you eating too?" Pretorius asked Proto.

Proto shook his head. "I'd have to take my real form."

"So what? We know what you look like, and so, I gather, does everyone at the spaceport."

Proto made a face. "I'd have to eat on the floor, surrounded by your feet. I'd prefer to eat in my quarters, as usual. I'm sure Snake will provide for me."

"As you wish," said Pretorius. He summoned the robot, ordered the same meal for Ortega that he had had, and then turned to the two newcomers. "Well?" he said. "What have we got?"

"I think you're gonna love it, Nate," said Ortega. "In fact, that's the real reason we're here. I could have waited for Snake to bring my dinner, but I knew you'd want to hear this."

"I'm all ears," said Pretorius.

"Nate, they're repairing a bunch of air shafts and ducts at the spaceport," said Ortega enthusiastically.

"Who is?"

"A neutral race that adapted and evolved from a world the Antareans colonized millennia ago. We didn't see them when we landed, because they were working in the chlorine-breathers' section. But now they're moving to the part where we passed through Customs. And they were in the Customs building. Their ship's parked there, near the building and away from all the other ships." He learned forward, grinning. "Don't you see? How do we go down two miles to the prison? We swipe their ship and their equipment. Even if they report it missing, news of it won't make it to the Coalition, and if it does, who'll think we stole it so we could break into the least accessible jail in the galaxy? And the Antareans aren't going to fire on neutrals they're related to."

"You know, Felix," said Pretorius, "sometimes I think there's hope for you yet. That's a damned promising first step."

"What do you mean, first step?" demanded Ortega.

"These guys may come and go freely inside the Coalition, but no humans or human stock work for the Coalition," noted Pretorius. "How do we disguise ourselves? Or do these guys wear such heavy, protected suits that all you can tell about them is that they're bipedal? I assume they're bipods. Will their protective suits function two miles deep?"

"That's all stuff to work out," said Ortega gruffly. "The main thing is that we can get a safe ship and most of the equipment we need."

"No argument there, Felix. But there are a lot of details to work out."

"Including the most important of them all," said Pandora.

"Oh?" said Pretorius. "And what is that?"

"Madam Methuselah was wrong about Nmumba being in the tunnel. I assume you're going to want to stop by McPherson's World, find out what went wrong, and find out if the real Nmumba *is* in that prison." She paused. "How can we make sure your information is right this time?"

# 24

"**G**ot some goodies," announced Snake as she walked into the guesthouse's lobby.

"I never doubted it," replied Pretorius. "Where'd you stash them?"

"They're out back, under a tarp. They'll keep until dark."

"You're sure?"

Snake smiled. "There was a month's worth of dirt on the tarp."

"Okay," said Pretorius. "I've rented us a suite with a pair of bedrooms—one for the ladies, one for the gents. Come on, I'll show you where it is."

"Has Proto decided whether he's a guy or a girl yet?"

"He's whatever we need him to be," said Pretorius.

Snake nodded her agreement. "As long as there are no sensors around."

They took an elevator to the third level, stepped out into a corridor, and walked about twenty paces to a door at the end of it. Ortega pulled it open.

"They're pretty primitive, aren't they?" remarked Snake.

"What are you talking about?" asked Ortega.

"Doors that don't recognize you and open as you approach," she answered, "elevators instead of airlifts, and I saw a couple of vehicles that actually required a driver. Primitive world."

"I'm sorry you disapprove," said Pretorius.

"On the contrary," she replied with a smile. "It makes it that much easier to plunder."

"Let's hope that you've done all the plundering that's necessary," said Pretorius.

"Oh?"

He nodded. "Felix and Proto found a ship that sounds perfect for us. Now that you're back, I'll be going over to the spaceport to see if I can buy it."

"And if not?"

"We'll steal it, of course," answered Pretorius. "But why put every police and military ship between here and McPherson's World on the alert?"

"So you *are* going back to Madam Methuselah's," said Snake. "I was going to mention it to you."

"Get in line," said Pretorius wryly. He got to his feet. "Well, I might as well see if we can get it through legitimate means." He looked around the room, and finally his gaze fell on Irish. "You come with me."

"Me?" she said, surprised.

"You."

"But I don't know anything about buying a ship."

"Then it's time you learned," he said, walking to the door. He opened it, waited for her to walk out into the corridor, and then followed her.

They took the elevator down to the lobby. Then Pretorius approached the desk, found out where to wait for public transportation, and a moment later he and Irish were gliding along a foot above the ground in an open-air vehicle.

It took them about five minutes to reach the spaceport. They got off the vehicle and looked around.

"That must be it," he said, indicating a medium-sized ship

with a capacity of perhaps ten adult beings of human or Moltoi size. "It's parked right behind Incoming Customs, and clearly it's not going anywhere, so that implies they're working right where they are."

"I don't see anyone moving around," noted Irish.

"Good."

"Good?" she repeated.

"It means Felix was right, and that they're working in some shaft or enclosed space somewhere, and that means the tools and equipment are built for it. We'll use what we can, and the rest at least will give credence to our cover story that we're working on the shaft or some structure far beneath the surface."

"*Is* that our cover story?"

"If we manage to get this ship, it is," he answered. "Well, let's see who owns the damned thing and what it'll take to buy it."

They walked behind the oxygen-breathers' Customs building and saw three humanoid aliens working inside a subterranean air shaft that clearly led to an underground level of the building. Finally one of the aliens, who had been lying on his stomach, manipulating something about eighteen inches below the surface, noticed them, stood up, and lumbered over. He said something that their t-packs couldn't translate, and Pretorius adjusted his mechanism to speak in Moltoi.

"Good afternoon," he said. "My t-pack is unfamiliar with your language, and I am sure yours does not speak Terran, but we are both on Moltoi so surely this language will work."

The alien fiddled with his t-pack, made a gesture of incomprehension, and summoned another member of his crew. Pretorius offered the same message, and this alien nodded, adjusted his t-pack, and replied.

"Please excuse my friend," he said through the mechanism. "This is his first trip off-planet." A pause. "Off our home planet," he qualified.

"I was just admiring your ship," said Pretorius.

"It functions very well for our particular duties," replied the alien.

"Will you be here—I mean, on Moltoi—long?"

"We should finish our work by sunrise tomorrow, and then we'll return home and await our next assignment," said the alien. "I will miss Moltoi. The people are very friendly, and the restaurants and bars go out of their way to accommodate travelers from other worlds."

"If you are leaving tomorrow, I have a proposition for you," said Pretorius.

"More work?" suggested the alien. "You will have to confer with our employer. But even if you reach an accommodation, it will be performed by a different crew. We have been working for eighty-two—no, make that eighty-three—days on this planet, and we need some time to rest."

"Actually, I have work crews of my own," said Pretorius. "What I would like to do is purchase your ship and all of its equipment."

The alien stared at him as if unable to comprehend what he had heard, and made no reply. Finally he responded. "You wish to take work away from us."

"Absolutely not."

"It is not a new ship," said the alien. "Why would you want it, and if you do not plan to take work away, why do you need all of our equipment?"

"I have mining rights on two uninhabited worlds," answered Pretorius. "I need a ship that can get my crew there, and I need instruments for them to use once they arrive. I am willing to sign a pledge that I will not seek work on any world where you do business."

"That does not seem unreasonable," replied the alien.

"To whom would I make an offer?" continued Pretorius. "Of course, the offer will include passage to your home world for you and your crew."

There was no reaction.

"And for five days for your entire crew on any world you wish to visit on your way home," added Pretorius.

The alien's eyes widened. "Come back in . . ." He uttered a figure that translated as forty minutes.

"We'll be inside the oxygen Customs building," replied Pretorius.

He and Irish made their way to the building, sat down, and tried to guess how much the aliens would ask for their craft. The alien was back in fifteen minutes with a price.

"I will have to consult with my employer," said Pretorius. "I assume your employer will accept the local currency."

"Yes."

"Then give us a few minutes. We'll meet you back at your ship."

"I shall be awaiting you," said the alien, walking off.

"Okay," said Pretorius, "let's go find a private room."

"What for?" asked Irish.

"You know that we can triple his price if we have to, and I know it, but why should *he* know it. Let him think it's a hard negotiation and maybe he won't jack up the price at the last second because we gave in too easily."

"I saw a room off to the left," said Irish, getting up and leading him to it.

"I wish they served coffee or some other mildly human drink here," he remarked as he followed her.

"They've probably got a couple that won't kill you," she said. "But I suppose that's not the same thing."

"Not quite," he replied with a wry smile. "Check your timepiece, and we'll leave in about ten minutes. Well, check that. *I'll* leave."

"Why am I staying behind?" she asked.

"To call me back when I've made it halfway to the exit," answered Pretorius. "They've got a member of their race watching us from over there by that Perigoni ship. Let 'em think I'm not a free agent, that if they start adding a few credits here and there to the price you'll call me back and they might blow a beautiful deal. They don't get any part of the purchase price for the ship, but—" he paused and grinned "—they want that five-day all-expense-paid vacation."

"Okay," she said, returning his smile. "I'm taking mental notes. I'm learning."

They waited ten minutes, then Pretorius left the room and began walking toward the exit, only to have Irish call him back with a stern expression on her face.

"I'll bet they're thinking it's falling apart, and wondering what they can do to put it back together again," said Irish.

"The only thing they can do is grab it and run," he answered. "Let's give them five more minutes to consider it, and then go make our offer."

And ten minutes later Pretorius took possession of a ship, and twenty thousand light-years away Wilber Cooper authorized what he felt was an outrageous payment for an alien ship possessed of no armaments.

# 25

Their first port of call, of course, was McPherson's World. Given where they began, they traveled a strange and circular route, but Pandora got them there in the most efficient way possible.

"Felix," ordered Pretorius as they touched down, "you're on guard duty until we get back."

"How can I guard you if I'm here and you're at Madam Methuselah's?" demanded Ortega.

"Not *me*," answered Pretorius. "Guard the ship."

"Nobody on this world has ever even seen this ship," said Ortega. "Who am I protecting it against?"

"Anyone who wants it, or wants to rob it. Don't forget how we've occasionally acquired a ship when we've needed one."

"Am I accompanying you like last time?" asked Proto.

"No need to," said Pretorius, shaking his head. "You already know what an Antarean uniform looks like."

"I assume I'm staying here too?" asked Irish.

He stared at her for a long minute. "You come along."

She shrugged. "Not that I wouldn't love to visit the most famous whorehouse in the Neutral Zone again," she said sardonically, "but may I ask *why* I'm coming?"

"I wish to hell Circe was here," said Pretorius. "But she's not."

"I don't follow you."

"I need to know if Madam Methuselah just had a lousy informant, or if she sold us out. Circe could have told me by the time I'd asked three questions." He frowned. "But Circe's dead. You're the closest thing we have to her."

She shook her head. "Circe was intuitive. I'm a scientist. I'd need to devise tests and measure reactions. It could take days, which I gather we don't have."

"I know, probably nothing'll come of it. But come along anyway. Just let me know if you spot anything unusual, anything out of the ordinary."

"In a whorehouse that's home to twenty races?" laughed Snake. "Perish the thought."

Irish shrugged. "I obey orders. You're in charge, so of course I'll come. But I doubt that it'll do any good."

"Truth to tell, I doubt it too," Pretorius admitted. "But Felix and the others can protect the ship—and if they can't, then I very much doubt that your presence would make a difference."

They exited the ship and walked the relatively short distance to the center of town, and to Madam Methuselah's. It was early afternoon, and the place was a little less crowded than the last time.

"May I help you?" asked a green-skinned golden-eyed Denebian hostess. "And your companion?"

"Tell the Madam that Pretorius is here."

"Is there any message?" asked the Denebian.

"Just tell her," said Pretorius.

The Denebian left without another word, and Pretorius turned to Irish. "If she's with someone else, we could have a short wait."

"She still . . . ah . . . ?" began Irish.

He shook his head. "Not that she isn't pretty enough, but I guess it palls after eight or nine centuries. Anyway, everyone else here is in the pleasure business. She's in the information business."

"Is she really that old?" asked Irish dubiously.

"See that painting?" Pretorius asked, indicating a portrait of Madam Methuselah in a feathered gown that hung over the center of the bar.

"Yes."

"Good likeness, isn't it?"

She frowned, wondering what the catch was. "Yes, it is."

"It was painted by Benoit Mancuso," said Pretorius. He smiled. "He died more than five hundred years ago."

She sighed deeply. "I never looked that good on the best day I ever had."

"Do you wish you had?"

She shrugged. "I never really thought about it."

"Then don't think about it now," he said. "You're attractive enough, but the service is paying you for what's between your ears."

A trio of Torquals, each of them ten feet tall and heavily muscled, entered, paused to stare at the two humans, then walked over to a section of the bar that had been raised for their race.

A robot approached Pretorius and Irish. "She will see you now," it said, turning and leading them to Madam Methuselah's office.

"Ah, Nathan!" she said as they entered and the door snapped shut behind them. "Back already? I assume your mission went well."

"Yes and no," said Pretorius.

Madam Methuselah frowned. "Explain, please."

"We got the man that your operative identified as Edgar Nmumba." He watched her face for a reaction. "He was a ringer."

"Truly?"

"Truly," said Irish.

She walked over to her desk, stared at her computer for a

moment, uttered a command in a language neither of her visitors had ever heard before, then looked up at them.

"He made a mistake," she said. "He will never make another. I am so sorry, Nathan! Of course you owe me nothing, and in fact I am deeply in your debt. That was the first misinformation—let me be blunt: the first *lie*—I have ever received from my operative in Antares."

"Have you any other operatives in that system?" asked Pretorius. "Because we still need Nmumba."

"I will get the information you need, and there will be no obligation on your part—no payment, no favor, nothing. Though," she added, "I would of course appreciate your discretion concerning this little glitch."

He nodded. "How soon can you let me know for sure where they're keeping him?"

"Within a few hours," she said. "And everything in this building is at your disposal—both of you—until I have what you need."

"If you've still got a restaurant toward the back, we'll take you up on that," said Pretorius. "Now, how sure are you that you can trust whoever you're going to get our information from?"

"Once Nmumba's location has been pinpointed, I think there's no chance of an error."

"You thought that last time," said Pretorius.

Madam Methuselah visibly winced. "I know. But conditions are different this time. I've had reports of your progress. You stole the false Nmumba and escaped with him. No one has reported that you have discovered the deception, that you have rid yourself of him, indeed that you are anywhere except on your way to Deluros VIII." She paused. "That means they have no further need of deception. They assume the first one worked, and since they are at war only with the Democracy and the Democracy has made its move, there is no sense creating a second ringer. Whatever my operative reports, I will stake my life on it."

Pretorius resisted the urge to reply "Yes, you will," and walked to the door, which irised when it sensed his presence. He motioned Irish to join him, then turned to Madam Methuselah. "Let us know as soon as you find out. We've already lost a few days."

"I know, and I apologize," she said.

Then they were in the corridor leading back to the main section of the building.

"Toward the left, as I recall," said Pretorius, taking Irish by the arm and walking to the restaurant.

Another Denebian girl showed them to a table, uttered a command, and holographs of menus appeared above the table, with mouth-watering representations of each item.

"Damn!" said Irish. "I don't recognize three-quarters of the dishes, but the ones I do know belong in a five-star restaurant."

"They don't stint here," said Pretorius.

They took a few minutes to order, and then he lowered his voice so only she could hear it.

"Well?"

"I think you can trust her. After all, she gains nothing by lying. Once is a blunder. Twice, on the other hand, invites retaliation."

"I've been relying on her for, hell, it must be twenty years now, and this is the first problem," he said. "And when you think of it, the poor bastard who gave her the information had good information. We didn't know our Nmumba was a phony until we were out of the system, and Lord knows we didn't just walk in, grab him, and walk out." He shrugged. "Well, what the hell—you work in this business, you accept that there are consequences for being wrong."

Their meal arrived, and they were about halfway through it when a Denebian girl—it could have been the same one; Pretorius couldn't tell them apart—approached the table.

"Madam Methuselah is ready for you," she announced.

Pretorius was on his feet immediately. "You want to finish?" he asked Irish.

"No, I'll come along."

"You sure?" he said. "We've decided she's going to be telling the truth, and even if she isn't we're going to have to believe her until we prove otherwise."

"I'm through, really," she said, forcing an insincere smile.

"Okay," said Pretorius. He turned to the Denebian girl. "We know the way."

The two of them walked through the main section of the building to the corridor that led to Madam Methuselah's office, and a moment later were standing inside it.

"I made absolutely certain this time, Nate," she said by way of greeting. "He's in the prison."

"Okay," replied Pretorius. "I figured that was what you'd find."

"I apologize again," she said. "I checked to see the last time I gave false information that I believed was true." A self-deprecating smile spread across her face. "It's been a *long* time."

"I'll bet it has," said Pretorius. "Well, we'll be on our way. We've still got our work cut out for us."

He and Irish turned and approached the door, which irised to allow them through. Just before he left the room he turned to face Madam Methuselah. "*How* long a time?" he asked.

She sighed deeply. "One hundred and twenty-seven years," she replied.

# 26

"Okay," said Pretorius as the ship took off from McPherson's World, "it's time to do some serious thinking. Why did they dig down two miles to begin with? Surely it wasn't just to create a jail that only holds one man. Hell, it has to have taken them long enough to dig that far down, whenever that was, they couldn't have known they'd have their hands on Nmumba when it was done."

"What difference does it make?" said Ortega. "We know he's there—at least we think we know it—and all that matters is that we've got to go down and pull him out."

Pretorius merely stared at him until he fidgeted uncomfortably, then spoke again. "If all they built was a theoretically impregnable jail, there's only one entrance and one exit. But if they decided to put the jail there because the space was available and wasn't being used for anything else at the time, that could make a huge difference in how we access it and, assuming we live long enough, how we escape from it."

"Well, if they had some reason to go two miles deep, there would have to be something there that they need," said Pandora. "Something *rare*."

"Why rare?" asked Snake.

"Because most things are far more easily obtained," answered Pandora. "It takes a lot of work and a lot of money to dig two miles deep, and to make sure the area at the bottom has breathable air and acceptable temperatures."

"Does anyone want to argue that?" asked Pretorius. "No? Okay, then—I want each of you to tie into Pandora's computer and see if you can come up with what their original reason for burrowing so deep might have been."

"And if we find it, what then?" asked Snake.

"First let's find it," said Pretorius. "Then we'll worry about it."

And within an hour, they *had* found it—or, more precisely, Irish had.

"I've got something very interesting here," she announced.

"Yeah?"

She nodded her head. "Have you ever heard of Mistalidorium?" she asked.

Nobody had.

"It's the one hundred and twenty-fifth element," she replied. "It's only known to occur in Nature on three worlds—and one of them is Antares Six."

"Mistalidorium?" repeated Pretorius. "What does it do?"

"It cures a cancer-like condition that plagues the inhabitants on Antares Three. That's probably why anyone was on Six to begin with: to mine it. From what I can find, it's exceptionally rare, occurs only in tiny quantities, takes all kinds of lab work to isolate it, and—" she smiled "—it occurs at a planetary depth of two to three miles."

"Son of a bitch!" said Pretorius happily. "If it's that rare and that vital, there *has* to be more than one shaft leading down to it."

"Make sense," agreed Pandora.

"So . . . is the jail connected to any of the other areas?" continued Pretorius. "I think it would almost have to be. You'd need a means of emergency evacuation if the shaft collapsed or filled with poisonous gas or fluids, and if the few areas at that depth are connected, it has to make distributing supplies a little easier."

"But we don't know that," said Pandora. "And we've dealt with enough alien societies to know that being logical has nothing to do with being true."

"Also," added Proto, "we're going to be seen. We may convince them that we're a repair crew or delivering foodstuffs or medications or whatever . . . *once* . . . but if there's no connection, we're going to have a very hard time convincing them twice."

"I know," said Pretorius. "We'll keep trying to find some other means in ingress as long as I think we can wait, and then, if we haven't found it, we go in the front door."

"Which they probably have covered six ways to Sunday," said Snake. "It was hard enough to rescue the ringer, and they *wanted* us to rescue him."

Pretorius shot her a smile that was half grim and half amused. "Did I ever say it was going to be easy?" he asked. He turned to Pandora. "I assume this isn't the only world where they mine this stuff?"

"No," she answered. "There seem to be half a dozen of them spread throughout the known galaxy."

"Any others in Coalition territory?"

"Let me check," she said, putting the question to her computer. "Yes, one. It's also mined on Beshar, the ninth planet orbiting a very large red star named Zhantagor."

"Well, that's a start," said Pretorius. "Have the machine tell us whatever it can about who mines it, how it's mined, what kind of special equipment they need, what particular dangers may be involved, everything it can find out. And," he added, "it wouldn't hurt to find out how and where they mine it on Antares Six."

"We already know they mine it here," said Snake.

"Yeah," replied Pretorius, "but we'd like to know *where* they mine it. It won't do us any good if it's at either pole, or just in one location halfway around the planet." He paused. "But I keep thinking that subway wasn't built just to endlessly transport a prisoner, or even a group of them, and if I'm right, then the only thing that seems to make any sense is that it connects with some kind of mining operation."

"But it's only half a mile deep," noted Snake, "and from what Pandora says, the mine for this Mistalidorium shit is two miles deep."

"That's why we need to find out more about it," said Irish. "Maybe they have to process it, rid it of some harmful element, do *something* before they bring it to the surface. Maybe they dig at two miles, but their lab is at half a mile. Easier to build it and access it if it's not all the way down."

"She's right, of course," said Pretorius. "It's worth waiting an extra few hours, or even a day or two, if we can find some connection, or definitely prove there isn't one."

"It's a pain in the ass," muttered Snake.

"True," he agreed.

"Well, then?" she asked hopefully.

"It's even more of a pain if they break him and you're one of the billion or so people standing under the next Q bomb," said Pretorius.

# 27

It was two hours later that Pandora looked up from the computer, frowning.

"Uh . . . we have a little problem," she announced.

"They don't mine it anywhere else on the damned planet?" asked Pretorius.

"Oh, *that*—I haven't been able to find out yet."

"Then what's the problem?"

"We're going to need another ship."

"Why?" said Pretorius. "We bought it, we've got receipts, ownership papers, everything."

"They've just declared that the entire Antares system is off-limits to all nonmilitary personnel, except for legal residents."

"Shit!" he muttered. "I knew it would happen, but I didn't think it'd be this soon."

"You knew *what* would happen?" asked Snake.

"They must have figured we'd rush the phony Nmumba back to Deluros and turn him over to the authorities by now," answered Pretorius.

"So?"

"So if Irish hadn't killed him, that bomb inside him would be exploding right about now, theoretically killing off a lot of the service's top brass—and they had to assume the second that happened we'd know it wasn't Nmumba and would be coming back for him, or to dump a few of our biggest bombs on the Antares system, especially on the heavily populated one, Antares Three."

"So do we find a way to drop a smart bomb down the shaft, assuming that it *is* a shaft?" asked Snake.

Pretorius shook his head. "No."

"It's the easiest way," she insisted. "And it's part of our job description: save him if we can, kill him if we can't."

"First we have to find out if they broke him," said Pretorius.

"What real difference does it make?" she persisted. "Either they got what they want or they didn't. Either way, it makes sense to kill 'em all."

"Snake, I do believe you are the bloodthirstiest human being I've ever met."

"You didn't answer me," she noted.

"We can't kill him before we know if our defense against the Q bomb is still viable, or if they've found a way to negate it," said Pretorius.

"What if he's already dead when we get there?"

"Then we have to assume they got what they want, and get word back to Deluros VIII."

There was a momentary silence.

"So we can't approach Antares even in this neutral ship?" said Ortega.

"Right."

"And we have to have a military ship."

Pretorius nodded his head.

"And you think six of us are going to steal a battleship or a destroyer?" continued Ortega.

"Of course not," replied Pretorius. "Not all military ships have crews of hundreds or thousands, especially here in the Neutral Zone, where they're not at war with anyone. There'll be a handful of small ships—survey ships, ships carrying medical supplies, ships with half a dozen peaceful functions. We'll just have to find one and appropriate it."

"You say that as if it's the easiest thing in the universe," noted Snake.

"No," he agreed. "But if you've got anyone you care for who's targeted by a Q bomb, it's the most important thing in *our* little universe."

Snake sighed deeply. "Point taken."

"You care about someone?" said Ortega, surprised.

"Oh, shut up," she said, glaring at him.

Pretorius turned to Pandora. "Start monitoring all the messages you can and see if you can spot us a reasonably small, reasonably close military ship."

"I'm good for another hour or two," she replied, "but then I've got to get some sleep."

"What kind of program are you using?" asked Irish.

"Commisky 738-B," replied Pandora.

Irish smiled. "I can work just about every Commisky program."

"You're an endless source of surprises, Irish," remarked Pretorius. "You killed a bad guy, and now you can find a ship carrying more of them."

"Only if it's out there and sending signals," she replied.

"Fine," said Pandora. "You want to use my ID or your own?"

"Better to keep yours a secret," she said. "Just program 'Irish' in for me."

"Are you sure?" asked Pandora. "Wouldn't you like something not instantly identified with you, just in case?"

Irish shook her head. "I wasn't Irish until I joined the Dead Enders, and I'm sure I'll never be Irish again once I leave."

"You come up with one or two more hidden talents and we may never let you leave," said Pretorius.

She turned to face him and return his smile, only to find out that he wasn't smiling at all.

"Okay," he said, getting to his feet. "I'm going to try to find something mildly edible in the kitchen. Pandora, go grab some sleep. Irish, remember that whatever ship you pinpoint for us, we're almost certainly going to have to take it away from its crew, so try to find us one that doesn't hold more than ten or twelve of the enemy."

"Right," she replied.

"And if you can find a medical ship, so much the better," he added. "I have a feeling that one of them can access areas where we'd have to fight our way in on a regular ship."

"I'll do what I can," said Irish.

"I'm sure you will," said Pretorius. "You haven't disappointed us yet."

"To hell with eating," said Pandora, walking off to her cabin. "I think what I really need is some sleep."

"If the food doesn't get much better, maybe I'll join you," said Ortega, heading toward the galley.

"The hell you will," said Pandora.

"I meant I'll go to sleep," he said. "In my cabin. Alone."

"Stick to that," commented Pretorius, "and she just might let you live."

He ordered his meal, picked it up, and carried it to one of the two tables. Ortega joined him a moment later.

"Do you get the feeling," said Ortega, "that no matter what they say about breaking codes and assimilating alien cultures and all that other crap, the thing we do most often is steal goddamned ships?"

"Sometimes it feels that way," admitted Pretorius. "But my last three assignments had me and my team deep in enemy territory, where the quickest way to commit suicide would have been to be aboard a Democracy ship."

"Still . . ." muttered Ortega.

"Just be glad if that's the most difficult thing we have to do," said Pretorius. "I've been shot at, stabbed, bitten, and had my goddamned foot blown off three times—the real one once, the artificial replacement twice. You were on the last mission. Do you really think stealing a ship, even one with a military crew, is harder than replacing the enemy's most powerful and best-guarded general with a clone that we created?"

"No," admitted Ortega. "No, I suppose not."

"Hell, stealing a military ship is probably the easiest part of what lies ahead of us."

He had no idea just how prophetic a statement that was.

# 28

It was seventeen hours later that Pandora, back at the controls, announced: "I've got one."

"How big?" asked Pretorius, coming out of his cabin.

"Looks to hold maybe eight, possibly ten."

"And it's definitely military?" he asked.

She nodded her head. "Definitely. It's set down on Tabor II. From what I can tell the crew are all oxygen breathers."

"Can you determine what it set down for?"

She shook her head. "No. But I'm getting no life reading from the ship, which means they've all left it."

"And it's functional?" persisted Pretorius. "They didn't crash?"

"All of its systems seem to be operative."

"They haven't sent out an S.O.S. or answered one from the planet?"

"Not as far as I can tell," she replied.

"And it's definitely military?"

"It's not a warship," said Pandora, "but it's definitely a military ship."

"Okay," said Pretorius. "Let's get over there before they decide to leave."

"I've already adjusted course," she replied. "We should be there in about three hours."

"One more question," he said. "Is the planet populated?"

She frowned. "Yes, of course."

"There's no 'of course' about it," he answered. "If there's a population, clearly the Antareans are interacting with them, and that makes our job that much harder."

"I don't follow you," said Pandora.

"If they just landed on, say, an empty chlorine world to effect repairs or pick up some rare element they want or need, we could simply land next to their ship, move our gear into it, destroy this ship, and take off. But since there are sentient beings there, maybe even chlorine breathers, we have to assume that they know and interact with the Antareans." He paused. "And that means we have to kill the ship's crew. We can't leave them behind if they can report that we've stolen their ship."

"We'd better hope they're not too scattered over the landscape," said Snake.

"And that they don't have allies," added Proto.

"We'll worry about each problem as we come to it," said Pretorius. "The first order of business is to make sure your weapons are fully charged." He turned back to Pandora. "And your job, along with getting us there, is to determine the conditions—gravity, atmosphere, temperature, whatever we need to know. And try to determine what the hell they're doing on that planet, and where they might be if they're still out of the ship when we arrive."

"I'm working on it," she assured him.

Three hours later she was still working on it as they entered the Tabor system.

"Okay," said Pretorius as Tabor II came up on the viewscreen. "There's no sense setting the ship down until we know what's there and what kind of reception we might get. I think we'll take the sleds. Irish, you, Proto, and Ortega go on one, Snake and I will go on the other. Pandora, keep the ship in orbit, pinpoint any signals they try to send out, and keep in touch with me."

"What's the gravity like?" asked Ortega.

"About ten percent heavier than Standard," answered Pandora.

"And visibility?"

"Looks clear," she said.

"Okay," said Pretorius. "Let's get ready to go. Get into your protective suits, make sure your weapons are charged and that your oxygen tanks are full."

"Oxygen tanks?" said Ortega, frowning. "I thought this was an oxygen world."

"There are all kinds of oxygen worlds," replied Pretorius. "Trust me, you wouldn't like one with ninety percent oxygen in the atmosphere, any more than you'd like one with five percent."

A few minutes later they were riding their sleds down to the planet's surface, and a couple of minutes after that all five of the landing party were inside the Antarean ship.

"Well, that was easy enough," remarked Snake, taking off her helmet and deeply inhaling the ship's air. "Can't say that I admire their color sense. The whole goddamned ship is gray."

"There's always a possibility that they're color-blind," suggested Proto.

"After eating what we've been eating for the past few days, I can't imagine their galley will produce anything we can't metabolize," said Irish. "I look forward to tasting some of their foodstuffs."

Ortega shook his head. "Take it from me, no matter how they try to dress it up and color it, alien food is alien food." He made a face. "Gives you a new appreciation of the endless non-variety of soya products we have to eat on Democracy ships."

"So how many Antareans *were* on this ship?" asked Snake.

"I'd guess eight or nine," answered Irish. "Anything more and they'd be too cramped."

"Shit!" exclaimed Pretorius, who was examining the ship's control console.

"What is it?" asked Irish.

"The bastards activated an alarm system that radios them when the ship's been boarded. I don't know where they are, but they know we're on the ship, and *that* means they're not coming back, not right away."

"So what?" said Ortega. "We're in control of the ship. We'll just take off."

"We can't," said Pretorius. "Right now we could just be kids, curiosity-seekers, half a dozen other things . . . but the second we take off they'll know we've stolen their ship, and they'll alert the powers-that-be in the Coalition to keep an eye out for it and blow it out of the ether once they spot it."

"So what do we do?" asked Ortega. "We can't leave, and we can't just sit here and wait for them to return because they're not coming back while we're on the ship."

Pretorius sighed deeply. "We leave the ship and go out hunting for its crew."

"And kill them," said Snake.

Pretorius nodded his agreement. "And kill them."

# 29

It was a bleak, sandy world, reasonably flat except for the occasional enormous dune. The heat wasn't oppressive, and the gravity was a little lighter than Standard. Pandora had said there was a freshwater ocean, but it wasn't within a thousand miles of where they touched down.

"So where do we start?" asked Ortega as they left the ship. "Take our sleds and look for them?"

"No," answered Pretorius. "The sleds have no defense mechanisms."

"Then what do we do?"

"We remember that this is a neutral world. Pandora will direct us to the nearest locals, and we'll play it by ear."

"That could be miles."

"It could be," agreed Pretorius. "But I doubt it."

"Why?" asked Ortega.

"Because they could have set their ship down anywhere, and they chose this spot. That makes me think that whatever they're looking for—locals, animals, minerals—is nearby."

"And this sandy soil," added Snake, indicating the ground, "makes it very easy to track them."

"Perhaps we should spread out a bit," suggested Irish, "since they know we're looking for them."

"They do?" asked Ortega.

"Well, they know we're on the planet and have been in their ship," she replied. "The fact that the ship is still here would seem to imply that we're looking for them."

"And they shouldn't be too hard to find," added Pretorius. "All they have to do is check with some local source to find out that we came in a Coalition ship, not a Democracy one. There's no reason for them to think we're an enemy military force."

They walked for another fifteen minutes, and then Pandora got in touch with them.

"I think I know why they're here," she announced, "and if so, then I know where you'll find them."

"What have you got?" asked Pretorius.

"I've been doing a little research," she began.

"On Antareans?"

"On Tabor II," she replied.

"And?"

"You ever hear of *crattius*?"

"No," said Pretorius. He looked at his team. "Anyone else?"

"I have," answered Proto. "But I confess that I've never seen or experienced it."

"*Experienced* it?" repeated Pretorius, frowning.

"I believe it's a stimulant for certain oxygen-breathing species," said Proto.

"He's right," said Pandora.

"They're here for drugs?" said Pretorius.

"With all due respect, there's nothing else on Tabor that's worth anything to anyone."

Pretorius scanned the barren landscape. "It can't grow in the ground," he said. "Nothing does, not around here—and if there's a garden spot anywhere on this planet they'd have set their ship down a lot closer to it."

"It's like Mistalidorium—it gets *mined*," answered Pandora.

"Based on what I can glean from the computer, the stuff is mined solely at the polar areas."

"That doesn't make any sense," said Pretorius. "We can't be fifteen degrees north of the equator."

"It gets mined at the poles," said Pandora. "But it gets processed in the cities—villages really. And you've covered about half the distance from the ship to the nearest village."

"So are they going to the village?" asked Snake. "I think it'd be more convenient to have a drop point."

"No, it makes sense," said Pretorius. "Having a drop point for off-worlders implies you hope they'll drop their money off at the point. Dealing with them face-to-face makes getting paid much more likely."

"Then why not set the ship down right at the village?" persisted Snake.

Suddenly Pretorius smiled. "Pandora, you still there?"

"Where would I go?" she asked.

"Is *crattius* legal?"

"Let me check." There was a brief pause. "It's legal on most worlds of the Coalition, but it's outlawed in the Antares system and about a dozen other worlds. And it's illegal to sell it to residents of those worlds."

"Thanks," said Pretorius. "That explains it." He turned to face his crew. "That means they're probably at the village—or else they've done their business and are on their way back to the ship. It also means they'll almost certainly start shooting the second they see us." He looked ahead across the bleak landscape. "And since we don't know when we're going to come upon them, I suggest that we spread out. No sense giving them one big target rather than five smaller ones."

"I think I can help," said Pandora's voice.

"Oh?"

"There's a gully off to your left. You're not that far from the village. If you can't see them yet, that's the most logical spot for them to be."

"Thanks," said Pretorius, heading toward the gully. "By now they have to know we've boarded their ship, but they probably don't know yet that we've come looking for them . . . so we have an element of surprise that should last about two seconds. Make your first shots count. I assume the locals don't want any trouble, especially since they don't know who we are or what legal authority we represent, but there's also the chance that they'll be so afraid of the consequences of being caught selling drugs that they'll join the fight on the Antareans' side."

"This should be a piece of cake," said Ortega. "We're out to kill, not capture, and we've got the element of surprise on our side."

"Before you get too confident," said Pretorius, "remember that whether they're buying drugs or not, they're trained military men."

"Or military *things*," added Snake.

"Whichever," said Pretorius.

They reached the edge of the gully in another five minutes.

"I hope to hell Pandora was right," said Ortega.

"We'll know soon enough," said Pretorius, lowering himself to the ground and inching forward on his belly.

"Four of them," whispered Irish. "And maybe six locals."

"Okay, target the Antareans first, aim carefully, and fire on my signal," said Pretorius.

Suddenly they heard a raucous buzzing sound.

*"Goddammit!"* bellowed Ortega, blood spurting from his left arm.

"Fire!" yelled Pretorius, and as the others fired, Proto had his image stand up to draw the enemy fire, which didn't figure to touch him unless they aimed at the image's feet.

*"Son of a bitch!"* growled Ortega as laser beams dug into the ground near them and explosive projectiles burst just over their heads. "That was my only whole limb!"

"Stop moving and maybe you won't bleed to death before we can get you back to the ship!" snapped Pretorius.

"Got two of 'em!" hollered Snake.

"And I got one!" added Irish.

"Where the hell is the lookout?" said Pretorius. "The one who shot Felix?"

"It came from that sand dune," said Snake, pointing. "Now he's ducked behind it."

"It won't save the bastard!" yelled Ortega. "I'll kill him myself!"

"Just hold still!" said Pretorius, ripping off part of Ortega's shirt and trying to use it as a tourniquet.

"Got the fourth one!" cried Snake triumphantly.

"What about the locals?" asked Pretorius.

"Running like hell in the other direction," said Proto.

"Irish, get over here and go to work on his arm," said Pretorius. "I don't think it hit an artery, but there's a lot of blood."

Irish crawled over and took over trying to create the tourniquet.

"Snake, stay on guard in case some of the locals come back."

"Where are you going?" asked Snake as Pretorius stood up.

"I'm going after the lookout, the one who shot Felix," answered Pretorius, heading in the direction the shot had come from.

"Be careful," said Irish. "After all, he's the only one who hit us."

"He's the only one who had time to take aim," replied Pretorius, crouching and approaching the ridge where the shooter had been hidden. He found the tracks that were clearly Antarean, and began following them. After he'd gone a quarter mile he saw the sun glint off something at or near ground level, and he threw himself onto the sand as a beam of solid light passed three feet above his head.

He look across the sand, couldn't see his foe, but knew he had to be hiding directly behind a mound of sand, the only cover in that direction. He thought for a moment, then aimed his laser at the sand that was just behind the mound and fired it, moving slowly from right to left, turning the sand into a boiling, bubbling glassy semiliquid. He then did the same thing on each side of the mound.

"Okay," he whispered, "let's see you run through *that*."

The Antarean remained in hiding behind the mound, and Pretorius holstered his burner and pulled out his screecher—his sonic pistol. He put the power on maximum and fired it directly into the mound of sand. He held it steady for ten seconds, and suddenly there was a scream of agony, and the Antarean burst out from behind the mound, ran unthinkingly through the molten sand to his left, lost his footing, and fell with a splash.

He was dead before Pretorius walked up to make sure of that fact. He put a quick laser blast through the Antarean's head, just to be sure, then turned and walked back to where his party was waiting for him.

"You got him," said Snake. It was not a question.

Pretorius nodded his confirmation, then turned to Irish. "How is he?"

"Well, I've stopped most of the bleeding," she said. "There's no way we're going to get him to a doctor—at least, a human doctor—but I think he'll be okay. Nothing's broken. It's a flesh wound. We need to get it fixed, but once we do he should be able to use it." She shrugged. "How much he uses it depends on how much pain he can stand."

"It was my most useless part anyway," grated Ortega, grimacing. "Once we get back to Deluros maybe I'll trade it for an old-fashioned sword, or a device that can sense an enemy before the five senses I've got."

"Let's just concentrate on keeping you alive until then," said Irish, fashioning a sling out of what remained of his shirt.

"And the best way to do that is get back to the ship," said Pretorius. "Start walking. Pandora, set your ship right down next to the Antarean ship. First thing we'll need is any medical supplies that we have on either ship. Then we'll transfer all our gear, give you time to hook your computer up to the new ship, and then we're out of here."

"Sounds good," replied Pandora. "I should get there a little ahead of you."

"Good," said Pretorius. "When you do, go into the Antarean ship and open up a communication channel between me and the village. I don't know their ID for this, but the Antareans had to have it. I mean, hell, they wouldn't come here unless they knew they had a deal."

"I'll do what I can" said Pandora, and three minutes later Pretorius found himself speaking to one of the villagers.

"Why did you kill our friends?" asked the villager.

"They robbed us and tried to kill us," said Pretorius. "They were our enemies, but we have no quarrel with you. In fact, I have a proposal to prove our goodwill."

"I am listening."

"We have not touched any of the corpses. Once we take off, which will be momentarily, you can take your payment back from their bodies," continued Pretorius. "Not only that, but we will make your village a gift of our ship, which is worth many times what you were paid for the *crattius*."

"No one is that generous. What do you want in return?"

"Only your silence," said Pretorius. "You will tell no one that we took their ship."

"I agree," said the villager.

"We have a deal," said Pretorius. "I want you to know one more thing."

"Oh?"

"Yes. If you break the deal, if you tell anyone that we took the ship, we will come back and kill your entire village."

He cut the communication.

"Did you mean that?" asked Irish, who had been standing near him.

"No," he said. "If they tell anyone before we get to Antares, we'll get blown to pieces as we approach the planet. And if they tell anyone once we've got Nmumba and are back in the Democracy, who gives a damn?"

"You're almost as devious as I am," said Snake with a smile.

"All right," said Pretorius. "Next stop: Antares."

# 30

They spent half a day in orbit around Tabor II while Pandora acquainted herself with the ship's controls and codes, then began making their way to the edge of the Neutral Zone.

Pretorius wanted more information about the mining of Mistalidorium on Antares Six, but he was aware that time was running out, that no matter how tough Nmumba was, sooner or later he had to break, and given the length of time the Coalition had had to work on him, probably sooner.

"I've checked and double-checked," announced Pandora wearily, "but there's no chart, no map, no anything to show us how to get to the interior of the planet."

"If we have to go right down to the jail, we will," responded Pretorius, "but if there's a better way it's worth a little extra effort to find it."

"I'm telling you it can't be found, not from here," said Pandora.

"Then we'll have *them* direct us."

"What the hell are you talking about?"

"In the old days, when Man was still Earthbound, he had the Red Cross. These days we've got the E-Meds. They're a civilized society; they have to have something similar. If we can convince them we're part of that organization, that we've received a message about a collapsed tunnel or some such thing but the message was garbled or cut off before we were given all the details, they might very well tell us exactly how to get down there."

"Give me just a minute . . ." said Pandora, uttering a few commands to her computer. She looked up, smiling, in less than a minute.

"I was right," said Pretorius when he saw her face.

"It translates as the Traveling Hospital. They have some sixteen hundred ships, each a fully equipped hospital."

"Shit!" muttered Pretorius. "No way we're going to convince anyone this thing is a functioning hospital."

"No, but since it's military, it can pass as a transport to a military hospital," said Pandora. "No one expects a quarter-mile-long ship to land on rough terrain or inaccessible places, so each ship has a pair of transports for finding disaster victims and bringing them to the ship, or even just moving patients from one ship to another."

"Okay," said Pretorius. "Find the IDs for half a dozen of these little transports, and create one for us that seems like it's part of the same family, so to speak. We'll be military until we cross out of the Neutral Zone into Coalition territory, and then change us into a medical transport."

"All right," said Pandora. "Now we're almost certainly going to get permission to land, and get coordinates for the shaft leading to the mine if indeed it's traversable. If they want a face-to-face transmission, what are we going to do?"

"I'm working on it," replied Pretorius.

"We haven't got time to make one of us up as an Antarean," said Snake. "Proto would be right visually, but he can't speak the language. And not only would we waste time kidnapping one, but the moment we put him in contact with the planet he'd probably figure we were going to kill him anyway and spill the beans."

"I know," said Pretorius.

"Then what are we going to do?" she persisted.

"I just need a minute to think," he said, getting to his feet and walking to the galley, where he poured himself a flavored drink. As he lifted it up from beneath the spout, he saw his reflection on the polished glass just before he took a sip. He frowned, walked beneath a light, and stared at the glass again.

He promptly set the glass down and rejoined the crew.

"Proto," he said, "become a native of any of the Antares planets, whichever one you're most comfortable imitating."

Proto's middle-aged human was instantly replaced by a native of Antares Three.

"That's damned good," said Pretorius. "I can't tell you from the real thing."

"So what?" said Irish.

"She's right," said Snake. "We can't use him. You know that. He won't register on any security machine."

"He won't have to," said Pretorius.

"Bullshit," said Snake.

"I've seen that glint in your eye before," said Pandora. "What's up?"

"Proto, you don't . . . how can I put it . . . you don't hypnotize people into thinking you're a Man or an Antarean, right?" said Pretorius. "You just, in some way that none of us truly understands, project an image. Is that correct?"

"Yes," replied Proto, who looked as confused as the rest of them.

"And when you project an image before, say, a security scanner, it analyzes the space you seem to be taking up and reports that there's nothing there."

"Nothing above my actual body," said Proto. "That's correct."

"So if they can't analyze your image, if they can't examine the actual space you seem to be taking up, they can't conclude that you're not filling every cubic centimeter of it?"

"That's true," said Proto. "But where is this leading?"

"Felix," said Pretorius. "Go to the bathroom and bring back the mirror that's above the sink."

"I'll have to rip it out of the wall," replied Ortega.

"That's why I didn't ask Snake or Irish," said Pretorius. "Just get it."

Ortega went off to fetch the mirror, grunted in pain as he grabbed one side of it with his wounded arm, pulled it off the wall, and returned with it a minute later.

"Now hold it up in front of Proto," said Pretorius, standing behind the alien, whose Antarean image, along with Pretorius's, stared out from the mirror.

"See?" continued Pretorius triumphantly. "The mirror isn't a security device. It doesn't analyze what's in front of it, it just reflects it. We'll arrange it so that Proto is sitting in front of your control panel, in his guise as an Antarean. Felix will set the mirror down on Pandora's chair. Now, if we trained the sensor on Proto, it would know that he's not there and it wouldn't transmit his image, so of course we won't do that. We'll train it on the mirror, and it'll transmit exactly what it sees: an image of Proto and all the controls. We'll have to practice a bit, to make sure that the sensor shows nothing *but* the mirror, nothing behind it, and especially not the frame."

"Goddamn!" said Snake. "It might work!" Then she frowned and added, "If you're right."

"Barring a better suggestion, let's assume I *am* right," said Pretorius. "Irish, while we're adjusting the sensor and the mirror, use one of the auxiliary computer outlets and find three or four simple lines Proto can say or at least lip-sync to. We've received this signal, we need to coordinate, it's an emergency, if they die because you hassled us you'll be blamed in our report. . . . You can figure out the kind of things he has to say."

"Right," replied Irish, walking to a console about twenty feet away.

"All right," continued Pretorius. "Proto, grab a chair and set it up opposite Pandora's."

"I can't," answered Proto. "What you see is an image, remember?"

"Shit!" said Pretorius. "I keep forgetting. Okay, Snake, get the chair."

A moment later it was in position and Proto's Antarean seemed to be sitting down on it.

"Are you centered in the mirror?"

"Nathan, I'm only two feet tall. I can't *see* the mirror."

"Snake, get behind him and manipulate his chair until he's centered."

"Right," she said, and a moment later nodded her approval.

"Pandora, train the sensor on the mirror. Get it close enough that there's no chance of it showing any of the edges."

Pandora ordered the sensor to move slowly. "Snake, you'll have to tell me when it's centered."

"Right there," said Snake a few seconds later.

"Now let's just make sure this isn't an instantly fatal piece of foolishness," said Pretorius. "Snake, the sensor sees his image in the mirror, right?"

"I just said so, right," confirmed Snake.

"Stay there," said Pretorius. "Proto, get up, walk around the controls, and stand behind or beyond the mirror."

Proto did as he was instructed.

"Okay, Pandora—what does the sensor see now?"

"Just the mirror."

"Broaden the view so that it sees more than the mirror."

She did so. "Proto's not in it at all."

Pretorius smiled. "Then we're in business. Pandora, the ship's all yours again. Let us know when we're maybe fifteen minutes out from Antares Six. Irish, how's it coming?"

"I have half a dozen phrases, and as many requests for instructions," she said. "I'd write them down, but I think it would be better for Proto to hear them spoken, to get the inflections right."

"I agree." Pretorius turned to Proto. "Back to school you go. Irish will walk you through their dozen likeliest responses."

After another hour the ship was positioned where Pretorius wanted it, and Proto could come up with half a dozen responses, depending on what questions he was asked. Irish had also given him his first few sentences, which he could read off a screen before the sensor was activated.

"All right," said Pretorius. "No one except Proto speaks, and no one moves anywhere near the camera. Pandora, activate the communication system. Let's get started."

"Hello, the Mistalidorium mine. Hello, the Mistalidorium mine. This is Traveling Hospital Transport Ship 3011-A. We have received your signal and are on our way."

Instantly there was a message from the planet.

"Transport Ship 3011-A, we did not send for you. Explain your presence."

Pandora, unseen, activated a two-way visual contact.

"We received a message that a cave or a passage has collapsed. Some are dead, some buried. We will rescue and tend to the injured."

"*Again?* Are you sure? I have no report of it."

Proto repeated what he had said.

"It must be the mine that had the trouble a few days ago. You're better come down. We can worry later about why I didn't also receive the signal. Those damned miners are always summoning hospital ships before they make any kind of report to ground control."

"I need coordinates," said Proto. "Must I land on the surface, or can I fly directly down to the mine?"

"If it's as bad as the last time, you'd better go straight down," was the reply. "Sending the coordinates to your ship."

"Received."

"Will you need any help evacuating the wounded?"

"No," replied Proto. "This is our job. Onlookers will just be in the way."

"All right," said the officer. "Good luck."

"Thank you," said Proto, as Pandora cut the connection.

"They bought it!" said Ortega, removing the antigravity clamps on the mirror and carrying it back to the bathroom.

"Let's hope so," said Pretorius. He turned to Proto. "Keep in your Antarean form. If we run into anyone down there, we're going to have to pose as your prisoners."

"What do we do when we get down there?" asked Snake.

"We try to find out how to reach the jail," said Pretorius. "There's got to be a connecting passage, maybe more than one."

"We hit the atmosphere in another twenty seconds," announced Pandora, who had seated herself at the controls again. "I'm going to put it on visual. You'll see our target pretty soon." And finally: "There it is."

"Can we *fit* in that?" asked Ortega.

Pandora smiled. "It's bigger than it looks, Felix."

"Damned well better be," he said. "My goddamned arm is bleeding from carrying that mirror. Why couldn't they have hit me in the prosthetic one?"

"I'm glad they didn't," said Pretorius as Irish began cleaning the wound again. "It would have smashed it, and we'd have only your natural arm to depend on."

"I'm slowing down to a virtual crawl," announced Pandora. "We're about to be swallowed up by the shaft that leads down to the mine."

"I sure as hell hope he's worth stealing twice," remarked Snake as the ship vanished beneath the surface of the planet.

# 31

"How far down are we?" asked Pretorius.

"A little over a mile," answered Pandora.

"Even if they bought Proto's story, there are going to be *some* Antareans when we stop. It's the ingress/egress route, probably where they receive their supplies, maybe even near their living quarters, so we'd better be ready. Felix, how's the arm?"

"Sore as hell," replied Ortega, "but it won't stop me from using it."

"All right," said Pretorius. "We'll start by having Proto become a general. That should get them all to attention and saluting, which gives them one less hand to reach for their weapons."

"We kill everyone?" asked Irish, frowning.

"Proto's illusion will only last until he has to open his mouth, if that long," replied Pretorius. "And we *are* at war with these bastards."

"Besides," added Snake, "if we don't kill 'em all, you can bet your ass the survivors will radio ahead and they'll be waiting for us at the prison."

"Always assuming we can get to the prison from here," said Ortega.

"There's a way," said Pretorius with absolute certainty.

"What makes you so sure?" asked Ortega.

"Because we're at the same depth as the jail," answered Pretorius. "Why dig down this exact distance to put your cell block unless you were going to service it from one of the mines?"

"I dunno," said Ortega. "They could go uphill or downhill just as easily."

Pretorius shook his head. "They could have *dug* uphill or downhill when they were building it, but if they're ever under attack, they use a lot less power transporting things from the mine to the jail and back if they're doing it on level ground."

"I hope you're right," said Ortega. "But at the very least, we're going to put one mine's worth of these bastards out of commission."

"You sound a little bloodthirsty today, even for you," commented Snake.

"I've probably lost a pint or two of blood in that fight," growled Ortega, holding up his bandaged arm. "Someone is gonna pay dearly for that."

"We touch down in ten seconds," announced Pandora. "I assume they're monitoring us."

"Okay, Proto," said Pretorius. "Time to become a general."

The alien instantly appeared as an Antarean general.

"Looks good," said Snake. "And I'll bet they're not using scanners down here."

"They probably are," said Pretorius. "If it's worth mining, it's worth protecting." He turned to Proto. "Don't worry. They'll be so surprised to see a general down here, especially one they don't recognize, that even if they have a scanner they'll forget to look at it before we have time to get out and go into action."

"I hope you're right," replied Proto nervously.

"Just walk out when the hatch opens, and look smug and superior, like any general of any race."

"There are only three of them waiting for us," announced Pandora, checking her viewscreen.

"Good!" said Pretorius. "The rest are probably all working."

"Or just uninterested," added Irish. "I got the distinct impression that hospital transport ships are regular visitors here."

"I only know the sentences Irish taught me," said Proto. "How do I respond if one of them asks me a question, like what I'm doing here?"

"Not to worry," said Pretorius. "We'll do the responding for you."

"You're going to kill them all?"

"They *are* the enemy," replied Pretorius. "And more to the point, this may be our only escape route. I suspect any way up out of the jail is guarded and booby-trapped. I don't want any survivors calling for help or backup."

The hatch slowly opened.

*"Go!"* whispered Pretorius.

Proto stepped through the hatch, surveyed his surroundings, and stepped down to the ground. The three Antareans stood some fifty feet away, at what seemed to be the entrance to a cave or tunnel. Proto saluted them, they seemed confused but saluted him back, and then, before their arms could drop, all three fell over, the victims of laser fire from Ortega's and Snake's pistols.

"You okay?" asked Pretorius, jumping down to the cavern floor as the others climbed out of the ship.

"Yes," said Proto. "Just as well we shot them when we did. I must confess that I couldn't remember a word of Antarean once I confronted them."

"You'd have remembered if you had to," said Pretorius. He turned to Snake and Irish. "Better go pay the insurance."

"The insurance?" repeated Irish, a puzzled frown on her face.

"He means to spend an extra credit or two worth of power and make sure they're dead," said Snake, walking over to the three dead Antareans, putting the muzzle of her weapon up against each one's head in turn, and pressing the firing mechanism.

"What now?" asked Ortega.

"Now we hunt around for some way out of here on level ground, hopefully with some form of transportation we can use." He turned to Pandora. "How far would you say we are from the prison?"

She shrugged. "Perhaps fifty miles, maybe a little more."

"That's a long walk," said Ortega. "We *better* find some kind of train or shuttle."

"Start looking for it," said Pretorius. "Where the hell did these guys emerge from?"

"I think I found it," said Irish, indicating a narrow passage that led to a cavern that was illuminated by walls of some glowing mineral. "It's beautiful."

"Let's see if we can find anything resembling a map of this subterranean system," said Pretorius, following her into the cavern.

There were four awkwardly shaped desks made of alien hardwoods, each with an outmoded computer, each with an oddly structured chair created for Antareans.

"Not very up-to-date," noted Pandora.

"True," agreed Pretorius. Then he shrugged. "Still, how up-to-date do you have to be to dig a hole in the ground, or extract your cancer drug from . . . from wherever the hell it gets extracted from: walls, floors, whatever." He looked at the barren walls. "What we need is a map, something that'll tell us how to get to the jail. I suppose it's got to be in the computers, since these guys don't seem to have printouts of anything."

Pandora and Irish each activated a computer and began rummaging through the machines' memories.

"This would be a lot easier if they were programmed for Terran," said Irish after a few minutes.

"It's not that difficult," said Pandora, suggesting a different approach to her. "Piloting their ships has helped me understand something of their technology."

"It *is* easier when you've been flying an Antarean ship," agreed Irish. Then: "Wait a minute! I've got something here."

"What?" asked Pretorius.

"I'm not quite sure. Pandora, how do I transfer it to your machine?"

"Don't bother," said Pandora, getting to her feet. "I'll just come over." She walked across the room to where Irish sat and learned over her shoulder. "You're close," she said. "Very close."

"But how do I get past this defense wall?"

Pandora uttered a series of commands that had no effect, frowned, then uttered some more—and suddenly a hologram of a map hovered above the computer.

"There it is," announced Pandora. "The gold line seems to be the route for whatever supply vehicle can be accommodated down here. These four purple points are clearly mines, and that means that the single red point is the jail."

"Which mine are we in?" asked Pretorius.

She uttered another command, and finally one purple light began blinking.

"So if your estimate of fifty miles is right, each inch is about twenty miles," said Pretorius.

"So we're ready to bust him out!" said Ortega.

"Soon," said Pretorius. "We've got two things to do first."

"What are they?"

"We've got to bury the bodies, or at least stash them where they won't be found until we've freed Nmumba. There can be a number of reasons why they're missing, but only one why they're all dead from a laser pistol."

"Okay, we'll find a storage space to hide them," said Ortega. "What's the other thing we have to do before busting Nmumba out of jail?"

"Find out how the hell to get there," answered Pretorius.

# 32

"**H**ere's the entrance," announced Pandora, leading them to a tunnel at the back of the mine. "But as you can see, it presents a problem."

"The ship will never fit," remarked Ortega.

"That's the problem," she agreed.

"Clearly *something* traverses this tunnel, servicing the mines and the jail," said Pretorius. "Probably something that transports food and basic supplies." He frowned. "It makes our job a lot harder, because once we break Nmumba out of the jail, we're probably going to have to bring him back here to the ship."

"There might be ships at the jail," suggested Snake.

"I'm sure there are," answered Pretorius. "But the odds are that they'll be heavily guarded. This is just a mine; *that's* a jail, and it's holding what is, at least to the Antareans, the most important Man in the galaxy." He turned to Pandora. "Have you been able to pull up a *schemata* of the prison?"

"Not yet," she said. "I have a feeling there's some stuff they simply didn't want to put on a computer. But I'll go back and try to find it."

"I'll tell you what else we could use," said Pretorius.

"What?"

"The schedule for whatever's running through the tunnels. Can we summon it, or do we just wait for it to stop here on its regular route? And *does* it stop here? It's been almost an hour, and no miners have shown up. Maybe they've got a week or a month's worth of supplies down wherever they're digging, and just call for more when they need them."

"Right," said Pandora, nodding her agreement "I'll check on that, too."

Pretorius turned to Irish. "See if you can hunt up another computer here, and try to find anything that Pandora's not looking for—where the miners are, how many of them there are, and the shape of the transports, which I'll call trains for convenience."

"The shape?" repeated Irish, frowning.

"I want to know if we can hop off or climb out maybe half a mile from the jail. There might be a back door, and even if there isn't, I don't want us getting off at what passes for their station or loading docks."

She nodded. "I see. Okay, I'll find out what I can."

"I'm sure they've got dozens of security devices in the shaft from the surface to the jail," he continued, "but I have a feeling that they're less likely to anticipate a jailbreak engineered from the tunnel connecting the mines."

"Less likely is one thing," said Snake. "But ignoring it altogether is another—especially since we broke the phony Nmumba out of what they thought was a secure train."

"I know," agreed Pretorius. "This is probably the most inaccessible jail in the Coalition, or they wouldn't be holding him here. And I'm sure there's no danger-free way to get there. But this way seems less dangerous than a more direct approach—or do you think we could have gone down the shaft to the prison and met only three Antareans, none of them military?"

"No, of course not," replied Snake. "I'm just saying that we'd better not relax."

"Hey, I've got something!" said Pandora, staring at her screen.

"The jail?" asked Pretorius hopefully.

"No, the schedule."

"Just as useful."

"Give me a few seconds to translate it," she said, uttering a number of commands. "Okay, here it is. The transport—and I've no idea what it looks like or how accessible it is—comes by every six hours. If we want it to stop, all I do is have the computer instruct it to."

"Shit!" muttered Pretorius.

"What's the matter?" asked Proto.

"It means if we bust Nmumba out in, say, half an hour, we've got to hold his captors off for five and a half hours before we can get out of there." Suddenly another troubling thought occurred to him. "Say we stay alive and unapprehended for the whole six hours and another transport comes by," he said. "Can we make it reverse course and come directly back here, or do we have to ride it for the whole circuit and hit three other mines before we stop here again?"

Pandora put the question to the computer and looked up a moment later. "I don't know. I don't think it's ever been suggested."

"A simpler question is: does it have a reverse gear?" said Ortega.

"I'll try to find that out," she answered, "but I'll have to ask very carefully. If anyone or even any machine is monitoring this, too many questions of that type are a giveaway that something's wrong."

"All right," said Pretorius. "Don't worry about that. Just find out when the damned thing's due to stop here, and what speed it goes between stations."

A moment later she had his answer. "It's due in forty-one

minutes," she said, "and it will stop at the jail in just under ninety minutes."

"So it's going about a mile a minute," said Pretorius. "I don't think any of us except maybe Snake could jump off without breaking something at anything more than fifteen miles an hour. We'll see how suddenly or gradually it stops here when it arrives and assume it'll be like that at every destination, which'll give us a notion of how close or far from the station we'll be when we get off it." He looked around. "Any questions?"

"Yeah," said Ortega. "Do we shoot our way *in* as well as out?"

"I hope not," said Pretorius. "I hope there's more than one way in, I hope there's no guards at the door once the transport moves on, I hope a lot of things, but we'll have to play it by ear."

"So as I understand it," said Snake, "we find out where Nmumba is, we bust him out, we shoot anyone who isn't Nmumba, and we hope nobody will call in reinforcements for six hours."

"That's one scenario," agreed Pretorius.

"Give me a better one, just to cheer me up," she said.

"Okay. We find out how the controls work, we park the transport where we get off, we rescue Nmumba, take him back to the transport, and we're back here in an hour."

"*If* it goes in reverse," she said.

"If it goes in reverse," he agreed.

"And I assume if we're seen or confronted," continued Snake, "we have the general here—" she jerked a thumb in Proto's direction "—order them away."

"Either that, or he can explain that he's captured us and wants us in the same cell block as Nmumba."

"We'll have to hide our weapons a lot better if that's the plan."

"It's a possible plan," replied Pretorius.

"A thought occurs to me," said Proto.

"What is it?" asked Pretorius.

"We're missing an opportunity here," said Proto.

"What are you talking about?" demanded Pretorius.

"I should ride inside the transport, in the guise of an Antarean officer. I'm sure I couldn't fool their machines once we're inside the jail, but I could probably pull it off in the loading and unloading area, and if they even just stare at me for a few seconds as I walk away from the transport and they then question me, that will give you all the time you need to disembark. And if for some reason they see through our ruse and arrest me, don't try to stop them. Wire me for sound. If they arrest me I'll make my confession so odd that they won't kill me because they'll want to learn more—and in the process, you'll hear what I hear, and I'll be able to tell you what defenses they've got and where any weak spots are."

"I don't like it," said Pretorius. "You might fool them out in the tunnel, but the second you set foot inside you'll set off every alarm in the place."

"True," agreed Proto. "But if they incarcerate me near Nmumba, it will work to our advantage."

"Proto, you can make yourself look like a Man, or an Antarean, or a monster out of my worst nightmare, but when all the illusions are pierced—and they'll have systems that'll pierce them—you're just a pillow that's maybe twenty inches high that crawls on its belly. If they hit you once, it could kill you."

"Maybe I'm tougher than you think," said Proto.

"And maybe you're not as tough as *you* think."

"How do we wire him for sound?" asked Ortega. "It's not as if he's got a bunch of mechanical parts where you can hide a mike or even a camera, like I do."

"Kill the illusion and let me see you as you really are," said Pandora, and instantly Proto appeared in his true form. "I don't know," she said at last. "I can tie a mike onto you, maybe even find a way to stick it on your underbelly, but it'll show up the second they scan you."

"There's a way," said Irish.

"Oh?" said Pandora.

"How small is the microphone?"

"I can give him one the size of a thumbnail, but it'll still show up."

"These are scanners, not x-ray machines, right?" said Irish.

"Son of a bitch!" exclaimed Pretorius. "Pandora, if he swallows it, will it still pick up sounds?"

"It should function for maybe three hours, maybe a little less, before his digestive acids disable it," replied Pandora. "But I don't know if we'll hear anything exterior to his innards' growling and burbling."

"Let's find out," said Pretorius.

Pandora quickly disassembled one of the tiny computers that hung from her belt, then held up a silver object the size of a small thimble. "Okay, this is it." She placed it on the floor next to what she thought was Proto's head.

"Thank you," he said, slithering across the floor toward the microphone. When the last of him had passed over it, nothing remained on the floor.

"*Bon appetite,*" said Snake.

"All right," said Pretorius. "Proto, ambulate as far from us as you can, turn what passes for your back to us, and start speaking."

They all watched as the alien slithered across the floor until he was some forty feet away.

Pretorius frowned. "I don't hear a damned thing."

"*I* do," said Pandora. She took a small receiver out of her ear and handed it to Pretorius. "Try this."

"Okay, Proto," said Pretorius after inserting the tiny earphone. "Say something else."

"Can you hear me?" asked Proto.

"Plain as day," said Pretorius. He turned to Pandora. "Have you got any more of these receivers?"

"Just one more," she said.

"Okay, you and I will wear 'em. Proto, remember that. You can't communicate with Irish, Snake, or Felix."

"I'll remember," said Proto.

"All right. Pandora, can any of those computers that are holding your pants up give him a few lines in Antarean that he can say when we stop?" And silently he added: *if* we stop.

"What do you want him to say?"

"Give him a typical name, as close to an Antarean Jones or Smith as you can get. Have him bark 'Attention!'—and have him tell them that he has to speak to their supervisor, and that they should forget about the transport and follow him."

"Four, maybe five sentences," said Pandora. "Not a problem."

They practiced for the next fifteen minutes, until Proto felt confident and Pretorius decided that the inflections sounded right.

"Yes," said Proto after the final run-through. "I think I can do it."

They fell silent then, and Pandora and Irish went back to working the computers while they waited for the transport to arrive.

THE PRISON IN ANTARES

"Three minutes," announced Irish, getting up from her computer.

"Does it stop even if it's not bringing supplies?" asked Pretorius.

"Yes, it seems to run on a regular schedule. It not only brings supplies, but it collects raw Mistalidorium—or maybe the rocks that contain the Mistalidorium, it's difficult to tell based on this."

"You sure it's coming?" asked Ortega. "I don't see any headlight."

"It doesn't need one," said Pretorius. "There's no engineer, and for all we know, there's only one or two other transports in the whole system."

"It's slowing down," announced Snake.

"Okay," said Pretorius, stepping forward. "Let's go pull off a jailbreak that would turn even Jesse James and Santiago green with envy."

# 33

"It's stopping," announced Ortega.

"Quick, everyone climb aboard," ordered Pretorius. "Either flatten down on the top, or find some handhold on the side. All except Felix."

"What are you talking about?" demanded Ortega. "I'm part of the team. I'm going!"

"Of course you're going," said Pretorius, "but you and I have a job to do first."

"We do?"

"The damned thing's come to a stop. Whatever it's picking up or delivering, we killed the Antareans who were going to load or unload it. I have a feeling if we don't perform their function, the damned thing will never proceed, and sooner or later someone's going to notice."

As he uttered the words a panel slid back, revealing sacks of foodstuffs.

"Okay, pull 'em off and dump 'em on the ground," said Pretorius, grabbing a sack and tossing it back into the section they had just left.

"Damned stuff is cold," remarked Ortega after tossing a trio of sacks onto the pile Pretorius had started. "Frozen, I think."

"It'll be warm by the time someone finds it," said Pretorius. He pulled off one last sack and looked around. "Okay, it's empty. Climb on top of the car."

"Why don't we just ride in the compartment?" suggested Ortega.

"You mean, besides the fact that it's freezing?" replied Pretorius. "Felix, the damned thing is empty."

"So?"

"So how do we know it'll stop at the prison? Unless it's picking up something there, it might not—and if it doesn't stop, you can bet a year's pay that the door won't open. Now pick up Proto and carry him up top with you."

"I should have known," growled Ortega, climbing to the top of the transport. "We always get to do it the hard way."

"I would have thought the hard way was to be locked in a functioning freezer with a diminishing air supply," said Pretorius wryly as he reached the top of the transport.

"We're starting to move," said Irish.

"Everyone hold on tight," said Pretorius. "Who knows how fast the damned thing goes?"

They were suddenly enveloped by total darkness.

"You'd think they'd post an occasional light," complained Irish, peering ahead.

"There's no driver or engineer, no tracks or power lines, no forks in the road, so there's no reason to illuminate the route," said Pandora. "My guess is that the next light we see will be at the prison." She paused. "This might be a good time to ask what we do when we arrive."

"That depends," said Pretorius.

"On what?" asked Snake.

"On whether we stop or not. The transport's empty. If they don't have anything to load into it, it may not even slow down, and it almost certainly won't stop. That could make getting off more than a little dangerous." He paused. "On the other hand, if it *does* stop, there are likely to be armed prison guards loading a prisoner or something else onto it, and we'll be in a fire fight before we've even set foot in the jail proper."

"If we come through this alive, I want a bonus," muttered Ortega.

The transport came to a curve in the tunnel and all talk ceased while they concentrated on merely holding on.

"I'm still awaiting orders," said Pandora.

"If it doesn't stop, or it stops and there's no one waiting for it, we hop off, gain entrance to the jail proper as surreptitiously as we can, and try to figure out where Nmumba is. If they'll buy Proto as an officer, at least long enough to us to slip off unseen, so much the better. If not, and we have to kill our way to Nmumba, we will."

"And if it stops and there's a reception committee?" asked Snake.

"Then we fight our way in, and hopefully take a hostage or two who can save us the trouble of trying to find Nmumba if there's a maze of cells down here. All we know is that he's here. He could be the only prisoner, or one of a hundred or a thousand."

"More likely one of five or ten," said Snake.

"Why would you say that?" asked Felix.

"If they're feeding a thousand prisoners and their guards, there's no way this thing makes an empty run."

Irish nodded her head, though no one could see it. "She's got a point."

"Yeah. In fact, we'd better put you inside it. Officers don't ride on the tops of transports."

"The door will be sealed until it stops," said Pandora.

"There's more than one way to bust into a sealed room or transport," said Ortega. Suddenly they could hear his artificial arm spinning, and then came the harsh sound of metal drilling through metal. "One more minute," he grated, and heard a section of metal pop out. "Who needs two flesh-and-blood arms anyway? Nobody ever wounded *this* one."

"Proto, can you maneuver your way to it?" asked Pretorius.

"I don't think so," answered Proto. "I can barely hold on as it is."

"Not a problem," said Snake. "Proto, I think I'm just a few feet from you. I'm going to start crawling—well, *slithering*—over to you. Let me know when you feel my hand on you."

They were all silent for perhaps thirty seconds, peering into the darkness, trying without success to see what was transpiring.

"Now!" said Proto.

"Good!" replied Snake. "I've got one hand hooked over the hole that Felix made. Can you crawl alongside me, or even over me, to reach it, or should I drag you?"

"You'd better pull me over to it," said Proto.

"Okay," said Snake. "Got you. Let me know if I'm hurting you."

"No, I'm fine."

"Coming to the hole. The transport looks to be about ten feet deep. Can you take that kind of fall?"

"I truly don't know," answered Proto. "But we have to try."

"Just a minute!" said Ortega. "My arms are a hell of a lot longer than yours, Snake. I'll take it from here. This way the drop will only be maybe six and a half feet."

"Makes sense," agreed Snake. "Let me know when you've got him and I'll let go."

"Got him already. I'm positioned right at the hole, remember?"

There was a moment's silence. "Ready?"

"Yes, you can let go," replied Proto.

Pretorius thought he could hear a *thud*, but a moment later Proto's voice came up through the hole in the roof.

"Made it!"

"Nothing broken, I hope?" said Pretorius.

"I don't have any bones, remember?" said Proto.

"Still remember those sentences Pandora gave you?" asked Pretorius.

"Absolutely."

"I hope you're right," said Pretorius. "Because we're slowing down and I can see lights up ahead."

# 34

"**A**re we overlooking anything?" asked Pretorius.

"I wouldn't think so," said Pandora. "Whether or not they believe him when he climbs down, they're going to know the minute he's inside that he's an imposter."

"I know," said Pretorius. "But they won't spot the mike or whatever you call it right away."

"I have a question," said Irish.

"Shoot," replied Pretorius.

"Let's assume that we get into the jail intact."

"Okay."

"And let's further assume that we get Nmumba out from wherever they've incarcerated him, and that most—or at least some—of us live through it. We'll still be inside the most impenetrable jail in the entire Coalition." She stared at him. "Have you given any thought to how we escape from here?"

"I'm working on it," replied Pretorius.

The transport came to a halt, and Proto stepped out as the door slid open. The Antareans—there were five of them—froze, and one who was in uniform saluted and began speaking. Proto imperiously gestured for silence, repeated a couple of lines Pandora had given him to the effect that he needed to see their superior, and then walked toward the door to the interior, which vanished as he approached it.

He still looked like an Antarean general as he passed through the doorway, but suddenly three of the Antareans threw themselves at what they thought was his head and torso. They collided and fell to the floor, two of them unconscious, the third writhing in pain.

But the officer pulled his burner out and aimed it, not at what appeared to be Proto's head or heart, but rather at what seemed to be his feet, which meant that the scanner had not only told him that he wasn't facing an Antarean general, but was actually confronting a being that was at best two feet high.

He began asking questions, but Proto, who didn't speak Antarean, was unable to answer. He kicked Proto twice and asked them again, and it was all Pretorius could do to prevent Ortega from jumping off the top of the transport and racing to his rescue.

Finally the officer barked a command, at which his companion and the one who hadn't quite knocked himself out diving at Proto's image walked over and picked Proto up, carrying him off to the interior of the jail.

"I'm being carried straight in from the transport, which I will arbitrarily call North. Ten, eleven, twelve steps, and now they've turned east."

The officer growled a command.

"I think he just told me to shut up. I'd better, or else I won't be able to—"

There was a grunt, and then silence.

"We'd better go in after him," said Pandora.

"Not yet," said Pretorius.

"What the hell are we waiting for?" demanded Snake.

"In case it's escaped your attention, there are two Antareans lying on the ground between the transport and the entrance to the jail. Either they'll wake up shortly, or someone will be by to collect them."

"What about Proto?" said Ortega.

"He'll be fine," answered Pretorius. "They're not going to kill him before they find out who and what he is and what he's doing here."

"With the right torture device, that will take about ten seconds," said Snake.

"They've probably never seen a member of Proto's race," answered Pretorius. "I know that *I* haven't. And if they're not acquainted with any of them, they won't know what his pain threshold is or how to torture him. He's breached the most secure prison in the Commonwealth. I guarantee they're not going to risk killing him before they find out how and why he did it."

Snake was about to reply when four burly, uniformed Antareans emerged, walked over to the two unconscious bodies, lifted them up, and carried them inside.

"Okay," said Pretorius, climbing down off the roof of the transport half a minute later. "They should be on their way to what passes for an infirmary. Get down here quick."

"Why are we suddenly in a hurry?" asked Ortega.

"The transport hasn't moved an inch," explained Pretorius.

"So?"

"Tell him, Irish."

"The transport didn't stop because we were on it," explained Irish. "We know there was nothing to unload. That means they have something, perhaps a lot of things, to load onto the transport. They were delayed by the little scene with Proto, but now that he's been captured and the injured Antareans have been moved to safety, they should be coming back with whatever they plan to put in the transport."

"And if we get into a shooting match with them, we may win the battle, but they'll lock every entrance to the building and go on full alert, and we'll have lost the war," concluded Pretorius.

"So we rigged Proto to guide us, and now we're storming the place without knowing anything about its interior?" demanded Ortega.

"We're not storming it," explained Pretorius. "We're just getting out of the most obvious line of fire. Once we're inside, we'll do our damnedest to find a storage or supply room, something like that, and wait until Proto regains consciousness."

"And he'll say, 'I'm in a prison cell somewhere in the building. Find me,'" growled Ortega.

"It's okay, Felix," said Pandora before Pretorius could curse at him. "The thing he swallowed is emitting a signal that I can trace with this." She held up one of her tiny computers. "He'll tell us what he can, and we'll dope out the rest from his signal."

"Hurry!" snapped Pretorius. "Before they come or the door snaps shut."

He stood aside as his team entered, then stepped through the doorway just before it closed. They found themselves in a circular room, with passages leading to the right, the left, and straight ahead.

"Okay," he said. "Proto said they were carrying him straight ahead. That'd be the corridor opposite the transport. It either leads to the cells, or to the interrogation rooms, and that means it'll be better-protected than most of the place. So do we go right or left? There's no sense splitting up. Only Pandora can read and trace Proto's signals."

"This one," said Snake suddenly, heading off to her left.

"What makes this one better?" asked Pretorius as they all fell into step behind her.

"I see a vent in what passes for the ceiling," replied Snake. "It figures. There's no natural air circulation two miles below the ground. If you or Felix will give me a boost, I can probably fit in the ventilation shaft and follow it to see where it leads."

"Sounds good," said Pretorius as they reached the tunnel.

"Well?" demanded Snake as Pretorius walked past her.

"Let's see if this damned tunnel curves enough so that we're out of sight when they walk through the entrance," he answered. "If there's a vent here, there'll be more along the way."

They walked straight ahead for perhaps seventy feet, and then the tunnel curved gently to the right. They came to a storage room and entered it. It was filled with bags of torn clothes and blankets, and had another vent in the ceiling.

"This'll do," said Pretorius. "We're totally out of sight." He turned to Ortega. "Felix, lift her up and see if she'll need any tools to remove the damned thing, or if she can just pull it down or push it aside."

Ortega put his hands on Snake's hips and held her above his head. A moment later she pushed the vent loose and shoved it aside.

"Okay, I'm in," she said. "I don't suppose anyone's brought a headlamp?"

"Don't be silly," said Pretorius. "For all you know you'll be crawling or slithering over the guards' quarters. We don't need to let them know someone's up there by shining a light through the vent." He paused. "We'll be waiting for you in this room."

"All right, all right," said Snake irritably. "What exactly am I looking for? I mean, if this doesn't lead to Nmumba?"

"Empty secure rooms," answered Pretorius. "An armory. Other prisoners that we can set free to cause a distraction." He paused, thinking. "There's no day or night down here, so I imagine they work in two or three shifts. That means there's got to be a dormitory, living quarters, for those guards who aren't on duty. If you can pinpoint them, it could prove useful."

"Okay."

"And remember, you're just our eyes and ears, not our weapons. You look, you listen, and then you report back to us and tell us what you've seen."

"You know, Nate," said Snake, "you're no fun at all."

"I've been told that before," replied Pretorius. "Now get your ass in gear."

He found that he was speaking to an empty space.

# 35

"Do we know what kind of cells they have here?" asked Irish.

Pretorius shrugged. "Not a hint," he said. "Could be bars, or electricity, or a force field, or half a dozen other things."

"I'm more concerned with how we get back out of here once we've freed him," said Pandora.

"There are at least two routes that we know about," answered Pretorius. "The way we came, and the shaft that leads directly to it."

"You say that as if you think there might be a third way."

"I don't know of one," he replied. "But I wouldn't rule out the possibility. I mean, who the hell thought we could get to where we are now by entering a mine fifty miles away?"

They fell silent then, waiting to hear from Proto or for Snake to return. Pretorius posted Ortega by the doorway in case any Antareans approached it, but fifteen minutes later no one had come near it.

Then Snake returned, lowering herself until she was hanging by her fingertips. She released her grip, landing with the grace of an athlete.

"Well?" said Pretorius.

"If they've got any prison cells in this place, you can't prove it by me," she answered. "I followed the vent for maybe two hundred fifty, three hundred feet. At the end—not the end of the vent, just the end of my little exploration trip—I found myself over what seemed like an interrogation room. I was hoping they'd have taken Proto there, but it was empty."

"Then why do you think it was an interrogation room?"

"You ever seen a dining room with a Neverlie Machine?" she asked.

Pretorius considered what she said.

"I think we're okay," he finally replied.

"Okay?" said Snake, frowning.

"The Neverlie Machine gives you a helluva painful jolt every time you lie," he said. "But it doesn't work for all species. If they thought it would work on Proto, they'd have taken him there immediately, and you'd have seen him."

"Maybe not," said Pandora. "He's been unconscious for the past few minutes."

"Damn!" said Pretorius. "You're right. They might take him there after he's awake." He lowered his head in thought for a moment, then looked up. "It won't make any difference. The mere fact that they captured him in the transport tunnel means that by now they've checked with all the mines and they know that the one we came in through has got three dead Antareans . . . and since they've seen Proto as he really is, they know he didn't kill them or rip up the roof of the transport, and that he's clearly not alone. But that means we can't just sit here waiting to be discovered." He turned to Pandora. "How accurately can you pinpoint his location through the signal he's emitting?"

"I can get us pretty close," she replied. "But what I can't do is tell you who or what is between us and him."

Pretorius grimaced. "I hate to start marching down corridors and through rooms without knowing where the cells are. We'd be too damned exposed. Let's give him a few more minutes."

Suddenly Ortega waved his arm for attention, then put his finger to his lips.

"Of course!" whispered Pretorius. "They're going to load the transport."

The door was cracked open, and Ortega was peering through it. He extended his forefinger, then the middle and fourth finger.

Pretorius held up three fingers with a questioning look, and Ortega nodded. Snake drew her burner, but Pretorius shook his head and pointed to her screecher. She holstered the one and drew the other, and Ortega and Irish followed suit.

*Are they all here?* Pretorius mouthed the words.

Ortega nodded an affirmative.

Open the door.

Ortega walked through the doorway, which irised to let him pass through, and he, Pretorius, Irish and Snake all fired their weapons at the unsuspecting Antareans, who collapsed in a writhing, twitching heap next to various sacks they'd been carrying.

"Make sure they're dead," said Pretorius. "Then drag them in here."

"They're all dead," announced Ortega a moment later, dragging the first of the three into their room as Snake, Pandora, and Irish began dragging the sacks.

"Why the screecher instead of the burners?" asked Irish.

"A laser beam can put a hole in its target and scorch the walls behind it," answered Pretorius, "and we don't want to leave any blood or other marks to show that anything happened here. The screecher kills them with a barrage of solid sound; no wounds, no blood."

Ortega slung the second corpse over his massive shoulder, and dragged the third by an ankle. "Done," he announced, as the door closed behind him.

"Okay," said Pretorius. "They're only armed with their version of burners, so we don't need to appropriate their weapons. Check them for any communication devices, anything else that might prove useful."

They fell to examining the corpses. Suddenly Irish held up a small metallic card, some three inches on a side, with some odd symbols on it.

"What's this?" she asked.

Pretorius took it from her, studied it, and passed it over to Pandora. "Is this what I hope it is?" he said.

"I wish I had the ship's computer here," answered Pandora. "Still, maybe one of my little ones can confirm it."

"'Confirm it'?" repeated Irish. "It just looks like, I don't know, maybe an ID."

"Oh, it's an ID, all right," said Pretorius, as Pandora held it up before one of her tiny computers.

"What's so special about that?" asked Irish.

"Give me half a minute and maybe I can tell you," replied Pandora. She frowned, deactivated the computer she was using, then pulled another one from her belt and held the card up before it.

"Well?" asked Pretorius.

"Looks like it," she answered. "Give me another few seconds." Then: "Yes, we've hit pay dirt."

"Pay dirt?" repeated Irish. "What the hell is it?"

"It's an ID, of course," said Pandora. "But it's a very special ID. It gives him access to the cell blocks."

"Then what's keeping us?" said Ortega eagerly. "Let's get Nmumba and Proto and get the hell out of here!"

"What's keeping us," said Pretorius, "is that we don't know where the cell blocks *are*." He turned to Pandora. "I don't suppose that thing can tell us?"

She shook her head. "No. Which figures. Of course anyone down here would know where they are."

"Anything from Proto yet?" asked Pretorius.

"Not a word."

"Damn!" he said, frowning. "We'll just have to follow his signal, then."

"Why not wait for him to talk to us?" said Snake. "They wouldn't rough him up enough to put him in a coma. They'll want to question him."

"Personally, I'd love to wait for him to tell us how to find him," said Pretorius. "But we just killed three Antareans. How long do you think it'll be before someone notices they're missing and starts a search for them?"

"Okay," admitted Snake, "you've got a point."

He turned to Pandora. "Can you pinpoint his location?"

"I can come close," she said. "But what I can't pinpoint are any obstacles, natural or artificial, between us and him."

"And we don't know for a fact that he's near Nmumba," added Irish.

"We're going to have to assume he is until proven otherwise," answered Pretorius. He looked around the barren room. "Is there any way to hide the bodies and the stuff they were going to load onto the transport?"

"No benches, no chairs, no nothing," said Ortega. "I'd say we're out of luck on that front."

"Not at all," countered Snake. "I'm not climbing through this particular vent again if we're leaving the room, so we can stash them up there."

"Good point," agreed Pretorius. "Felix, give Snake a boost, and then you and I will hand each body up to her. Snake, if I have to stand on Felix's shoulders to help you pull the bodies through the vent until all three are up there, I will. Just let me know."

It took about five minutes, and Pretorius did indeed have to stand atop Ortega, but they finally got all three Antarean corpses hidden from sight.

"Okay, now let me heave these sacks up there, and we're done," said Felix.

"Wait a minute," said Pretorius. He stared at the sacks, frowning, for a moment. "Felix, see if the transport is still there."

Ortega walked to the entrance and looked out at the tunnel.

"Yeah, it's here."

"Good. Let's load the sacks onto it."

"Why?"

"There's no engineer or driver on that transport, we know that. So clearly it's programmed, and the fact that it's still here means that it's programmed to pick up those goods before it leaves."

"So what?" said Ortega.

"You know, I'm not following you either," said Pandora.

"Their security has been breached," said Pretorius. "They know that, because they've captured Proto. Now, if the three Antareans are missing *and* their goods never made it to the transport, they're going to assume Proto wasn't alone, and they're going to start looking for three dead men and whatever they were loading, and if you're looking nearby for dead men, you might very well check the vent." He paused. "But if you know the goods made it to the transport, then you're probably looking for three live Antareans who are off on their equivalent of a drunk, or maybe even hopped a ride on the transport. Anyway, you're less likely to check where we've stashed them."

"Until they start stinking," said Ortega.

"If we're not off the planet by the time you can follow your nose to them, we're in deep shit," said Pretorius.

"I would have thought being two miles deep on an enemy planet with no means of getting off it qualified as deep shit," remarked Snake.

Pretorius was about to argue when he decided that he agreed with her. "Okay, we'll be in deeper shit," he said, looking around. "They knew the second Proto was inside that he wasn't an Antarean, which means they've got some scanners near the entrance. We don't want to destroy them; that's a dead giveaway. Pandora, can you neutralize them for maybe a minute, send out some static, something like that?"

"I should be able to, as long as it's just for a minute or two," she replied, manipulating one of her computers. "Okay—go!"

They quickly loaded the sacks onto the transport, which began moving a few seconds later. Then they reentered the prison, and Pretorius turned to Pandora.

"All right," he said. "Which way?"

She studied the tiny computer she held in her hand. "That way," she said, pointing to her right.

"There'd better be a tunnel or a door there," said Ortega.

"It'd be nice," agreed Pretorius, walking over. "Yeah, it's a tunnel. Pandora, can any of your machines tell us if we're being watched once we enter it?"

"Probably," she replied. "It depends on what kind of equipment they're using, whether it reads motion, or heat, or even takes holos, though it's so dark I doubt the latter."

"They've got normal-sized eyes," said Irish, "which means they don't see any better in the dark than we do."

"Okay," said Pretorius, "the longer we stand here talking, the more likely it is we're going to trip some alarm. Let's get moving."

One by one, they entered the tunnel.

# 36

"Are you getting any life readings?" asked Pretorius after they'd proceeded a quarter of a mile.

"Some," answered Pandora. "But they're pretty much spread out, and they're too small to have the body mass of Antareans. I think they're the equivalent of rats."

"I hate rats!" whispered Irish with a shudder. "Ours *or* theirs."

They followed a curve in the tunnel, and suddenly Pretorius stopped. "Lights up ahead," he announced. "Anything showing up on your machine?"

Pandora shook her head. "Just what I've been getting all along."

"Just the same, let's approach it quietly. And if you haven't pulled your weapons out yet, now would be a good time."

They continued walking forward, and soon found themselves in a dimly lit natural chamber.

"How many ways out of here?" asked Pretorius, looking around.

"Four tunnels," said Snake. "No, make that three. We just came out of the fourth. It doesn't lead to anything but the transport."

"So do we just take one and see what happens?" asked Ortega.

Pretorius shook his head. "No," he answered. "With no map, we're as likely to walk in on the jailors' quarters or mess hall. We don't need much to go on, but we need *some* indication, however slight, as to where the cells are." He paused. "Failing that, I at least want to know where they *aren't*."

"Well, we can't stay *here*," said Snake. "If Antareans didn't pass through it regularly it wouldn't be even this dimly lit."

"Well, damn it all!" exclaimed Pandora, staring at her machine. "I think I've found that better way."

"What is it?" asked Pretorius as they all turned to face her.

"I only looked briefly at the life readings before," she said. "They were all spread out. They're *still* spread out, but they're converging on something at the end of the right-hand tunnel. Not fast, but definitely moving."

"The kitchen," suggested Irish.

Pretorius nodded his agreement. "Makes sense. There's nothing to eat down here, even for their equivalent of rats. It makes sense that whenever they smell or sense or somehow know the kitchen's in use again, they'd make a beeline to it—or if not to the kitchen itself, then to the general area, looking for scraps."

"And if the kitchen's in use . . ." began Ortega.

"They're going to be delivering food to the prisoners," concluded Snake.

"Right," said Irish. "Hell, even if most of it's for the guards, we know they have at least two prisoners—Nmumba and Proto."

"We know they have *one* prisoner," said Pretorius. "We *hope* they have two or more."

"They wouldn't kill him before they questioned him," said Snake. "And look how long Nmumba's held out."

"I hope you're right," said Pretorius. "But never forget that Proto isn't Nmumba. He's the only member of his race we've ever encountered, and we don't know what his pain threshold might be."

"If he'd broken instantly, they'd have been searching where the transport is and all the nearby hiding places," said Ortega. "You're underrating him."

"I'm just saying that none of us knows how much pain he can

bear," replied Pretorius, "and we'd be foolish to pretend otherwise."
He turned to Pandora. "The right-hand tunnel?"

"Yes."

"How far down?"

"I can't tell from here," she answered. "We'll have to start traversing it before I can find out where it ends. Also, I'm assuming that the kitchen is at the end of it, but it might not be. If I can find the point where the mice, or whatever they are, all converge, *that* will be the kitchen."

"All right," said Pretorius. "Let's go."

They went about thirty feet and stopped.

"Damn!" muttered Pretorius. "Now there's no light at all. We're going to have to feel our way along the sides of the tunnel until we get to some light. We don't dare use our own."

They proceeded slowly and carefully, keeping in physical contact with the tunnel wall, for perhaps two hundred feet. Then the tunnel curved gently to the right, and they could see a light some four hundred feet away.

They had covered half the distance when something launched itself at Pretorius, who went down under the force of the attack. He saw a pair of ravening jaws reaching for his throat and managed to hold them off until Ortega raced up, held it aloft with his natural hand, extended a huge blade from his artificial arm, and beheaded it.

"What was *that*?" whispered Irish.

"I'd say it's the Antarean equivalent of a rat," replied Snake. "Huge eyes, because it lives underground. Probably weighs about thirty pounds, which is strange, since there's not much to eat down here."

"I beg to differ," said Pretorius, getting to his feet. "Its size means that there *is* something to eat down here besides table scraps. Whatever it is, we'd better keep an eye out for it."

"Let's get moving again," said Pandora with a note of urgency in her voice.

"What is it?" asked Pretorius.

"Six or seven of the things are approaching this spot," she said, holding up her computer. "Probably they smell the blood where Felix beheaded it."

"Okay, let's go," agreed Pretorius. "Felix, bring up the rear. No sense letting them rip one of us up before you can kill them."

They began walking silently through the tunnel again, and came to a stop when they were within a dozen feet of a lighted chamber.

Pretorius sniffed the air, and made a face. "It's a kitchen, all right," he whispered. "Nmumba couldn't live on a diet of this shit. I assume it's for the guards, or for some nonhuman prisoners. Let's hope it's the latter."

"Why?" whispered Irish.

"Because after we kill everyone in there, we don't want the guards to come around asking why their meal is late." He turned to Pandora. "How many life-forms?"

"Two in the chamber, one just beyond it."

"Damn!" muttered Pretorius. "Let's wait and see if he comes back into the kitchen. If one of these two screams and he runs for help, we're in big trouble."

They held perfectly still for almost three minutes.

"I've got a feeling the rats are getting anxious," whispered Snake.

"Don't worry," answered Pretorius. "If they'd ever gotten away with killing anyone this close to the chamber, they'd have been all over us already."

Another minute passed, and then Pandora put her computer back on her belt.

"He's here!" she whispered.

"All right," said Pretorius. "Can you scramble any security they have here? We only need a minute, two at the outside."

"I don't know," answered Pandora. "If it's the same system as out at the transport, I can probably mess it up for ten minutes."

"Let's hope it's the same," he said, "because there's no turning back." He faced his team. "No survivors—and just as important, no noise."

He turned and raced into the chamber, screecher in hand.

# 37

There were two Antareans wearing food-stained clothes, and another one in uniform. Pretorius shot the uniformed one before he could react. One of the two cooks hurled a cutting instrument at Ortega, but he blocked it with his artificial arm as Snake killed the cook with a laser blast.

The other cook raced for a door, and Irish trained her screecher on the back of his head and fired. He collapsed without a sound.

Pretorius placed his finger to his lips, gestured for Snake to make sure all three Antareans were dead, and then opened the door that the cook had been running toward. He stuck his head out, then signaled the others to follow him.

They came to a fork in the tunnel and paused, wondering which way to go. Then Irish gestured for their attention and pointed to a tiny bit of food on the floor of the left-hand tunnel, food that had obviously spilled off a cart or a tray. Pretorius nodded his agreement and headed down the tunnel in question.

The lighting was dim but visible, and they proceeded for another eighty feet to a closed door. Pretorius looked questioningly at Snake, who approached the door as he stepped aside.

She bent over and studied the lock and the handle for a long moment, then stood up.

*It's not locked,* she mouthed the words.

Pretorius frowned and considered his options. He didn't want to go through the doorway with weapons firing, not until he knew what they might be firing *at*. He and Pandora had picked up a few words of Antarean, but their voices didn't have the right tonal quality, and he was certain they couldn't answer any questions that might be asked through the door.

"Snake," whispered Pretorius, "I don't see any hinges. Does it open away from us?"

She shrugged. "It could open away, or iris, or just vanish."

"Felix, pound on it. Bust it down if you can."

Ortega stepped forward, pounded the door with his fists—one real, one metal—and then hurled himself against the door, which opened instantly. Pretorius saw two armed and uniformed Antareans racing toward him, and spotted enough holos of prisoners on the left-hand wall to determine that this was an observation station for the prison guards.

All five of the team took aim at the two guards, killing them on the spot.

"Pandora!" said Pretorius. "You're the computer wizard. See if you can make heads or tails of their machines. We especially need to know how to find Nmumba's and Proto's cells, and how to see if any of the guards are converging on this room."

"I'll do what I can," she said, walking over to a pair of computers that faced the wall. "My experience aboard one of their ships should help."

"Felix," continued Pretorius, "find someplace to hide the bodies. Irish, give him a hand."

"If they know we're here, they're going to know we've killed the guards," said Irish.

"True," admitted Pretorius. "But if Pandora can hide our presence from any prying spyware, the last thing we want is for someone to trip over a pair of bodies on the floor."

Ortega and Irish dragged the bodies to a closet, opened it up, didn't see anything worth appropriating, and stuffed them into it.

"How's it coming?" Pretorius asked Pandora.

"I've found a row of cells," she answered. "But I don't know yet where it is, or if it's the only one."

"Are they occupied?"

"I'm working on it," she replied. "This is a little more complicated than the software that ran the ship." Then, a few seconds later, she added: "No bars. Three walls and a force field."

"Can you kill the force field from here?"

"Almost certainly," said Pandora. "I just have to find the right command."

"We can't wait too much longer," said Pretorius. "We've killed five Antareans. Surely one of them must have had to report to his superiors by now."

"Wait!" she exclaimed. "I'm getting something!"

All eyes turned to her as she rapidly fed commands into the machine.

"Got him!" she said triumphantly.

"You're sure it's Nmumba?" said Pretorius.

"There are only seventeen prisoners in the whole jail, Nate!" she exclaimed. "Nine Denebians, three Kaboris, two Torquals, one Antarean, and a Man! It's got to be him!"

"That's sixteen."

"The other has to be Proto," she said. "Even the scanner can't identify his race."

"How do we get there?"

"Proto's still emitting signals," she replied. "We'll home in on them with *this*." She indicated a mini-computer on her belt.

"And can you kill the power to the force fields?"

"One thing at a time," replied Pandora. "Please don't speak to me. I'm speaking code to the computer, and every time I answer you in Terran of course it doesn't understand me and I have to start over."

"Sorry," said Pretorius. He walked across the room, folded his arms, and waited.

"What the hell are Kaboris doing here?" asked Snake. "They're part of the Coalition too."

"Beats me," said Pretorius. "You can ask them when we get to the cell block."

"Maybe I will," she replied.

He stared at her for a long moment, and then smiled.

"Oh, shit!" said Snake. "I know that expression—and every time I see it, it means there's going to be more trouble for me."

"We're two miles deep in an enemy stronghold, and our ship is fifty miles away," said Ortega. "Just how much more trouble can you be in?"

"All right!" said Pandora. "I know how to kill the force field!"

"Okay," said Pretorius. "Just point the way."

She shook her head. "I'm coming with you."

He frowned. "We need you right here at the computer."

"If Proto's signal is accurate, and there's no reason to believe it isn't, there are three coded doors between here and the cell block," she said. "By the time I show you how to manipulate the codes on one of these—" she held up one of her tiny computers "—we could be there and on our way back."

"Can you kill the force field with that?" said Pretorius.

"Absolutely," she answered. "I've tied it in to their big one."

"All right," he said. "Let's go. Lead the way."

"Follow me," she said, walking to what seemed a solid section of wall at the back of the room. She uttered a low command and a broad section of it slid back to reveal yet another dimly lit tunnel.

"Quickly!" Pretorius said to the others. "Who the hell knows how long the wall stays open?"

The tunnel went straight ahead for perhaps fifty feet, and then they came to a door. Pandora uttered the proper code, the door irised, they stepped through, came to a second door in just a few yards, and repeated the procedure.

Pandora stopped after they went another hundred feet and came to a third door.

"Okay," she said. "The cell block is just beyond this door. And if I'm interpreting the computer correctly, we can kill the force field for all the cells at once, or just for individual cells of our choosing."

"Open it," said Pretorius.

She uttered a final command, the door spread apart to let them through, and they found themselves in the cell block. There were twenty-four cells, twelve on each side of the tunnel, each equipped with a chair and a bed or their equivalent, none of them occupied by more than a single prisoner, seven of them totally empty.

The second the prisoners saw them, all except Nmumba and Proto rose as one, approached the force field, and began asking questions in their native languages. When they received no response they began yelling and screaming.

Pretorius stopped in front of the one cell that held a Man. He was the spitting image of the false Nmumba they had stolen days ago, and Pretorius gestured for Pandora to kill the force field at the front of the cell.

"He's going to be weak as hell," said Irish. "Snake, give me a hand with him."

They walked into the cell, helped Nmumba get shakily to his feet, and supported him as he went out into the aisle between the two sets of cells.

The screaming on the part of the other prisoners had reached a crescendo, and Pretorius stepped a few feet away from his team, faced one set of cells, and raised his voice.

"Does anyone here speak Terran?" he asked.

"I speak the languages of *all* the prisoners," replied the Antarean.

"Ask them if they'd like us to kill the force fields on *all* the cells."

The Antarean relayed the question, and while Pretorius couldn't understand the words, the response was wildly enthusiastic.

"Tell them that in exchange for that, they do not touch any Man who is with me. That's my offer."

The Antarean put the proposition to them, was almost overwhelmed by the enthusiastic response, and relayed it to Pretorius.

"Okay, Pandora, kill the fields."

"You're sure?" she said. "I have a hard time considering this group as men—well, *beings*—of honor."

"They're beings of vengeance," replied Pretorius, "and they've got nothing against us."

She shrugged. "You're the boss."

And an instant later fourteen prisoners were racing down the tunnel, lusting for blood and freedom. Only Proto, once again appearing as a middle-aged man, and the Antarean remained where they were.

Pretorius stared at the Antarean. "You didn't go with them," he noted.

"You helped me," he replied. "I have an obligation to help you."

"The others didn't feel that way."

"They are ungrateful scum," said the Antarean contemptuously.

"Have you a name?"

"Kramin," replied the Antarean.

"And you feel obliged to help us?" said Pretorius dubiously.

"I wanted no part of this war. I was a professor of alien languages when they conscripted me. I was given no choice."

"What's a professor doing in a jail cell?" asked Pandora.

"You've heard of the Battle of Sikandor IV?"

"I think everyone has," replied Pretorius. "You were there?"

"I was there. In the midst of the worst firefight, our commanding officer started to flee, taking with him all our medical supplies—so I killed him." He gestured to his cell. "This is my reward."

"I can hardly blame you for killing officers," said Snake.

"I have befriended Edgar, whose treatment was more severe than any of the others," said Kramin. "He is my only living friend."

"And you're willing to help him?" asked Pretorius.

"That is why I did not run away with the other prisoners."

"Kramin," said Pretorius, "I think you just made six new friends."

# 38

"First things first," continued Pretorius. "Can Nmumba walk on his own power, or does Felix have to carry him?"

"I can walk," said Nmumba. "I can't vouch for my stamina, and I certainly can't run, but I can walk."

Pretorius turned to Proto. "How about you?"

"I'll be all right," answered Proto. "When it became obvious I didn't speak their language they stopped beating me and threw me in a cell. I assume they were trying to find someone who spoke my race's native tongue." He paused. "I never spoke a word of Terran to them," he added proudly.

"You're sure you're okay?" persisted Pretorius. "We may need you to get out of here."

"I'm sure."

Pretorius turned to Kramin. "I don't imagine you know your way around this place?"

"Not well," admitted the Antarean. "They've taken me to two different interrogation rooms, but that's all I've seen." He paused briefly. "Well, except where they docked the ship that brought me here."

"And where was that?"

"I believe I can lead you there, though we'll almost certainly encounter opposition along the way."

"We could also fight our way there and find that there's no ship," said Snake. "I mean, how the hell long does it stay after it's disgorged its prisoners?"

"They had two ships already here when mine landed," said Kramin. "They were heavily armed. I assume they're there to repel any attacks."

Pretorius turned to Pandora with a questioning look. "Could you fly one?"

"How different can it be?" she replied.

"Okay, lead us there, Kramin," said Pretorius. "Or, rather, tell us how to get there and walk in the middle of our group so we can protect you. After Nmumba, you're the one being we can't afford to lose."

Kramin began uttering directions, which led them through a different series of tunnels than those they had come by. Now and then there were artificial barriers, but Pandora was always able to unlock them or make them recede.

After a few minutes they heard some rabid screaming.

"What's that?" asked Pretorius.

"The Denebians, yelling and cursing in their native tongue," answered the Antarean. "Either they've found some of their jailors, or their jailors have found them."

After a minute the screaming stopped.

"Sounds like one side won," remarked Ortega.

"The jailors," said Pretorius. "Unless the Denebians found a cache of weapons somewhere."

"Or maybe one side just frightened the other side away," said Snake. "Damn it! I wish we were in the good old days, when a gun made a *bang!* and we knew for sure what was happening."

"Those good old days ended more than four thousand years ago," noted Irish.

"And we pretty much know what happened," said Pretorius.

"The same thing that happens every time one side has weapons and the other doesn't."

They continued on, and in another quarter mile they came to a solid door.

"This is one of the interrogation chambers," announced Kramin.

"I hope it's empty," said Nmumba weakly. "I need to sit for a minute or two."

"We all hope it's empty," said Pretorius. "Pandora, do your thing."

She softly uttered commands into her computer, and the door vanished. The chamber was about forty feet on a side, with a table, half a dozen chairs, a heavy door at the far end, and a Neverlie Machine.

"Did they use that on you?" Pretorius asked Nmumba as the latter sat down, exhausted, on the nearest chair.

"Almost every time," he answered.

Irish walked over and examined the machine's controls. "It's not set at Lethal," she announced, "at least not for Men. It might kill a Denebian or a Bortoi at this level."

"Have you experienced it too?" Pandora asked Kramin.

"Yes," he said. "But only as punishment. I never hid or denied my actions, so I had no secrets to reveal to them."

Pretorius waited until Nmumba gestured that he was ready to walk again, and then said, "Pandora, the door?"

She help the computer up to her mouth, spoke her commands, and the door at the far end slid into a wall. They walked through and found themselves in a continuation of the corridor.

"Straight ahead, I presume?" said Pretorius.

"Yes," said Kramin. "And unless I misremember, it should go uphill just a bit."

THE PRISON IN ANTARES

Within fifty yards the tunnel did indeed angle up slightly. And before they'd gone another fifty, they heard two agonized screams.

"The Torquals?" suggested Snake.

"I don't think so," replied Kramin. "Torquals have much deeper voices."

"Then maybe they got a couple of guards," said Ortega hopefully.

There was a third scream.

"The Kaboris," announced Kramin. "There is no one left now except ourselves and two Torquals."

"They're not going to prove much help," said Pretorius. "They're as unarmed as the rest of them, and they're so tall they're going to be moving hunched over if they don't want to keep cracking their heads against the top of the tunnel." He turned to Pandora. "A thought occurs to me."

"Yes?"

"You're in touch with the computer that controls the cells and all these doors, right?"

"Well, with the one that's currently operative. There are backups, of course."

He frowned. "So even if you had a way to wipe this one clean . . ."

"Another one would kick in two seconds later."

"And if you wiped *that* one too?"

She shook her head. "It would respond to the same commands, but a different ID and password."

"Okay. I should have known it couldn't be that easy."

"I keep looking for those oversized rats," said Ortega, "but the place seems to be free of them."

"My guess is that they can smell the blood of the Denebians

and the Kaboris," said Snake. "They probably racing to the dinner table right this moment."

"How much farther?" asked Pretorius.

"We follow a fork to the right and we should be at the second interrogation room," answered Kramin.

They came to the fork in less than a minute, and shortly thereafter Pandora entered the code that opened the room.

"This one's a little smaller than the first," noted Ortega.

"Still got a Neverlie Machine, though," added Snake.

"And a pitcher of water, if anyone wants a drink," said Irish.

"No!" said Nmumba. "Don't touch it!"

"Poison?" asked Pretorius.

"No, they don't bring you to this room to kill you. But that stuff will burn away your tonsils and half your tongue—or at least it feels like it when they force you to drink it."

Pretorius turned to Kramin. "You had to drink it too?"

"I think drink is the wrong word," answered the Antarean. "I've had it poured down my throat."

"Nice playmates, your countrymen," remarked Pretorius.

"I'm sure yours would be much the same if they had an Antarean who was on the brink of developing something even deadlier than the Q bomb."

"I hope we never have to find out," said Pretorius. He looked around the chamber. "I see two doors at the back of the room. Which one do we take?"

"I've only had my back to them, and I've only heard one open a single time, to allow a pilot and her crew through," answered Kramin. "I believe they were coming from a slightly higher level, because they kept referring to being 'down here.'"

"It's *all* 'down here' if you were above the surface until you landed," said Pretorius. "Pandora, can you produce a diagram, a *schema*, *some*thing that you can turn into a holograph?"

She softly issued some commands to her computer, and a moment later a holograph of the interrogation room and its approaches and exits hovered a few feet above the floor.

"I think we go through the door on the left," she said. "It leads downhill, but the one on the right doesn't lead anywhere. It's like they meant to dig or extend the tunnel that led us here, but there's the door and nothing else, as if they decided this was far enough."

Pretorius was silent for a moment. He studied the holograph once more, and then spoke. "Open the door on the right."

"But it doesn't lead anywhere," protested Pandora.

"Then what harm can it do?" he asked.

Pandora shrugged. "What the hell, it only takes a few seconds."

She uttered another command, and the right-hand door vanished, revealing a well-lighted tunnel continuing the slightly uphill curve that had led them to the chamber.

Pandora stared at her computer, even tapped it twice with a forefinger. "Something's wrong with the damned thing. It never showed anything beyond this door."

"That's because no member of the staff here had to know about it, though obviously some did, when a pilot or a member of his crew came through here. But they made sure that if anyone ever busted out of a cell and got access to any computer in the place, the computer wouldn't show him that there was anything behind this door." He turned to Kramin. "This leads to the ships, right?"

"I have to assume so," answered the Antarean.

"Then let's go."

Pretorius, screecher in hand, walked through the doorway and began the gently uphill climb, followed by the rest of his crew. The tunnel proceeded in a straight direction for perhaps eighty yards, took a hard left turn, then curved to the right again.

After they had proceeded almost half a mile the tunnel became wider and was even better lit.

Pretorius rubbed a couple of fingers against a wall, then studied them.

"Phosphorescent coating, of course," he whispered. "We feel it's getting brighter, but if you were coming down here out of a ship, it's getting duller as your eyes begin adjusting to the darker conditions." He wiped his fingers off on his pants leg. "It means we're going in the right direction."

In another two minutes the lighting was brighter still, and they could hear voices up ahead. Then, finally, they could see the end of the tunnel, and a large area, perhaps a quarter mile across, where they could see portions of two ships at rest.

"Proto," whispered Pretorius, "get rid of the image, and just slither ahead until you can get a clear view of the place. They're less likely to spot the real you than any of us."

"Right," said Proto as the middle-aged man vanished and the cushion-shaped alien ambulated forward some six feet past Pretorius. "There are four—no, make that five—Antareans that I can see in the open space. There seems to be an office, or some kind of room, off to the left. I can't see into it, but it's very well lit, so I assume there are Antareans in it."

"Anyone in the ships?"

"Not that I can tell."

"Okay," said Pretorius. "Hold still another minute or two, and see if you can spot any movement *behind* the ships."

Ninety seconds later Proto spoke again. "There are at least three more behind the ship, possibly as many as six. The ships are both poised under a broad shaft. I can't see more than seventy or eighty feet high, but based especially on what Kramin told us, that figures to be the shaft to the planet's surface. If it isn't, then I've no idea how the ships got here in the first place."

"Okay," said Pretorius. "Snake, Felix, Pandora, take everything that's left of center, for lack of a better way of describing it. Irish, you and I will take the right. Nmumba, you're in no condition to fight, and Kramin, I'm not going to ask you to kill your own species."

"I've already killed a member of my own race," said Kramin. "That's why I'm here, remember?"

He held out his hand for a weapon, and Pretorius handed him his burner.

"Remember," said Pretorius, "we want to do this quick. We've got to get onto a ship before any reinforcements get down here." He double-checked the charge on his screecher. "Let's go!"

They emerged from the tunnel, weapons blazing. Four Antareans fell instantly. A fifth one screamed for help before collapsing, and three more raced out of the office, weapons in hand.

"Felix!" yelled Pretorius. "Concentrate on the ones from the office!"

Four more Antareans fell before the barrage before they could even identify who was firing at them, but the three new ones turned their fire on Pretorius and his crew, who hit the dirt while still returning fire.

"Goddammit!" growled Ortega.

"You hit?" asked Pretorius without taking his eyes off the enemy.

"No," said Ortega. "My burner's stopped functioning. Somebody toss me a weapon."

Proto crawled a few feet ahead of him. "I'll buy you some time," he said—and instantly he projected a creature out of every race's worst nightmare, some ten feet in height, half that in width, with a trio of saber-toothed heads possessed of glowing, malevolent eyes, and waving shining claws that seemed to have been fashioned for tearing its enemies painfully apart.

"Goddamn, but that's good!" cried Ortega as Snake tossed him a burner. He got to his feet behind Proto's monster. "Let me get a little closer."

"Get down, you idiot!" yelled Pretorius, as three weapons were trained on where they thought the heart of Proto's image might be, and since it was only an image, all three shots went right through it.

One went over everyone's heads. Another was wide. But the third ripped into Ortega's neck, severing the jugular and almost decapitating him.

He flew backward and landed at Nmumba's feet.

"I . . . forgot," he mumbled, and died.

Pretorius and Snake killed two of the three Antareans from the office, and then Kramin nailed the third.

"Choose a ship—quick!" said Pretorius.

"The one on the right," said Pandora, running toward it.

"Irish and Snake, help Nmumba! Kramin, give me a hand with Felix."

"But he's dead," said the Antarean.

"He deserves better than what they'll do for him," said Pretorius, lifting Ortega's body by the armpits. Kramin took his feet, and within a minute they had loaded his body onto the ship and were climbing aboard themselves.

"You'd better be able to work this thing!" said Pretorius.

"Not a problem, as long as there are no obstructions in this shaft," answered Pandora.

"Has this thing got a bomb we can leave behind and set to explode?"

"Probably," she said. "But it could take me five or ten minutes to find it and activate it. Do you want to take that long?"

"Hell, no!" said Pretorius. "Just get us out of here!"

And less than a minute later the ship emerged from the shaft and headed straight for the stratosphere and beyond.

# 39

They were two days out of the Antares system. Their ship had been sighted and pursued twice, but both times they were able to elude the Coalition ships that were after them.

Finally Snake approached Pretorius while he was in the galley, trying to decide which type of Antarean food would upset his stomach less.

"Gotta talk to you, Nate," she said.

"Yeah?"

"It's about Felix," continued Snake. "He's not turning into any nosegay. I think we're gonna have to dump him."

"Dump him where?" asked Pretorius, frowning.

"No particular place. Jettison him the way you did Circe."

"That was at the beginning of the assignment, and there was no way we could handle the body until we got back home. But we're only maybe three days from Deluros."

"At least move him out of the cabin he's in and down to storage."

"OK, I'll have Kramin give me a hand."

"We should have drafted that bastard ourselves," said Snake. "He works harder than anyone else onboard." Then she smiled and added, "Except me, of course."

Pretorius chose a meal, took one bite of it and dumped it, and settled for the Antarean equivalent of coffee, which was neither warm nor caffeinated, but at least had a flavor that wasn't too off-putting. He carried his cup back to the main deck and sat down.

"Take a break," he told Pandora. "I'll take over for a few hours."

THE PRISON IN ANTARES

"Thanks," she said, getting to her feet. "I could use one."

"Anything I should be watching?"

"Small ship about eighty thousand miles off the port bow," she replied. "No armaments that I can tell." She looked at her screen again, then smiled. "He's gone. Must be a wormhole over that way that's either not in this ship's memory, or at least that I can't read."

Pretorius sat down at the controls and sipped his not-quite-coffee. A few minutes later Kramin emerged from his cabin.

"Just the man—well, the Antarean—I was hoping for," said Pretorius.

"Is anything wrong?" asked Kramin.

"My friend Felix is becoming offensive," explained Pretorius. "You and I will move him from his cot down into the storage department."

"Why not just cast him adrift?" suggested Kramin. "He won't know the difference."

"No," agreed Pretorius. "But *I* will." He got to his feet. "Come on."

It took them a few minutes to move Ortega's body to the storage area in the ship's belly.

"I've been meaning to ask, if it's not a sore point," began Kramin, looking at Ortega's artificial arm and legs, "but who did that do him?"

"He lost one leg in the Battle of Tomaris III, the other one when he stepped on a mine on Windfall, and the arm got cut up pretty badly in personal combat during the Siege of Mariposa."

"And yet he kept reenlisting," marveled Kramin.

"He believed in his cause," answered Pretorius. "Just as you believe in yours."

"Me?" repeated Kramin.

"They beat the crap out of you on a regular basis, and yet here you are helping their enemies when you could have gone free."

Kramin uttered a hoarse laugh. "What would be the point of going free on Antares Six?"

"You could have asked me to set you down on another world," said Pretorius. "You still could."

"Let's get Edgar home first, and then I'll worry about it."

"Was it as rough as I think it was?" asked Pretorius.

"Probably," answered Kramin. "I'd prefer not to talk about it."

"Sorry," said Pretorius. "We're through here. Let's get back up to the main deck."

A moment later Pretorius was back at the control panel while Kramin returned to his cabin. He checked to make sure the ship Pandora had been tracking really had vanished into a wormhole, determined that there were no more ships, military or otherwise, within range, and finally looked up to find Irish standing next to him.

"Yes?" he said.

"I've had three four-hour sessions with Edgar," she replied, "and while he's in poor shape physically, he's got a truly remarkable mind. It's as strong as ever, and I'll stake such reputation as I have that he told them nothing."

"And he's definitely the real thing this time?"

She nodded. "Definitely."

"So we're not only bringing him back, but we're also coming home with a turncoat who should be able to tell them quite a bit when he's debriefed."

Irish shifted her weight uncomfortably. "I've been meaning to ask you about him," she said.

"About Kramin?"

"Yes."

"Okay, shoot," said Pretorius.

There was a pause as she chose her words carefully. "Do you find it a little odd that he chose to come with us?"

"The alternative was staying in the damned jail or being shot as an escapee."

Irish shook her head. "We'd have let him off on some other Coalition or neutral world. Hell, we still could."

"You're condemning loyalty to a friend," said Pretorius.

"Am I?" she replied.

Pretorius was silent for almost a full minute. Finally he spoke. "He *did* know exactly how to lead us out of there, which fork to take. And he's in pretty good shape considering all the pain and punishment he claims to have suffered. Still, that's pretty far-fetched."

"I'm just sharing my observations," said Irish. "I'm not accusing him of anything . . . *yet*."

"We'd better find out before we're inside the Democracy," said Pretorius. "He's in his cabin. Tell him I want to see him up here."

She nodded her head and went off to get Kramin, who emerged a moment later and accompanied Irish back to the bridge.

"I'm sorry to bother you," said Pretorius, "but we've got a little situation on our hands."

"Situation?" repeated Kramin.

"It seems the Democracy is not allowing any more Antareans to enter it. I've contacted them and vouched for you, and I know I can get Irish and Pandora and Snake to vouch for you too, but they were pretty adamant. So I think, for safety's sake, I'm going to drop you off on a neutral planet. We're entering the zone in a couple of hours. Is there any particular planet you'd like?"

"I thank you for your concern," replied Kramin, "but Edgar is my friend. I'll take my chances."

"I realize you may have burned your bridges insofar as the Coalition is concerned—"

"I'm a convicted murderer and traitor, as well as an escaped prisoner," said Kramin. "You should welcome me with open arms."

"The Democracy doesn't want an Antarean murderer and the Coalition doesn't want a traitor," said Pretorius. "That's why a neutral world makes the most sense."

"No! I will not desert my friend!"

"All right," said Pretorius. "We'll set down on Cordoba IV. They're neutral, they have an atmosphere and gravity that can support us both, and they have a hospital where both of you can get treatment. That should be acceptable to all involved parties."

"He is a human!" protested Kramin. "He needs human doctors."

"There are probably some on Cordoba."

"He is too important to take that risk. You should take him only to the finest specialists in the Deluros system!"

"And you were counting on that, weren't you?" said Irish.

Kramin was motionless for an instant. Then he uttered a savage, inarticulate scream and dove for her, but Pretorius already had his screecher out, and a wall of solid sound crashed into the Antarean's head, knocking him sideways into a wall. Before he could get to his feet Snake had her burner out and delivered the fatal shot.

Pretorius walked over and stared at the corpse, then turned to Irish.

"I owe you," he said. "I actually bought into that act."

"He was good at his job."

"He wasn't the only one," replied Pretorius. "I'm glad you're with us.

"So should we cart him down to the storage area?" asked Snake.

"I hate to have Felix share a room with him," said Pretorius. "But yes. We can't leave him up here, and maybe they can learn something more from him where we're going."

"Let's just get there quick," said Snake. Pretorius looked at her questioningly. "You're the guy who never loses a team member," she concluded bitterly. "When they start handing out medals, just make sure they give one to Felix and another to Circe."

# EPILOGUE

**T**wo months had passed. Nmumba had been nursed back to acceptable if not glowing health, and was once again working in his laboratory. Ortega had been buried in his family's plot, and the others had put their lives in some semblance of order when Pretorius was summoned to Wilbur Cooper's office.

"I want to congratulate you once again, my boy!" said Cooper enthusiastically. "That was a Grade-A piece of work, though by this time I suppose no one should be surprised by the results you get. Just a tremendous job!"

"May I speak frankly, sir?" said Pretorius.

"Absolutely!"

"Then cut the bullshit and tell me why you really sent for me."

"All right," said Cooper, his demeanor suddenly businesslike. "How soon can you and your Dead Enders be ready for another assignment—a very urgent one?"

"It depends on what the problem is," said Pretorius.

"Do you remember the Michkag clone, the ringer you installed in Orion last year?"

Pretorius frowned. "They discovered what he was and killed him."

"Nice guess," said Cooper. "I only wish it was right."

"Oh?" said Pretorius, arching an eyebrow.

"The bastard has turned!"

"Turned?"

"He decided he *likes* being a general," growled Cooper, "and he's not going to help us defeat his own race. He's a brilliant strategist, and thanks to being raised here he knows more about how we think and react than any other alien in the whole Coalition. It turns out he's been feeding us false data for months. He's currently the best-protected being, human or alien, in the whole Coalition. You and your Dead Enders are going to have to kill him before he costs us this goddamned war!"

"Where is he?" asked Pretorius.

Cooper waved his hand in a gesture that encompassed roughly half the galaxy. "Out there somewhere," he said.

# THE ORIGIN OF THE BIRTHRIGHT UNIVERSE

I t happened in the 1970s. Carol and I were watching a truly awful movie at a local theater, and about halfway through it I muttered, "Why am I wasting my time here when I could be doing something really interesting, like, say, writing the entire history of the human race from now until its extinction?" And she whispered back, "So why don't you?" We got up immediately, walked out of the theater, and that night I outlined a novel called *Birthright: The Book of Man*, which would tell the story of the human race from its attainment of faster-than-light flight until its death eighteen thousand years from now.

It was a long book to write. I divided the future into five political eras—Republic, Democracy, Oligarchy, Monarchy, and Anarchy—and wrote twenty-six connected stories ("demonstrations," *Analog* called them, and rightly so), displaying every facet of the human race, both admirable and not so admirable. Since each is set a few centuries from the last, there are no continuing characters in the book (unless you consider Man, with a capital M, the main character, in which case you could make an argument—or at least, *I* could—that it's really a character study).

I sold it to Signet, along with another novel titled *The Soul Eater*. My editor there, Sheila Gilbert, loved the "Birthright Universe" and asked me if I would be willing to make a few changes to *The Soul Eater* so that it was set in that future. I agreed, and the changes actually took less than a day. She made the same request— in advance, this time—for the four-book Tales of the Galactic Midway series, the four-book Tales of the Velvet Comet series, and *Walpurgis III*. Looking back, I see that only two of the thirteen novels I wrote for Signet were *not* set there.

When I moved to Tor Books, my editor there, Beth Meacham, had a fondness for the Birthright Universe, and most of my books for her—not all, but most—were set in it: *Santiago, Ivory, The Dark Lady, Paradise, Purgatory, Inferno, A Miracle of Rare Design, A Hunger in the Soul, The Outpost,* and *The Return of Santiago*.

When Ace agreed to buy *Soothsayer, Oracle,* and *Prophet* from me, my editor, Ginjer Buchanan, assumed that of course they'd be set in the Birthright Universe—and of course they were, because as I learned a little more about my eighteen-thousand-year, two-million-world future, I felt a lot more comfortable writing about it.

In fact, I started setting short stories in the Birthright Universe. Two of my Hugo winners—"Seven Views of Olduvai Gorge" and "The 43 Antarean Dynasties"—are set there, and so are perhaps fifteen others.

When Bantam agreed to take the *Widowmaker* trilogy from me, it was a foregone conclusion that Janna Silverstein, who purchased the books (but moved to another company before they came out) would want them to take place in the Birthright Universe. She did indeed request it, and I did indeed agree.

A decade later I sold another *Widowmaker* book to Meisha Merlin, set—where else?—in the Birthright Universe.

And when it came time to suggest an initial series of books to Lou Anders for the brand-new Pyr line of science fiction, I don't think I ever considered any ideas or stories that *weren't* set in the Birthright Universe. He bought the five *Starship* books, and after some fantasies and Weird Western excursions, he—and his successor, the wonderful Rene Sears—commissioned the Dead Enders series to be set there as well.

I've gotten so much of my career from the Birthright Universe that I wish I could remember the name of that turkey we walked out of all those years ago so I could write the producers and thank them.

# THE LAYOUT OF THE BIRTHRIGHT UNIVERSE

T he most heavily populated (by both stars and inhabitants) section of the Birthright Universe is always referred to by its political identity, which evolves from Republic to Democracy to Oligarchy to Monarchy. It encompasses millions of inhabited and habitable worlds. Earth is too small and too far out of the mainstream of galactic commerce to remain Man's capital world, and within a couple of thousand years the capital has been moved lock, stock, and barrel halfway across the galaxy to Deluros VIII, a huge world with about ten times Earth's surface and near-identical atmosphere and gravity. By the middle of the Democracy, perhaps four thousand years from now, the entire planet is covered by one huge sprawling city. By the time of the Oligarchy, even Deluros VIII isn't big enough for our billions of empire-running bureaucrats, and Deluros VI, another large world, is broken up into forty-eight planetoids, each housing a major department of the government (with four planetoids given over entirely to the military.)

Earth itself is way out in the boonies, on the Spiral Arm. I don't believe I've set more than parts of a couple of novels on the Arm.

At the outer edge of the galaxy is the Rim, where worlds are spread out and underpopulated. There's so little of value or military interest on the Rim that one ship, such as the *Theodore Roosevelt* of the *Starship* series, can patrol a couple of hundred worlds by itself.

In later eras, the Rim will be dominated by feuding warlords, but it's so far away from the center of things that the governments, for the most part, just ignore it.

Then there are the Inner and Outer Frontiers. The Outer Frontier is that vast but sparsely populated area between the outer edge of the Republic/Democracy/Oligarchy/Monarchy and the Rim. The Inner Frontier is that somewhat smaller (but still huge) area between the inner reaches of the Republic/et cetera and the black hole at the core of the galaxy.

It's on the Inner Frontier that I've chosen to set more than half of my novels. In 1968's *Space Chantey*, the brilliant R. A. Lafferty wrote: "Will there be a mythology of the future, they used to ask, after all has become science? Will high deeds be told in epic, or only in computer code?" I decided that I'd like to spend at least a part of my career trying to create those myths of the future, and it seems to me that myths, with their bigger-than-life characters and colorful settings, work best on frontiers where there aren't too many people around to chronicle them accurately, or too many authority figures around to prevent them from playing out to their inevitable conclusions. So I arbitrarily decided that the Inner Frontier was where *my* myths would take place, and I populated it with people bearing names like Catastrophe Baker, the Widowmaker, the Cyborg de Milo, the ageless Forever Kid, and the like. It not only allows me to tell my heroic (and sometimes antiheroic) myths but also lets me tell more realistic stories occurring at the very same time a few thousand light-years away in the Republic or Democracy or whatever happens to exist at that moment.

Over the years I've fleshed out the galaxy. There are the star clusters—the Albion Cluster, the Quinellus Cluster, a few others.

There are the individual worlds, some important enough to appear as the title of a book, such as Walpurgis III, some reappearing throughout the time periods and stories, such as Deluros VIII, Antares III, Binder X, Keepsake, Spica II, some others, and hundreds (maybe thousands by now) of worlds (and races, now that I think about it) mentioned once and never again.

Then there are, if not the bad guys, then at least what I think of as the Disloyal Opposition. Some, like the Sett Empire, get into one war with humanity and that's the end of it. Some, like the Canphor Twins (Canphor VI and Canphor VII) have been a thorn in Man's side for the better part of ten millennia. Some, like Lodin XI, vary almost daily in their loyalties, depending on the political situation.

I've been building this universe, politically and geographically, for a third of a century now, and with each passing book and story it feels a little more real to me. Give me another thirty years, and I'll probably believe every word I've written about it.

# APPENDIX 3

# CHRONOLOGY OF THE UNIVERSE CREATED IN *BIRTHRIGHT: THE BOOK OF MAN*

| YEAR | ERA | STORY OR NOVEL |
|------|-----|----------------|
| 1885 A.D. | | "The Hunter" (IVORY) |
| 1898 A.D. | | "Himself" (IVORY) |
| 1982 A.D. | | SIDESHOW |
| 1983 A.D. | | THE THREE-LEGGED HOOTCH DANCER |
| 1985 A.D. | | THE WILD ALIEN TAMER |
| 1987 A.D. | | THE BEST ROOTIN' TOOTIN' SHOOTIN' GUNSLINGER IN THE WHOLE DAMNED GALAXY |
| 2057 A.D. | | "The Politician" (IVORY) |
| 2403 A.D. | | "Shaka II" |
| 2908 A.D. | | 1 G.E. |
| 16 G.E. | Republic | "The Curator" (IVORY) |
| 103 G.E. | Republic | "The Homecoming" |
| 264 G.E. | Republic | "The Pioneers" (BIRTHRIGHT) |
| 332 G.E. | Republic | "The Cartographers" (BIRTHRIGHT) |

| | | |
|---|---|---|
| 346 G.E. | Republic | WALPURGIS III |
| 367 G.E. | Republic | EROS ASCENDING |
| 396 G.E. | Republic | "The Miners" (BIRTHRIGHT) |
| 401 G.E. | Republic | EROS AT ZENITH |
| 442 G.E. | Republic | EROS DESCENDING |
| 465 G.E. | Republic | EROS AT NADIR |
| 522 G.E. | Republic | "All the Things You Are" |
| 588 G.E. | Republic | "The Psychologists" (BIRTHRIGHT) |
| 616 G.E. | Republic | A MIRACLE OF RARE DESIGN |
| 882 G.E. | Republic | "The Potentate" (IVORY) |
| 962 G.E. | Republic | "The Merchants" (BIRTHRIGHT) |
| 1150 G.E. | Republic | "Cobbling Together a Solution" |
| 1151 G.E. | Republic | "Nowhere in Particular" |
| 1152 G.E. | Republic | "The God Biz" |
| 1394 G.E. | Republic | "Keepsakes" |
| 1701 G.E. | Republic | "The Artist" (IVORY) |
| 1813 G.E. | Republic | "Dawn" (PARADISE) |
| 1826 G.E. | Republic | PURGATORY |
| 1859 G.E. | Republic | "Noon" (PARADISE) |
| 1888 G.E. | Republic | "Midafternoon" (PARADISE) |
| 1902 G.E. | Republic | "Dusk" (PARADISE) |
| 1921 G.E. | Republic | INFERNO |
| 1966 G.E. | Republic | STARSHIP: MUTINY |
| 1967 G.E. | Republic | STARSHIP: PIRATE |
| 1968 G.E. | Republic | STARSHIP: MERCENARY |
| 1969 G.E. | Republic | STARSHIP: REBEL |
| 1970 G.E. | Republic | STARSHIP: FLAGSHIP |
| 2122 G.E. | Democracy | "The 43 Antarean Dynasties" |

| | | |
|---|---|---|
| 2154 G.E. | Democracy | "The Diplomats" (BIRTHRIGHT) |
| 2239 G.E. | Democracy | "Monuments of Flesh and Stone" |
| 2275 G.E. | Democracy | "The Olympians" (BIRTHRIGHT) |
| 2469 G.E. | Democracy | "The Barristers" (BIRTHRIGHT) |
| 2885 G.E. | Democracy | "Robots Don't Cry" |
| 2911 G.E. | Democracy | "The Medics" (BIRTHRIGHT) |
| 3004 G.E. | Democracy | "The Politicians" (BIRTHRIGHT) |
| 3042 G.E. | Democracy | "The Gambler" (IVORY) |
| 3286 G.E. | Democracy | SANTIAGO |
| 3322 G.E. | Democracy | A HUNGER IN THE SOUL |
| 3324 G.E. | Democracy | THE SOUL EATER |
| 3324 G.E. | Democracy | "Nicobar Lane: The Soul Eater's Story" |
| 3407 G.E. | Democracy | THE RETURN OF SANTIAGO |
| 3427 G.E. | Democracy | SOOTHSAYER |
| 3441 G.E. | Democracy | ORACLE |
| 3447 G.E. | Democracy | PROPHET |
| 3502 G.E. | Democracy | "Guardian Angel" |
| 3504 G.E. | Democracy | "A Locked-Planet Mystery" |
| 3504 G.E. | Democracy | "Honorable Enemies" |
| 3505 G.E. | Democracy | "If the Frame Fits . . ." |
| 3719 G.E. | Democracy | "Hunting the Snark" |
| 4026 G.E. | Democracy | THE FORTRESS IN ORION |
| 4027 G.E. | Democracy | THE PRISON IN ANTARES |
| 4375 G.E. | Democracy | "The Graverobber" (IVORY) |
| 4822 G.E. | Oligarchy | "The Administrators" (BIRTHRIGHT) |
| 4839 G.E. | Oligarchy | THE DARK LADY |
| 5101 G.E. | Oligarchy | THE WIDOWMAKER |

| | | |
|---|---|---|
| 5103 G.E. | Oligarchy | THE WIDOWMAKER REBORN |
| 5106 G.E. | Oligarchy | THE WIDOWMAKER UNLEASHED |
| 5108 G.E. | Oligarchy | A GATHERING OF WIDOWMAKERS |
| 5461 G.E. | Oligarchy | "The Media" (BIRTHRIGHT) |
| 5492 G.E. | Oligarchy | "The Artists" (BIRTHRIGHT) |
| 5521 G.E. | Oligarchy | "The Warlord" (IVORY) |
| 5655 G.E. | Oligarchy | "The Biochemists" (BIRTHRIGHT) |
| 5912 G.E. | Oligarchy | "The Warlords" (BIRTHRIGHT) |
| 5993 G.E. | Oligarchy | "The Conspirators" (BIRTHRIGHT) |
| 6304 G.E. | Monarchy | IVORY |
| 6321 G.E. | Monarchy | "The Rulers" (BIRTHRIGHT) |
| 6400 G.E. | Monarchy | "The Symbiotics" (BIRTHRIGHT) |
| 6521 G.E. | Monarchy | "Catastrophe Baker and the Cold Equations" |
| 6523 G.E. | Monarchy | THE OUTPOST |
| 6524 G.E. | Monarchy | "Catastrophe Baker and a Canticle for Leibowitz" |
| 6599 G.E. | Monarchy | "The Philosophers" (BIRTHRIGHT) |
| 6746 G.E. | Monarchy | "The Architects" (BIRTHRIGHT) |
| 6962 G.E. | Monarchy | "The Collectors" (BIRTHRIGHT) |
| 7019 G.E. | Monarchy | "The Rebels" (BIRTHRIGHT) |
| 16201 G.E. | Anarchy | "The Archaeologists" (BIRTHRIGHT) |
| 16673 G.E. | Anarchy | "The Priests" (BIRTHRIGHT) |
| 16888 G.E. | Anarchy | "The Pacifists" (BIRTHRIGHT) |
| 17001 G.E. | Anarchy | "The Destroyers" (BIRTHRIGHT) |
| 21703 G.E. | | "Seven Views of Olduvai Gorge" |

# NOVELS NOT SET IN THIS FUTURE

ADVENTURES (1922–1926 A.D.)
EXPLOITS (1926–1931 A.D.)
ENCOUNTERS (1931–1934 A.D.)
HAZARDS (1934–1938 A.D.)
STALKING THE UNICORN ("Tonight")
STALKING THE VAMPIRE ("Tonight")
STALKING THE DRAGON ("Tonight")
STALKING THE ZOMBIE ("Tonight")
THE BRANCH (2047–2051 A.D.)
SECOND CONTACT (2065 A.D.)
BULLY! (1910–1912 A.D.)
KIRINYAGA (2123–2137 A.D.)
KILIMANJARO (2234–2241 A.D.)
LADY WITH AN ALIEN (1490 A.D.)
DRAGON AMERICA (1779–1780 A.D.)
A CLUB IN MONTMARTRE (1890–1901 A.D.)
THE WORLD BEHIND THE DOOR (1928 A.D.)
THE OTHER TEDDY ROOSEVELTS (1888–1919 A.D.)
THE BUNTLINE SPECIAL (1881 A.D.)
THE DOCTOR AND THE KID (1882 A.D.)
THE DOCTOR AND THE ROUGH RIDER (1884 A.D.)
THE DOCTOR AND THE DINOSAURS (1885 A.D.)

# ABOUT THE AUTHOR

Mike Resnick has won an impressive five Hugos and has been nominated for thirty-two more. The author of the Starship series, the John Justin Mallory series, the Eli Paxton Mysteries, and four Weird West Tales, he has sold seventy science fiction novels and more than two hundred and sixty short stories and has edited forty-two anthologies. His Kirin-yaga series, with sixty-seven major and minor awards and nominations to date, is the most honored series of stories in the history of science fiction. Visit him at his website, http://mikeresnick.com/, on Facebook, www.facebook.com/mike.resnick1, or on Twitter @ResnickMike.

*Photo by Hugette*